Penguin Books

The Pure Land

David Foster was born in 1944 and spent his early childhood in Katoomba in the Blue Mountains of New South Wales. He trained as a scientist at Sydney University and the Australian National University and spent 1970 in the United States as a Fellow of the National Institute of Health, and 1978 in Europe as a recipient of the Marten Bequest for Prose. When first published in 1974 *The Pure Land* shared the first *Age* award for the best Australian book of the year, and his novel *Moonlite* (1981) won the National Book Council Award for Australian Literature. He is married with six children and lives in the southern highlands of New South Wales.

By the same author

The
PURE·LAND

David Foster

Penguin Books

Penguin Books Australia Ltd,
487 Maroondah Highway, P.O. Box 257
Ringwood, Victoria, 3134, Australia
Penguin Books Ltd,
Harmondsworth, Middlesex, England
Penguin Books,
40 West 23rd Street, New York, N.Y. 10010, U.S.A.
Penguin Books Canada Ltd,
2801 John Street, Markham, Ontario, Canada
Penguin Books (N.Z.) Ltd,
182-190 Wairau Road, Auckland 10, New Zealand

First published by The Macmillan Company of Australia Pty Ltd, 1974
Published by Penguin Books Australia, 1985
Copyright © David Foster, 1973

Offset from the Macmillan hardback edition
Made and printed in Hong Kong
by LP Printing Limited

CIP

Foster, David, 1944–
The pure land.

First published: South Melbourne: Macmillan, 1974.
ISBN 0 14 007700 6.

I. Title.

A823′.3

should he choose to live here? I have lived these past years, thought Manwaring, most happily in the mist myself. Amidst these alien firs, these guest houses styled California and Ritz, Carrington, Hydro Majestic, I have found my home.

We are suffering a superabundance of calliopsis and crimson rosella this summer, people are blinded by so much crimson, indigo and yellow of the yellowest imaginable, even black wattle cannot match such yellow. Sun glasses must soon be worn, pensioners must soon discover gay floral smocks to match the season. And all weathered emotions, suitable to mist and occlusion, be swept away, if only temporarily . . .

And where should *I* go, thought Manwaring, conscious of the absurdity of his own appearance in the sunlight. Sunlight which more than dazzled, which distressed him, with his thick lenses and foreign appearance, his dark humours. A man that wore a suit on a picnic, the strap of his Kodak camera rubbing against the chain of his watch. But in the mists, he felt appropriate. A favorite portrait had him lifting stones in the Cox's River, seeking frogs for his daughter's billy can.

A great romantic, a bird returning, Manwaring had returned, alone, without his wife, to live out his life in the upper mountains. His twelve year old daughter was boarded at the convent school. His wife, who disliked the cold, disliked Manwaring's choking emotionalism even more, finding him, without their daughter, impossible to endure. In his late forties it seemed to her that almost any event, taken at random, could elicit from him those familiar hoarse sobs and copious tears: he would even cry over his own photography. It was a tendency much deplored in his mother, a stout European lady long dead, but in himself he regretted it even more deeply than he did his peregrine eyes and hawk nose. When younger, in his twenties, he had struggled insatiably with books he could not understand, as though intuitively aware that in such books, if he could only decipher them, lay an oppressive counter-weight to sentimentality. But he had had little education, and the struggle had been abandoned. Outside of photography, his profession, he now no longer read.

ONE

Chapter 1

If I have recollections, thought Manwaring while drinking
his morning coffee at the Paragon—and thought no more.
There is a park in Blackheath called Memory Park, I'll sit
there. The rest is silence. At three thousand feet we enter
the high mountains so called—though in places this might
raise a smile— from which the sky is seen as a most brilliant
blue. Contrast the white cumulus, the yellow calliopsis—a
patch of colour in summer, an intrusion of colour, a mountain
rosella, flashing crimson and blue, startled into a mist. From
his plucking at a cotoneaster in a garden or a park I have
startled him into a mist—his rightful habitat. Why else

Inevitably he began, in his late thirties, to show that familial surfeit of emotion that to his wife, prim elder daughter of shopkeepers, seemed like a suppuration capable of drenching in spurious significance each and every event. At last she had fled in desperation to a sister in a beachside suburb of Sydney (Bondi, that other pole from Katoomba), and Manwaring had stood in their garden, a treasonous Ruth amidst the corn, staring at the poinsettias and hydrangeas, unfamiliar, no longer liking the salt air, the city as pale as its sky. He decided to return without her. On 'The Fish' that night, in what little light remained, he watched the crimson rosellas fly from the tracks to stud the still yellow fields of the higher ridges like opal chips tossed onto a bedspread. But he had been chiefly gladdened by the purple rain clouds that had come across the Grose Valley, the bleak mists enveloping him on the train like a mother embosoming an ugly son. His bird was not the mountain lory after all but the yellow-tailed black cockatoo, harshest, ugliest and most laborious in flight of all mountain birds. Where else could such a bird survive? He felt, as usual, an irresistible surge of emotion, a love for his mountains so fierce, so ridiculous, that its irony, its absurdity, attended it like the overtones of a musical note. On arriving in Katoomba he separated himself from the daily commuters by the eagerness of his stride and went directly to his studios. Sifting through sepia positives in an effort to re-establish himself at once, he took by chance a glass plate of Memory Park—a muddy pond, possibly a small reservoir, held by a weir of grass surmounted by a track with a small trestle bridge, the background dotted with spurs of dark fir and incongruous summer houses—and in white ink wrote upon it—Memory Park. Memory Park. Until the plate was completely obscured.

In the Paragon café where he went almost every day from the Astor Flats on his way to work, he sat the following morning looking out at Katoomba Street through the closed doors of the café. The rain had gone, but the Paragon, dark on the brightest day, belonged to his perpetual winter. He sat at a banquette under a Grecian frieze showing a dog *guardant* and smelt the fresh chocolates being carried past. Constantine, who carried them, wished him good morning.

He wondered how long until the whole town knew the truth. He could say, with some truthfulness, that cold winters had not agreed with his wife. The fire being on all but three months of the year, he could explain, and the steps to the Astor Flats so very exposed to the wind—Mrs Manwaring had trouble climbing them—they would understand that the prejudice of his wife against the town was only a symbol of her prejudice against him. There were many though in the same situation, sent by their firms from Sydney to an eventual domestic exile. He would not draw too much attention. Already he had decided that should Kodak wish to move him he would resign and set up in business for himself, stay in the mountains permanently. He saw no reason to change his mind now, simply on account of his wife's leaving. The photography of the mountains was, from a commercial viewpoint, his alone, and he ran the only photographic workshop in the entire area. At the top of Katoomba Street, in the pharmacy from which a flight of stairs led to his rooftop studio, many of his postcards stood for sale on a circular stand. These, according to plan, would soon circulate from similar stands in newsagencies and pharmacies throughout the entire Blue Mountain area. Each card bore quite conspicuously his name (in white ink) and also his inimitable style, a mysterious air, owing in retrospect something to the deep burnt sienna of the prints, but going deeper, under the gums as it were to chalets beneath, as though a European principality had somehow been broken up and concealed in valleys and behind ferns, and the tourist game lay partly in the guessing where. Bridal Veil, Linda Falls, Ruined Castle, Orphan Rock (motto of the Paragon: 'Stands Alone' proclaimed each chocolate box) never looked, as amateurs had begun to discover to their surprise (and cost), quite as they did in prints by Manwaring, even when developed by Manwaring's workshop on Manwaring's plates. Indeed, through an examination of Manwaring's saturnine photography alone it was possible for the tourist to construct for himself a town, together with most of its environs and many of its inhabitants, if not the real Katoomba, in some ways preferable.

Less sunny perhaps, but infinitely more romantic. The tourist who bought Manwaring's cards took away in his memory a palimpsest on which Manwaring's account, written in the more durable script, was bound to prevail. Not that Manwaring loved the tourists—he detested them. After all, most who came to enjoy a stroll in crêpe or worsted along some mountain path were not liable to be moved to tears by the experience.

The local Chamber of Commerce had shown its appreciation of Manwaring's talents when, in the face of some vehement opposition, it had persuaded the Council to agree to a proposal (acknowledged to have originated in Manwaring) to floodlight during the tourist season certain of his favorite portraits—Leura Cascades, Katoomba Falls, the Three Sisters. And even the scheme's detractors had to concede in the result an imprevisible *power* totally alien to the transmogrification they had feared: it seemed that Manwaring touched the great pulse through no intention of his own. Sales of his floodlit portraits eclipsed sales of all his previous work combined. Of themselves, the floodlit sites became a considerable tourist attraction. Kodak advised the seeking of further outlets, and his wife shortly afterwards left him, aware that another year would see her husband's fortunes settled and hers with them.

Stirring his Turkish coffee, a black slurry in which the grounds had settled to fill half the cup, Manwaring's thoughts turned back to his daughter. The decision to place her in the convent had been his wife's—of all places, a Catholic convent —but he reflected with satisfaction that he would now reap the benefit of it. During the acrimony of the preceding weeks he had frequently asked: but if the girl meant so much to you, how come you sent her out of the house in the first place? A torrent of vituperation had always followed in which the question drowned. But now, in solitude, solace and creator of his broken marriage, he found again and again arising the spontaneous thought, an Excalibur out of the lake of his confusion: he had never been in favour of the scheme that removed from him his only child. Advantages—what greater advantages can any girl enjoy than a life with her own family? She'll be gone soon enough, he had stressed in frequent conversation on the topic with his friend Danny Evans—sixteen years goes so fast—how much longer is sixteen years at our age for example? Then an empty house and no chance of filling it. His premonition had been surprisingly accurate. But his wife hit cruelly at his social vulnerability—a question of social position, she called it. You want your daughter to go without the way you went without? God forbid that any daughter of mine should not be given every opportunity of growing up into a young lady. She'll get elocution lessons, piano, violin, dancing—everything you can't give her she'll get up at the convent.

But can't she be a day girl? He felt that he *had* gone without, though probably no more than most, constitutionally unable to defend himself against such charges. Yet his mother had done her best.

The advantages are after hours only and day girls are looked down upon. No—she must board.

So he had taken Janet from the primary school and personally enrolled her at the convent. In tears, both he and his daughter. The nuns, he suspected, were now attempting to convert her to the Catholic faith. If anything annoyed him about the place, it was this! But how his wife, penetrating in her insight, had laughed when he mentioned it to her!

Con*vert* her! From *what*?

It's a case where nothing could be better than something he replied, the issue already a sea of confusion for him. He left the room and stood in the empty bedroom where the passive outline of, for example, a wardrobe, gave him comfort. When people start to talk he used to say to his friend Danny Evans, I have to leave the room. Pray God I never suffer total blindness.

Janet, he'd said to her soon after her enrolment during one of their weekend walks together—the nuns are very nice and there's no doubt they know what they're doing, but when it comes to religion I'd like you not to listen too closely. As a matter of fact I asked that you be granted exemption from all religious observances, but the Holy Mother tells me it's out of the question.

She had smiled—in a way he didn't much like. On their very next walk she had a tiny crucifix around her neck, so small and depending from such a fine chain that had he not brushed it with his mouth on greeting her, he might never have noticed it at all. He would never have seen it. He realized it was the way of such objects to grow larger with time.

Sipping his coffee, he watched the sun come out to illuminate directly the face of the café. Several pensioners could soon be seen, drawn out from doorways like moths to loiter in their moth-eaten coats, staring at the fine display of chocolates in the Paragon window while waiting for the shops to open. Bread and suet, thought Manwaring, taken back to his own boyhood. It had become more penurious over the years. When the tourists were not there, Katoomba could be seen to have the oldest and poorest population of probably any town in New South Wales. How appropriate that he should have come to live there; and yet why? What had he ever done? Why should he be one of them? Not merely one of them, but able to anticipate desires yet inchoate in their ancient and diseased breasts. Worse than one of them. Floodlighting. He was not always unaware of the perilously delicate direction and condition of his art. Yes, there was something lacking, but what. Nothing he could supply, so why worry. *How* worry, when there was no *object* to the worry? A line of thought burrowed along for a while, then worried itself to death. Or died of exhaustion.

You're an old woman Manwaring, said Danny to him at regular intervals in their relations. After lodge meetings, over photographs—Danny being a photographer too—any occasion which could make Manwaring loquacious could make him mawkish. For though teetotal (in fact, a Rechabite from a prenatal undertaking—such motherly psychogenetic insight! Maybe, after all, not so insightful. All Manwarings feared alcohol, and those of the family who drank had apparently all become alcoholics. This was what his mother had told him. He saw them in his mind's eye, sprawled over Alpine trestles in high mountain inns, weeping through villages, pursuing innkeepers to relate a conviction that van-

ished at the lip or drowned in thick cakes of saliva. All that
he knew about the Manwarings he had from his mother.
His own father had died in an accident shortly before his,
Manwaring's, birth. The Swiss family Manwaring. Sometimes
Manwaring wondered whether he was not illegitimate and
the Manwaring family a complete concoction)—nevertheless,
talk and the reflection contingent in talk could make him so
drunk that he would frequently, after sufficient talk to a
sympathetic audience of one—a friend, his daughter, in error
his wife—display maudlin intoxication: yawn, stumble, weep.
His gait on his way home would grow provocative towards
ladies and his manner, to the trained hypothetical eye, infin-
itesimally less mild. His lenses afog with tears wrung it
seemed from no particular lament, but from the great
primordial ground of non-rational sorrow in which he seemed
cursed, thanks to his putative lineage (—with what strange
transplanted emotions was he confronting the mountain gums
and valleys he photographed? His jumble of emotion greyed
towards enlightenment)—with an inordinate subconscious-
ness. In vino veritas? Is a man more himself when drunk or
sober? The answer comes where the memory fails would
say Danny, no Rechabite, such a cunning aspect of the
brewer's art. Am I then proof of the wisdom or folly of drink,
thought Manwaring, raising himself high—high above the
highest pine on the highest ridge just for a second; looking
down into all saloons and public bars.

Such an old woman. He had probably said it first and
Danny taken the phrase up. But each time the cruel words
were uttered or recalled he realized their ever-deepening
pertinence. There were even times, quiet moments (if he
feared anything in his wife's departure it was quiet moments,
dark, quiet moments in which self disgust rose like bile to
fill his nights), when he wondered what in God's name lay
ahead of him. To Danny alone he made some half-cries for
help. Seeing in idolatry a rationale. Danny, he would say in
the man's unhearing ears; what am I to do? What is to
become of me?

Strange the old world ring his words had even for him. As
though it had all happened and been spoken of numberless

times. But Danny, whose face was generally supposed to have lost its capacity for expression in that apocryphal Welsh mine from which he had reportedly clambered and quit at the age of twelve—a fiction now believed even by himself—could only shrug and distort the corners of his mouth. The question, the *ground* behind the question—only posed when Danny was drunk—Danny would drink and Manwaring get drunken—seemed far too amorphous. As a Catholic, Danny might have advised Manwaring to see a priest. A church that flaunts its irrationality may be assumed to do so at least partially for the comfort of such men as Manwaring. But the local priest was an irrepressible man who drank heavily and followed the dogs, and the nuns, as Manwaring and Evens both knew, were sweet, docile women, whose religion consisted in rote learning and blind obedience. Still, much better for Janet that way. The Protestants were not worth worrying about. And Manwaring, however much he and his mother were Jews, regarded himself as a Protestant. He detested Catholicism. It would have been better to have seen a psychiatrist, better yet a neurophysiologist, but it was an age in which religion enjoyed a vogue. Still, see anyone Manwaring had a conviction, and it'll do you no good whoever you see. Interview the Holy Ghost, it'll do you no good. At least he thought not, he hoped not. He enjoyed his condition in a way. It predetermined him. And, or because, he had no questions really formulated.

As such an old woman about the town Manwaring might as well have worn a badge stating 'unclean'—fogged spectacles, timid abstentionist banter, yet with such mannerisms as, for example, the grasping of an acquaintance's arm or shoulder in no way *sexual*; in fact, by virtue of hinting at passions deeper than sexuality capable of terrifying the average male or female well and truly—excepting maybe a lump of self-styled Welsh anthracite like Danny—'unclean': and indigenes hastened atavistically from a contagion they could not possibly have contracted, and which, if they could have, in an as it were *innocuous* dose, might have benefited them immensely anyhow—so his spouse left, with a lavender handkerchief pressed firmly to her nose—and Manwaring squirmed over coffee. How distasteful. His bowels were going to cause him trouble again . . . same old story . . . He knew though that if he were unclean then the rest of the town had a right to wear the sign 'Proof Against All Manner Of Dirt'. Which would save a lot of misunderstanding all round. Silence some nasty tongues. Thoughts came down a vertex from early life; occasionally a voice advocating complete and total self reliance. Whose had that been?

See the gangrene? Live with it boy, be proud. Jealousy everywhere you look.

But he felt his nemesis, whatever it was, how*ever* it had to be described, closing in on him; a malaise of the spirit, inoperable. Thick like coffee grounds. There seemed no escape.

Go see a doctor, his wife's parting response from the bay window of the Bondi estate. She thought he had some cancer he wouldn't discuss. He'd used the word once in a figure of speech, and she'd fastened onto it.

A mutilating operation? I'd rather die whole, who wouldn't? He joked, tried to speak another language with certainty, but the only certainty now was that Janet would have him alone, a responsibility he thought he'd have preferred to do without.

Morning. The morning after. The morning after the morning after. A glance at his watch told him the pharmacy would now be open. He called over the proprietor, a Greek with a sigmoidal back and a wife who wore always an overcoat.

Mr Manwaring?

I don't think I can drink the rest of my coffee, Con. But I want you to know it's delicious. I have an upset stomach today or something.

Ah. Sorry to hear it. Some peppermint?

Constantine offered a peppermint—one on the house. Manwaring took it. In the gush of peppermint he longed to confide in Constantine that his wife had deserted him. But looking up he saw such sad immigrant eyes behind spectacles nearly as thick as his own, he was put off. Definitely not the right man to confide in . . . A miracle of self possession. Another alien. Blinking and sucking, Manwaring opened the doors to the café and walked the fifty yards or so up Katoomba Street to his studio. The postman's horse made hoof strikes on the pavement that echoed up and down the canyon walls.

Chapter 2

Now driving a car, Manwaring grimly and with much trepidation and grasping at the steering wheel ascended Victoria
Pass. The cooling water had already boiled twice and it was
feared quite reasonably by Janet, who was sitting next to her
father in her most beautiful summer dress, that the brakes
alone would not hold the car in the event of any further
stoppage, already imperative as judged by the clouds of
steam issuing from beneath the bonnet. They had mistakenly
left behind the wheel chocks at their second stop and to
return for them was, as her father had indicated, quite
impossible. A literal cart before the horse. Manwaring's fears,

in fact, were less of killing them all (Danny, unperturbed, sat puffing at his pipe in the back seat, one arm upon their hamper, enjoying the view towards Mount York), than of abusing his daughter for neglecting to collect the chocks, and thereby casting a pall on the picnic. Manwaring's knowledge of engines was such that he had no fear of the consequences of overheating in itself; he simply assumed that steam issuing from beneath the bonnet created an undesirable driving hazard. Anyway, there was no more water to be had.

Oh Daddy, cried Janet, can we *ever* make it to the top?

Manwaring raised his eyebrows, a gesture less quizzical than lugubrious, and anyway lost beneath the frames of his glasses. He thought it probable that they would—one generally muddled through—notwithstanding the groaning of the clutch, already engaged in first gear. He had been advised by the garage proprietor from whom he had rented the vehicle to ascend the pass backwards—there being a better purchase apparently in reverse than in first—but the prospect of having to steer while looking over his shoulder had daunted him too much. Approaching now the road to Mitchell's Ridge he knew they were almost there, they had almost made it. How hot the day was. And yet how simply the drays had ascended, onwards from the days of Cox. And in any weather!

Every Sunday, whatever the weather, Manwaring and his daughter spent their day together. It was their habit, their one tolerable day of the week. It was also a concession not generally made towards convent boarding pupils, but so adamant had been Manwaring at the time of Janet's enrolment, that the nuns, rather than lose her, had agreed to breach a point. The fact of her religion, or lack of it, had no doubt assisted them in this decision, as for the rest of the girls most Sundays consisted in religious devotions of one kind or another, with the occasional supervention of a strictly chaperoned stroll around the evening streets. Sometimes Janet and her father stayed at home in the flat, talking, looking at photographs and books on photography and consuming the never ending stream of food in lieu of love that came on trays from the kitchen. For the girl this was a cruelty that, irredeemably, neither Manwaring nor his wife fully appreciated, the tendering of her birthright as a Sunday treat, but luckily, it was the kind of hurt that awaits adulthood for its full implication to be seized upon. At other times, weather really permitting or not, they went for walks along the mountain trails (Prince Henry Walk, Federal Pass), with Manwaring forever scaling crags and pulling threads in his cloth to find the right angle—for he always took his camera with him, and if the day was right, then his photography had to take precedence, despite his great paternity, over their walk; a precedence that Janet, to her credit, never resented, knowing that the presence of the magic camera transmuted her father from the lolly-offering figure of fun that all her schoolfriends laughed at, to a figure of undeniable if indefinable status.

And sometimes Manwaring lavishly hired a car and drove his friend and his daughter, the only two fellow humans he loved, on a picnic. His wife habitually refused to leave the flat except to shop, a blessing neither he nor his daughter drew the other's attention to, but for which each felt deeply grateful. In order for Sunday to be selected as a picnic day, certain criteria had to be met: the day had to be fine (though preferably dull), Manwaring's bowels trouble free from at least the preceding Friday:—and a host of multifarious mental indefinables satisfied. In short, he had to feel really *good*, quiescent, he had to feel like going on a picnic. Regrettably, only one precondition had been met, and then only just, on the Sunday after his wife's grand gesture: it was indeed a beautiful cloudless day; the clarity of which, if the photographer approved, the man distrusted— an unfortunate dichotomy but seemingly inescapable—he felt distinctly unwell and had circumstances been in any way otherwise he would have known from the moment his eyes had opened that the day was no day for a picnic—a presentiment events were certainly confirming. Not yet eleven and already course altered twice and the car ready to stall at any instant. He hadn't yet told Janet of her mother's actions— (there had, of course, been talk from her of an intention of writing to Janet, but more probably she would wait until the end of term garnering spleen for an all out attempt to pluck the child from him forever)—and he wished to avoid telling her, at least for the present. Until, that was, he had sorted out how it was to be done. Until how it was to be done had, as it were, descended to him in bright print. The day would spell to Janet, he realized around six a.m., on first light through the blinds of his transfigured flat, either a walk or a picnic. And a picnic would be best, because Danny came on picnics, though not on walks, And Danny, even at his most taciturn, could draw a conversation away from dangerous straits by his very presence. Manwaring knew how very easily *he* could be washed away by the gentlest freshet. The poignancy of the situation might well overwhelm him.

The rataplan of the pistons increased as they surmounted the pass. Janet sighed a large feminine sigh of relief: start-ling Manwaring by this reminder of their merely physical jeopardy.

Never do that to me again Janet, he said in his severest tone after a short equipoising silence.

Sorry, she answered, regretting that he regretted the picnic: I don't know how I came to forget to pick them up.

No, no, insisted Manwaring, I don't mean the chocks: I mean that if you hadn't insisted on the Cox's River to begin with we'd never have had to go down the rotten pass in the first place.

But the Megalong will be best, said Danny, defacing the resultant hiatus: the girl was quite correct to change our minds. And what's our hurry anyhow? We have the whole glorious day before us.

He removed his pipe from his teeth as though to raise it in an affirmative gesture, but seemed to feel an impediment. Manwaring was poisoning the air.

At their customary picnic site on the Cox's River (they usually picnicked, on Manwaring's insistence, in such cold weather that ascending the pass created no difficulties)—there had been another car. Manwaring, on seeing this, had, in an action so uncharacteristically fast as to seem reflex, immediately turned the steering wheel hard about and still in gear put the car into a culvert. The explanation he gave, when eventually he extracted them, was that, intending to brake, he had depressed the accelerator in mistake for the clutch—a patent physical impossibility. His action at the wheel he could and did not comment upon and Janet, acting through instinct to protect this outburst of paranoid resentment, this remarkable but general obsession with privacy, smoothed away the incident by suggesting a return to the Megalong Valley instead. Not many were game to drive down to Megalong, and Manwaring, who fancied himself a bit of a driver, was more than happy to oblige.

It is on our way back after all, agreed Danny in his most irritatingly factitious brogue, thoroughly in compliance, a great lover of motoring for its own sake, shortly after they began back. But Manwaring still ached to vent some spleen at the turn the world was taking; he couldn't resist a parting shot at Janet.

—*I* didn't suggest the Cox, said Janet though, in simple truth and finality: *you* did. For answer Manwaring, once through Mount Victoria, opened the throttle until the bodywork of the vehicle shuddered. They continued thus all the way back to Mount Boyce. Danny opened his window the better to enjoy the stiff breeze. Janet sat quietly, too sensible a girl to sulk, her head averted, her hands upon her lap. Thirteen, darker even than her father and without his nose, bound to grow into a talent and beauty by any estimate. Pretty as a picture and so clever, so understanding, with it. They drove, Manwaring striving to control the car and at the same time, his bowels, his spleen, his gall—fearing as though at any moment he might burst asunder, puncture his hernia belt, shower youth's beauty and excellence with the unwholesome muck his aged guts were beginning, on their descent towards death, to secrete.

What we need, obtruded Danny, casting his customary block of granite upon the etiolations of Manwaring's silence: is a wireless in this car. Surely for what we pay (—he paid nothing) they could see their way to a wireless?

Manwaring, again at a loss, belched, took peppermint from the glovebox, opened the driver's side window, clenched his teeth, broke silent but malodorous wind.

A wireless is just what we *don't* want, he managed at last to reply, indignant at Janet and Danny though knowing that they couldn't know what he knew, if only because he hadn't told them—but leaving aside his wife, he was annoyed that they couldn't see his predicament. Was it *that* invisible? His more than physical agony? His failure to thrive?

We come on drives to get *away* from city noise and confusion, at least that's my idea of it.

Katoomba, the city.

2KA, Voice of the Mountains, said Danny. In alluding to the recently established radio station, his voice (the true voice of the mountains) expressed his pride, his beatitude in progress.

Manwaring began instinctively to concentrate upon the scenery. Focussing upon that which did not progress. So sharp, so *dazzling* was the sunlight that several times he had mistaken the shadows of the roadside guide posts for snakes. His nerves no doubt, but the lack of penumbra was uncanny —his professional interest was aroused: thank God: as if by autosuggestion his gastric agony subsided. At times Manwaring's nervous system did this to him, converting the neurasthenic into a giant optic nerve like the axon of a squid, unable to form judgements, incapable of understanding distinctions.

They crossed the line at Blackheath and turned left towards Shipley. Danny gazed foward in great good humour towards one particular weatherboard house, scrupulously maintained in white with a hedge of rhododendron, and requested that Manwaring blow the horn. This Manwaring refused to do, but Janet, grateful for the levity, began some persiflage over Danny's well known proclivity towards the fairer sex. Highly amused, the two of them proceeded to rupture Blackheath's Sunday morning silence with their laughter: Manwaring, the better to conserve fuel, had switched off the engine and was silently coasting, at not much better than walking pace, down towards the Megalong turnoff. Janet's laughter welded one extra link in a concatenation of bird song, mostly currawong, that edged the road and filled the sky: she soared above Danny, remarkably deep and extemporaneously sexual, forever shifting forward in his seat, to Manwaring's mild annoyance, to speak into her ear.

The saccadic scanning of Manwaring's eyes began to drop in frequency; the adumbration of his particular euphoria; at times, if left uninterrupted and for no particular reason, he could attain a trophotropic de-rousal towards the level of an overdose of tranquilizer—unfortunately, the hairpin bends on the descent into the Megalong Valley, in commanding his wholehearted attention, precluded any but the foretokening. But he knew it, recognized its approach, whatever it was— and it always lasted a day—was he going mad he wondered? Losing his sanity? He set about attempting to enjoy the sensation.

The car continued to descend, with the screeching of the brakes, and Janet's peals of excitement following their increasingly providential negotiation of each bend, sounding in the otherwise perfect stillness like the protracted rape of a bellbird by a currawong. As Manwaring had still not switched on the ignition, the brakes faded towards their mid-descent, and the resultant pitch and rate at which they rounded corners created the occasion for increasing ribaldry between the passengers, who took the car's speed as evidence for Manwaring's improving, if characteristically maladroit and avuncular, high spirits. Naive of cars and their hazards, trustful of her father, Janet, joined soundlessly by Danny, continued in her reckless tossing about; Manwaring, meantime, a man on the edge of a trance, continued to strike for admission on the door of his other world. His lips quivered, his eyes moistened. Relentlessly, he wrenched at the wheel. Janet shrieked a warning to him as a lyre bird, tail erect, sprinted across the road before them. Danny, with considerable *sang-froid* under the circumstances, attempted to draw attention to the fantastic white palisades of the Hydro on the Medlow Bath bluff a thousand feet above. But Manwaring scarcely heard; he stared ahead of him as though through sheer concentration he was confining their centre of gravity over the perilous track. Mermaid Cave on the left. Down through the rainforest. They made it, and stopped. Looking back, towards the thicker forest above, they

saw the clouds of dust they had raised hovering like a
rebuke above the road. It was so still; not so much as a
breath of wind. Beside a huge tree and still in the rainforest
they gently opened the doors. And stood looking around
them. The car was covered in dust. Both men thought with
concern, Manwaring in a maternal daze, of the photographic
equipment in the boot.

Well, said Danny with approbation: quite a precipitous
descent you gave us there, Manwaring. Nothing like a car
for safety.

No, I don't suppose so, said Manwaring, his eyes now
relentlessly in scan, searching the forest, the plain below, in
the manner of a threatened gazelle.

Come on Daddy, said Janet, taking his unresisting hand
and making as if to embark upon a trek. But, flaccid and
languid as his hand felt, she could not make it move.

Raising his head and flaring his nostrils, he sniffed the air.
What is that I smell, he asked. Not barbecue I hope Evans?

Evans disclaimed responsibility, but agreed it was barbecue.

No, not barbecue: probably something dank in the forest,
said Janet, tired of mollifying them.

I say we go down to the creek and set ourselves up there,
said Danny, growing restless himself. Never mind about
barbecues up here, it's far too dark. On the other hand, there
is the chance of a few good shots on a day like today down
by the creek.

It was unanimously agreed upon, once they were all back
in the car, that the rainforest, floored under its panoply of
tree fern and liana in a perpetual mulch of rotting fronds and
leaves and reticulate with streams of about six inches width
and depth, was too dangerous a proposition for Manwaring's
plaid rug, even thrown upon the rare clearing. Besides; each
man had remarked with great, with over*whelming* candour
and satisfaction, upon the prettiness of Janet's dress, which
they did not wish to see dirtied. Indeed, Janet's pretty dress
had been, the whole drive out, their staple of conversation.

They continued down (Manwaring now holding the car
in first gear, so that they descended at a veritable crawl as

detrimental in its way to the clutch as their previous descent had been to the brakes)—and eventually rainforest gave way to rough pasture of a sort and the familiar tall eucalypts where the land had not been cleared, and here and there on the cleared ground grazed pollard Herefords. The sun beat down less frequently obstructed, with the sharpness of new autumn and the heat of summer. Yet—and this Manwaring had somehow sniffed out up in the forest, as a dog might a bitch in heat—there was something un*canny* in the quality of the light on the valley floor. It had a *golden* quality, not uncommon at dawn on bedroom walls (slat-patterned) and rocks in the unpolluted high mountains—(Megalong, though a valley floor, was still well above sea level and the air limpid like that over the ridges, though lacking to an extent the blue haze due to eucalypt oil found in the other valleys)—but un*usual* at midday. Manwaring could not remember it quite so remarkably golden at that hour. He glanced continually at his fob watch in disbelief. Janet noticed that both Danny and Manwaring were beginning to fidget and glance at their fob watches. And in fact, predictably for Janet, when eventually they arrived at the creek—Manwaring had to be reminded to stop there—having driven the car up a steep bank to hide it, for privacy's sake, behind some wattles, the first items to be removed from the boot were the cameras and the photographic paraphernalia generally—quite bulky too—not the foodstuffs.

Can't we eat first, pleaded Janet, ravenous adolescent, but Danny and Manwaring had, each in a vaguely comical manner, stepped away in differing directions from the car towards the perimeter of wattle and tea tree, cameraless, gingerly, like figures on a moving film. They stepped as though on a foreign planet, confident of their mass, uncertain of their weight. Once or twice she saw them look at one another in an obsessively neutral manner, betokening she imagined, great wonder and curiosity. But at no time did their glances synchronize.

Curious colour in the sky, said Danny at last, breaking an awkward silence with less than the epiphany he felt it merited, returning for his tripod, now quite bathed in gold.

The sort of tint you expect in the Mediterranean area. (At once the mystery seemed appropriately accounted for by all —but the sensation of *adequacy* faded . . .). Quite bizarre. And then he spoke to Janet, setting up his tripod as he spoke.

I'd like *you*—(and your father if he'd be so kind)—to stand over there near that tea tree.

Manwaring could now only just be seen from the car, making his way incongruously (suit and hat) but certainly through a stand of wattle, in a hesitant but determined manner.

Danny had specialized in portraiture, Manwaring confined himself as far as he could to landscape. It was in part this lack of common ground that permitted no taint of professional hubris to mar their friendship, and indeed, their eventual choice of specialization (for they were the only professional photographers in the upper mountains) had probably developed a little through a desire not to encroach upon each other's territory, if mainly through temperamental proclivity—Manwaring was ill at ease with people while Danny enjoyed them to excess—for Manwaring *had* taken portraits, and Danny landscapes, but each had, as though by agreement, ceased to do so. There was no future in it, that much each could see. Manwaring's subjects, in Danny's eyes, stood stiff and unpliant, resentful of their backdrops, while, to Manwaring, Danny's nature studies were stultified and barren sets, devoid of interest, dull as the Nullarbor, awaiting to eternity the entry of a subject. For his living, Danny stood with tripod and camera and equipped with black, burnous-like hood on the steps at Echo Point, nearby a man sized red mountain devil (head shaped to resemble the luciferean nut of the mountain Lambertia), of his own construction, next to which, with much hucksterism, he posed his usually juvenile subjects. Mount Solitary across the Jamieson Valley in the rear, but it was not Manwaring's Mount Solitary as far as Manwaring could see. But no matter.

Manwaring appeared not to hear Danny's plea to pose, or else chose to ignore the first call and the second.

*Dad*dy!

The third call came from Janet, and that made all the difference.

The sense of paternal duty, the only emotion that conflicted with Manwaring's instinctive *urge* towards the bush (one could imagine him emerging totally naked at some point further down the valley having shed clothing along the way by means of some purely natural process), brought him back out of the bushes to the car. He kept looking anxiously at the sky—as indeed did Danny, now busying himself with an exceedingly complicated and archetypical light meter—fearing that at any moment luminal normality might reassert itself in all its new-seen mediocrity. Yet it did not, and Manwaring for one knew it *would* not—so slowly moves the sun, the only apparent parameter implicated—no cloud whatsoever in the sky—he had, over and above, the feeling that the luminal phenomenon would last the day out with his euphoria and vanish in the dusk wherein his euphoria would also vanish, hurling him back into his habitat; the world of quotidian triviality. He intended to keep Janet at home with him that night, at least it was an inchoate plan he had nurtured, and explain to her the startling new domestic situation. That would make the nuns think, for it was his wife who had been the Catholic. In the meantime, the preternatural illumination had drawn the attention even of Janet.

Why is it so *golden* Daddy?

How the devil should I know, said Manwaring with immense ill grace as he sought to obey the imperious directives of Danny's shutter-free hand, issuing from a hunched shoulder already draped in a cloth so black it soaked up one patch of their precious gold like a cerement thrown down from the cliff; ordering him hither and thither, now to his daughter's left, next to her right. Next he made them move up and down the rise. Nor could he altogether dispense with his customary commercial patter.

Watch the little birdie, he cried fluttering several hoary fingers and simultaneously shuffling his feet in a dance-like measure to Janet's spontaneous amusement but Manwaring's growing impatience.

Get on with it man—Manwaring found himself irresistibly falling into Danny's pellucidly affected brogue—I've pictures I want to take myself.

The shutter was at once depressed and the plate—which Manwaring would later develop—imprinted for all perpetuity. Regrettably, none of the golden light would be able in any way to be captured on film, a fact both photographers seemed suddenly, as though with the depression of the shutter, simultaneously to appreciate—in a silent, impotent despondency. Ah, if there were only some way of capturing *colour* on film! At least in the dawn the shadows were long. But at the present, the noon, with the sun directly at its meridian and no extent in the umbral worth mentioning, how could they record the singularity of this one day over all other cloudless days? Days of like luminous intensity but not golden? Who would believe them later? Who could know what the light had been like? Who . . . ? Breaking from the pose—(the photograph, a complete failure, subsequently disclosed a scowling and incipiently shifting Manwaring, eyes half closed in exasperation, and Janet very acutely and slyly conscious of her dress, displaying it with her hands in a semi-curtsy; on her face even more strongly than usual for some reason an expression of her naive, open-lipped narcissism—infuriatingly sexual) Manwaring moved down the rise.

I think you mucked it up chaps, you moved just as I pressed the shutter, said Danny reproachfully to Manwaring. But Manwaring was rapidly gathering his own gear in order to get out before being imposed on again.

Well that may be, but it's only my impatience to get up the creek myself, he answered. How long can these conditions last? I'll be back shortly: Janet dear—I can leave you with Danny to get the dinner on can't I?

He stood for the moment, his hand already holding back a branch of the peripheral tea tree, ready to leave, his face, directed towards his daughter, displaying a sweet, impish, costive smile. It vanished as he turned, and he went away.

He's like a busy little boy, thought Janet, and he wants *me* to be his mother. It was not fair to have so unfatherly a father on top of so unmotherly a mother. At length though, with Danny, she set about finding sticks to set their fire with; but in no great urgency, because they both knew they couldn't expect to see her father for at least an hour, and that when he did come he would sit, hardly speaking, not hungry, a thorough wet blanket and drugged with the efforts of his labours and the certain knowledge that virtually none of them would seep through to emerge in those finished products, those final prints. By rights his efforts at times like these ought to have yielded masterpieces, but they did not, and, notwithstanding everyone else's opinion to the contrary, he knew they never would. It seemed in vain to examine vexatiously his equipment (for who had better?), to rebuke in themselves his sere, beloved landscapes. The fault had to be supposed to be within himself: That was the rule. But *how* to grope? *What* to grope after? On the other hand, the ardor, the *venery*, seldom eluded him. What every development denied, each fresh plate promised anew.

Shortly after moving from view of the car Manwaring laid down his camera very cautiously and urinated behind a bush. Perhaps some of his restlessness had owed its origin to a distension of the bladder, he reflected; how just like life that would be—but *no*; covering the moist soil catlike with leaves, he walked down to the creek, to sprinkle, in a hygienic gesture, some water upon his hands: it was a dirty business. *No*, he felt as strong a sense of urgency towards the landscapes awaiting him up the creek as ever. Happily, he began again with considerable stealth; stalking he knew not what. The creek was clear and cold and pouring amongst boulders smooth and gilt in the sun like nuggets. A view down across the creek, framed by gums, on one side the rough pasture constituting a holding, with mountains in the background—and the sky above—would make (if somewhat an unoriginal for him) a *glorious*, a classical study—but for some reason Manwaring was not even tempted that day. His breath came quickly in excitement as he moved on through the scrub. It was as though he could smell out a subject further down; perhaps a vista at present unimaginable to him would await him in all its splendour, in the way that such vistas have of suddenly unfolding, hidden on a walk trodden countless times and equally possibly by countless men with cameras, around a corner, under a bush, it would be there. Glorious natural surroundings flora and fauna. It was true that the end result was generally, in fact inevitably a disappointment, but with the equipment available to him what else could it be? Clumsy great glass plates, wretched choice of light and contrast—he too had to accept the limitations of his medium, just as in walking he had to accept the limitations of his rapidly eroding body (for which he felt a violent disliking). That there lay no choice in the matter didn't make it any the easier to accept.

He knew of a bridle path a little way up from the creek on its more bushy side, and determined to use it. His sense of urgency must have been extreme to outweigh his natural reluctance to be caught in the bush, because riding parties from the Hydro frequently sauntered up and down the creek, and indeed some of the horse dung on the track seemed quite dangerously fresh. He stopped to examine one especially conspicuous and odious residue, composed largely of what he took to be undigested chaff. While it did not steam, as he believed fresh horse dung would, he felt that if he were to take it in, for example, his hands, he would find it warm to the touch, far warmer than could be accounted for by spontaneous combustion, or the heat of the sun which was falling full upon it. And suddenly, something about the *colour* in the day, a reverie, the dung, the golden . . . made him feel well within him the familiar urge, crying to escape, an urge sometimes interpretable as one to soil his hands, a lust towards unity, piercing the gaiety of his hunting mood like a well flung outsider's spear, more beautiful in its construction than his own: Sometimes, when similarly possessed, he chopped wood in the yard at the back of the flats till his bones ached. In death, to gasp out: well flung, sir. Removing his camera by its strap for the second time and laying down the rest of his photographic impedimenta, he stooped down, then finding this tiresome, squatted, and picking up one lump of dung, held it in his hands and with all the fascination of a three year old for his own motions began to knead it, admiring the variety in its texture, a veritable diapason from liquid to quite literal granite. What these horses eat. It was indeed warm and fresh. He inhaled deeply of its aroma, not so really unpleasant. Pleasant? Unpleasant? His poise on the verge vanished as thought or reflection led him further along what seemed to him by now a familiar tram track he could well afford to uproot. His daughter Janet was keen to own a horse, but, aside from the preclusive practical difficulties (the nuns, for instance, would never countenance it), he considered it, as befitted a man of his age and disappointment in life, quite improper for a girl at or about her menache to sit astride a horse. So. Laying down the dung and giving his hands a perfunctory and self-defeating wipe together, he moved forward once more into what breach he wondered, what further follies. Don't make too much of this episode, his inner voice cautioned in reference to euphoria and its attendant strange vagaries, interpret it and it pales into enigma, leads to self-reproach . . . But there persisted *physical* proof, for how his hands now badly needed washing! Curious emotions rolled around, self-mockery alternating with despair. Something to do with the countryside. Yet to reach the creek, though its song, its golden, joyous, infinitely winsome and beguiling song still filled his ears, was now far from convenient. Soon, the faltering of his steps predicted, this transcendental earthlust, this suspension of all normal taboo-etched behaviour that had permitted him to clasp the horse dung would vanish, and the odour on his camera and accoutrements, when he came to manipulate them as he knew he soon must, would later just stink, just that and no more, in his nostrils and embarrass him not to mention Janet and Danny. Euphoria of its nature left no trace but took up where it left off in another time, another context, didn't take a barbecue into its account, as though belonging to another scale of consciousness, another scheme of things entirely. The ineffable stillness of the valley at high noon, made him when he stopped walking look upwards at the trees, their silvery leaves. A flock of darting silver-eyes with tinkling bell chirpings created the only interruption in his silence, and their movements, outside of his own footsteps and the unavoidable snapping of the occasional twig as he brushed by it and broke it off, the only movement outside of the still moving stream. He could not see clearly, even with his powerful glasses, but it was all in front of him, far too clear and bright for his liking, in fact he liked, he had always liked, the duller days better. He felt, increasingly, and at the moment, overwhelmingly, less mockery in the duller day, golden days seemed meant for golden youths, a pox upon them, and he had to admit a more than trifling discomforture as he stood there, which did not emanate from his bowels entirely but from the knowledge rather of his age and ugliness. Yes, they should have been relative, quite meaningless qualities there in the bush and in the absence of present comparison, but they were not, they remained inflexibly absolute, quite indelible. His heart sank at this insight, so he was only a grey lick-spittle from his maker's mouth. And everywhere the forest existed to mock and mirror him. There was something freshly unendurable about a day so horribly perfect—something in him leapt in a familiar response, but the wall of total *enlightenment* he could not surmount: He leapt, leapt like an exhausted hare darting at a fence, conscious of his fibre weakening, his chance of escape, pursuit, whatever—lessening. In some strenuous earlier leaps during full maturity though he had taken maybe some glimpses over the other side: that was when they had all least understood him . . . Insanity, drunkenness—his soul was not up to them, couldn't take these prescribed cathartics. His green supposed motherland would only create in him, he knew, agonies of repugnance, which was why he had shown, to his mother's regret, no semblance of interest in the place . . . But why think of this now? Better to eke out existence here, he had reasoned, amongst these ugly yet strangely familiar spindles, these low, wretched, weathered cones and beaks of mountains, absolute travesties by international standards. But God, determined never to be taken lightly, could lazily create even of this valley something too beautiful for him to withstand. His inadequacy petulantly rattled round in the beauty of fresh Megalong like a marble in a bottle; and of course he had to hunt for the dung heaps.

Too much thinking, thought Manwaring, too much mute change and alteration in life style—and look at the change in a man. Once I could have had true happiness here, but since Friday, a veritable quantum leap back, a change came over me, and I am no longer even a simulacrum of Adam in Eden. Henceforward, my landscapes will probably resemble those of the tourist: desultory, and verging on uninterest. From being merely *vaguely* unpleasant and discomforting, fine days are now intolerable, a large, leering rebuke on the part of the cosmos that I can no longer, never mind find, but not even properly *seek* rest.

Yet the fact remained: even on the mountains there was bound to be the occasional bright day. So where to next? Van Diemen's Land, final outpost and assignment, *anus mundi?*

Aware only of a regret that he had not kept the stinking dung about him in its entirety, perhaps thrust it into a pocket which was probably what God had wished, he began back down, back down the track, off the bridle path again (too obvious), back towards the creek. A journey of probably less than twenty yards. And then he heard a noise made by a horse, or possibly more than one horse. Which stopped him dead in his tracks. Until he heard the disturbingly proximate whinnying of this horse, he had not been worried about how far up the track he could go in anonymity. It certainly stopped him in his tracks, it brought him up sharply. He stopped, dead in his tracks. The stream, the silver-eyes, then again the voice of the horse. Ne-igh-hg! Manwaring's hands began suddenly to stink. Also to shake when the horse's foot stamped down heavily. A task of Hercules for him not to bolt straight back to the barbecue. But adrenalin filled him, rooting him on the spot. He lay down in the mud, terrified yes, but feeling certain that either his prey was closing in on him, or he on it. Or did it matter, or did it have a meaning at all. A voyeur again, sneaking up on adults. Near-novel sensations. The most recent incidence of this behaviour since around the age of eleven, this recidivous cat. A pataphysical joke? Death in the offing, a recapitulation in the manner of a drowning on this day, this chosen day, in this gold. He

flashed out a quick response to fate's suggestion, which was
—before I get home tonight the car I predict will roll off
the road back up and I shall drown in six inches of water,
head depressed by progressive metals, noises rushing in my
ears like laughter. The wrong response, came the voice, guess
again, *keep* guessing. *No*, said Manwaring of the many
voices, too impatient to keep guessing for a lifetime any
longer: prefer now to rush in sight unseen, message misunderstood. Golden beauty had unriveted him at last.

For a while he lay until his breathing came less loudly:
ugly, ugly breath. Then he began ludicrously creeping
towards the horses—he reckoned them only about fifty yards
or less up the track, which shortly in front of him (for it was
only a few yards to his right) curved sharply to avoid a
fallen tree too big an obstacle for any horse to negotiate in
a leap—wondering if this was indeed the source of the scent
he had seemed to scent all the way from Mount Boyce. His
photographic equipment trailed ventrally beneath him ruff-
ling the leaves—in fact it would have been quieter to walk
—but nothing in comparison to the silver-eyes, now above
him in profusion. Crawling, span almost complete? Dharma
wheel about on the recycle? His terror had banished all
thought he might have had of seeking time out to wash his
brown, malodorous hands, so close now to his adequate nose
as he crawled. Indeed, it was as if their stench made him
more feral, he likened them in his mind to the ochre mark-
ings on the warlike aboriginals.

Even a lion will turn from an aggressor to lick itself clean,
but Manwaring had no feeling for such diversions. The
bush through which he made his clumsy way was totally
dry a foot or two above the ground, yet the ground through
which he crawled was waterlogged. By now he was liberally
coated in mud as well as horse dung. The rains of the
recent weeks, and it took time for the vegetation to respond,
quite properly, had left the ground saturated. Although he
had spent, as it seemed to him, a lifetime in the bush, he
knew the botanical name of no plant, nor had he any
curiosity of any scientific sort whatsoever. He did not know
which berries were poisonous and which were not. Or

which wood he could burn wet, or any bushlore at all. If dropped in the middle of one of his favorite valleys he would have perished in a week or less: and if there was something shameful in all this ignorance and no doubt there was, then how come he had theretofore understood no rebuke from the forests as he went about his photography? He had to be deaf as well as blind. To be a monkey or a wild man or even a pioneer necessitated no camera, but a rapacious intent. Without his camera he was scarcely even a man. An empty tripod. He had heard that such was the patience of aboriginals that they would wait for up to a week for one another at preordained meeting places, having no closer way among themselves of specifying a tryst. He had felt envy. But at that moment, while crawling, he lost his own awareness of time altogether. And naturally did not notice. The irony of it. The forest, like a woman, probably preferred him on his hand and knees.

He continued through the bush, which he was seeing for the first time as a mere obstruction; that is, he did not see it very well at all. Then at once, in a sort of clearing ahead of him, he saw horses, two, tethered to a tree on the far side. He recoiled—these were the ones to be wary of, they would sniff him out first. Probably take him in his present condition for one of their own. How humourous. But even myopic Manwaring could see they were nought but two riding school hacks, bent in the middle and utterly contemptuous no doubt of human intrigue. Chosen perhaps for this very purpose. People who ride such horses take no notice of them irrespective of what sort of ruckus they kick up, because they don't understand the ways of horses as Manwaring did, which is, through instinct.

Then he saw two people, a man and a woman, both young. They were standing almost directly between the horses and himself, locked in a standing embrace. For some reason, this surprised him. Perhaps because the horses were at the far side of the clearing he had expected to find their riders in it. In fact, they were on the near side of the clearing and the clearing was empty. They stood, awkwardly striving to maintain a doomed vertical stance, part way in and out of the bushes, evidently seeking instinctively some camouflage in what they proposed. He listened to their occasional foot shifts, then, without thinking about it, stood up an order to be able to see them more clearly. Just by turning they could have seen him, but they didn't turn. The girl had on jodhpurs and a sweater the colour of a tank. Occasionally the horses looked across at all three of them. There was a verbal silence—an occasional word of conversation between the lovers perhaps, thought Manwaring, but no; they were beyond words. Only the sound of the stream, and the restless champing of the horses, and the footsteps of the lovers, and the silver-eyes. If there had been speech, it would not have surprised Manwaring to have heard a foreign tongue. Calmly he picked up his camera with his filthy hands, and waited. And as the couple's foreplay intensified and it became apparent that they intended to copulate, he suddenly, in once fine burst of liquid gold, and to his great surprise, ejaculated into pants already stiffening in mud and dung.

If he could have smiled he would have—but he knew instead he would laugh. Loudly. He felt good. He didn't laugh, instead he became extremely serious, all eyes. He watched as the youth with great clumsiness removed the girl's sweater and brassiere and watched her breasts tumble out. He was glad then that his own irrelevant appetite had already been sated, because in his objectivity her breasts seemed to him the very items the sunlight had been searching for—lasciviously the gold stretched into them, clasped them even more hungrily than did the man, getting between his fingers, an interloping Manwaring followed. The man cried out as if in exasperation, began to grab at the breasts, and to lick them. The whole sublime business seemed then to take on an atmosphere just a little ridiculous and Manwaring found himself able to take a photograph. The considerable noise of his fossicking about seemed not to be noticed: the lovers' senses were quite dead, save to one another. Manwaring felt that they would probably have smiled across at him anyway, lazy golden smiles that would drift like blown kisses, there was such good humour in the air. He would have smiled back. He felt an entitlement, like a tree trunk, or, alternatively, they seemed a mirror to him—as in a stream, he saw in them his own reflection. Suddenly, he realized they were totally naked and serious, thoroughly documented, and in the beginnings of full intercourse. Gently, slowly, he watched what he could see of the man's lance, the girl making the softest of moaning noises throughout. How this endeared her to Manwaring and her lover both. It did not seem as if it could be their first act of intercourse for the day, so prolonged were their agonies, so long a time did it take for them to ascend to a climax. When it came, it was well nigh perfect and mutual (or as far as Manwaring could judge, having never seen a woman in orgasm before), and at another time he might well have been extremely jealous of their obviously thorough knowledge of one another— he even had a sudden horrible thought that they might be man and wife! But it was improbable, they were both so very young, and there were no stretch marks anywhere on the girl's gleaming, sweat-enchanted skin . . . During intercourse, they had frequently and with a terrible urgency altered their relative dispositions, and Manwaring had tried to catch each nuance. Finally, he had photographed the girl coiled in a last, pleading *fellatio* over the dead Priapus (her buttocks, damascened with clutch marks and bearing twig impressions then full towards him)—and found himself out of plates. He sat down abruptly in relief; it did not occur to him to consider whether he had been acting correctly in photographing an act of intercourse—it had simply seemed the natural thing to do, and so he had done it. Recrimination did not enter his head. As a matter of fact, when the girl had stepped, with magnificent aplomb, out of her pants (her face with its ineffable expression of disdainful concupiscence startling in its resemblance to one of Janet's habitual faces), the first waftings of her smegma mixed in with the eucalypt oil—pheramone no doubt responsible for his own gratuitous climax—had been instantly recognizable to him as the very scent he had tracked all the way into the valley. He was all nose, he always had been. He was proud too to have traced his scent so unerringly to its provenance—and even beyond, because, not strangely, when stretching up his neck he saw the two, finally replete, laying in one another's arms, he found himself in tears—there had been, he had undergone —what? A wrenching, a tickling, there had been an impetus like the sloughing of a cicatrice within him which seemed to create a painful plenum out of area that had previously been all vacuum. He had diverted primal energies into himself, and vaguely understood that he would later have to take the consequences; but they, more painful still, could wait. For the moment, enjoyment only. He badly wanted to walk across and embrace the two of them lying there, his children, to thank them with all his heart. However something warned him that the man would spring up from another world and kill him, strangling out a mad laugh. Don't die just yet, continued to caution his inner voice of conscience, sneak away successfully and stick around, live a little. Perhaps you deserve it, this one last fling.

He turned in sudden disrupting consternation at the immediacy of what he'd left behind—the barbecue! How dreadful if Danny and Janet were to come searching for him up the bridle trail! Looking over, he saw that the amorous couple had lazily arisen and, making no attempt to gather their clothes, were wandering hand in hand and with much delicacy for the lady's feet, down towards the creek. No doubt going for a swim. He fought a sudden impetus to race downstream and drink. When he judged them well away, however, he beat his way instead back out to the path—stumbling over the vine of a paddy melon as he did so—and hurriedly began back to the car. Acting to cut off any intruders. He wished a few minutes later he had kept one plate if one plate only for the expression on his daughter's face as he thrust his leering, freshly Pan-like visage, stinking terribly, through the boscage on the camp's perimeter. Danny was standing some yards further down, his back to Janet as he lit a pipe, as though lighting a pipe constituted some sort of indecency. She screamed, and

Manwaring laughed. A laugh they had hardly expected from him, and at which he himself was astounded—and not a little proud. It was so gutsy and so earthy, it seemed like a second ejaculation catching him unawares.

Had a little accident people, he explained. You'll have to excuse me if I wear my rug on the way home.

He later wrapped up his trousers (filthied in a fall, as he put it) and buried them in the sand. The night was altogether different, filled with low, reasoning tones as he and Janet discussed what they had to discuss concerning their future and their past.

Chapter 3

What worries me most, said Manwaring one evening three weeks later, quite his old self again, is the possibility of falling in love with another woman—if you can imagine that. I don't think I would want to go through with it.

Danny, suppressing amusement at Manwaring's choice of the word love to describe his relationship with his wife, took a pipe from his mouth, and said: There's no need to marry them you know. I have managed very successfully without that. When you speak of going through with it, do you mean marriage?

Yes, I'm afraid I do.

Danny knew his friend well. Manwaring meant marriage all right, he loved the very thought of marriage. Love and marriage, hack and trap. Something terribly amiss in his upbringing—perhaps his mother, in herself a surfeit of women?—but nothing he could put a precise finger on. An imprecise fist suggested itself instead, but how come anyway this nympholepsy for married bliss? Why so, why why why? Is it impossible to learn through experience? That morning he had seen in the mirror, for the first time, clearly, as with unscaled eyes, not knowing whether to laugh or scream at the effect, how even his *physical profile* was beginning to resemble a question mark. Time was quite short and life was very precious—too precious to waste any longer. His own marriage, horseless carriage in the modern tradition, had been singularly free of love from its consummation; he had apparently battered any physical existence it may have had into a moribund pulp with his early clamorous hungerings to subdue the *physical* i.e., that which he had seen as merely the giant outside the castle guarding over the *spiritual* inside . . . an attitude the utter falsity of which he was in the midst, he felt, of perceiving now, and which provided his days now with possibly their only strength. The body *was* the mind—but how painful it made looking in the mirror, what a joke it made of his life-long parlour games! The physical side of his marriage he remembered as his wife's eyes—not her breasts or anything else—her eyes; filled with misunderstanding and dumb resignation, her dumb, wounded eyes. Intending only caresses he had inflicted manifold hurts on her, like the ham-fisted ogre of a fairy story. He might easily have seen in his release—just that, a release, and looked foward to a lifelong swearing off. But his emotions towards his wife had never been released, and his feelings towards marriage never adequately expressed. He could see a woman he loved easily consuming his lifetime, twenty-four hours a day, a dangerous, time wasting situation. Perhaps he had really missed his mark entirely, perhaps he had really been intended as a great lover. Mercifully, such insights come too late. The question was though, what are women *after*? Or was it perhaps a

mistake to consider them generically at all. His mistake with
his wife had lain in supposing that she had felt as he had.
What an odd woman she had been too, how hard to draw
out emotionally. A judicial separation had been arranged, in
deference to the strictures of her religion—already, so soon
. . . though he often wondered what religion represented for
her, and why she had clung, with such fervour, to a church
so full of simony, venality, hagiolatry—words failed him—
as almost to stand as the perfect example of that which it
stern-in-the-face each Sunday stood to condemn. Is all the
world mad but I? Or am I blind to what all the rest of the
world see in painless clarity. The spiritual side of her nature
—if indeed she possessed one, which he would have doubted
but found himself forced to deduce—was hidden, always
kept jealously from him, a miniscule back-of-the-moon to his
full-flowering turgid sun. He supposed it represented to her
what life itself represented for him, for every Sunday had
seen her at mass, piously clasping her psalter and reciting
gibberish; only instead of world-sickened *Weltschmerz* as in
his own case (Janet had been begotten, as through prayer,
in an explosion of desperate, viable, seed, maybe his last
viable seed)—she had clung to a crass, blind meliorism, in
which all went to Heaven who could be frightened into
kowtowing to a few oversimplified rules and regulations—
and that, of course, excluded him: how infinitely more
appealing he personally found those heresies that promised
annihilation to the devout and rebirth to the reprobate!
Marriage was adjured, divorce proscribed. So that was that.
He had married the first adult claimant to his affections, a
Catholic, vulnerable as a wide-eyed bream amidst a school
of sharks, and now, if he wanted divorce and the obloquy it
would bring him, he would have to fight for it. Janet had
astounded him by initially expressing a preference for seeing
them divorced—but he later suspected only because of the
added status that probably accredited to any child of
divorced parents in the baby blue eyes of her peers—he
certainly wanted it. Janet later renegued. But one part of
him (the tiny voice of reason) recognized judicial separation
as a most convenient damper really, a ready-made mora-

torium on all his perenially callow yearnings, his massive capacity for implicating himself in undesirable situations.

I don't have your tough mind Danny, but how the deuce I wish I did!

Was that enough? Such false fervours . . .

You're your own worst enemy Manwaring—Danny had a million clichés ever at his lips, forthright, he never spared another man's feelings if he could help it—if you want to be tough, *be* tough and stop this miserable puling . . . Kick them out of your bed and tell them to go to the blazes. They'll respect you the more for it you'll find. They're quite perverse, and at your age you shouldn't be thinking in terms of young girls. There are plenty of married ladies of about our age whom you will find not averse to a little side issue. I'm speaking perfectly frankly now. In fact, I'll defy you to name one whom, when approached in the correct manner, would offer resistance of more than a token nature!

Leering foward, as good as his word and about as ponderously platitudinous, he stared in defiance at Manwaring, with just a hint of a fear that Manwaring caught but did not understand and could no longer be bothered with. If Manwaring had said for example, my wife, what would have Danny answered then?

But it was useless. Manwaring's most immediate problem lay not in getting them out of bed but in getting them into it. He broke into a despondent laugh—such advice his friends gave him! If approached in the correct manner! Was it not obvious a *lifetime* of experience lay in that disingenuous phrase, impossible ever to be translated! What is this difference, he would have liked to have asked Danny only he could never phrase things rightly; what is this difference at this level which purports to call a prick a prick and the one as good as the next—between the next prick and the one? And don't try to deny that the difference exists, because it represents *all* that is different between you and I! So while obviously I lose, I win in this sense: *you* cannot satisfactorily lock out the heart and turn yourself into a complete non-man and non-animal, because who goes into even a brothel blindfold? We make love when we are lonely, and seek to create more company for ourselves, and everyone knows that the best company is family . . . And to cross out the *love* in the making love is to me like trying to enjoy freewheeling your pushbike down a steep mountain in the morning knowing you will have to trudge it back up that night—it may or may not be the correct approach but some people just cannot manage it. *Finis.*

But he said nothing. Sex was warfare, Danny a shirker, to have seen the sets of animated genitalia out-thriving, out-living their caballeros to insinuate themselves into their inevitable household pre-eminence—this was the fortunes of war. But Manwaring seemed forever prepared to back into the breach.

They were having an evening drink in Manwaring's now filthy flat. Manwaring, settled under Danny's protective aegis, was beginning to acquire a taste for liquor. Danny, seizing the opportunity, had set out to make a man of Manwaring. The very manner in which he approached his task though told Manwaring the difficulties he foresaw. *He* responded to a challenge *pro rata*, a true man, in situations where Manwaring would have rinsed his hands in despair. And yet what could he possibly hope to accomplish? A large bottle of Johnny Walker, three quarters empty, stood on the mantlepiece and Danny poured them nips. Time alone would tell.

Manwaring stared at the carpet. How much he lacked self confidence. Why was it always *he* the subject of discussion and ultimately disapprobation. Was Danny supposed to be fault free? Danny was a thoroughgoing drunkard and bloody profligate; and yet in a more fundamental sense than Manwaring, he *was* fault free—and carried himself accordingly! Manwaring supposed the critical factor lay in the how one carried it off. Danny, in never doubting himself for a minute, presented a coat of mail to the half-hearted upper mountain quidnunc. So you are all that you *appear.* And Danny, who represented to Manwaring all that was best and toughest in bachelordom, had to listened to.

The difference between you and me Evans lies in our approach. He noticed he was slurring his words. He was in

fact beginning to know drunkenness, and to like it. How
had he held it off so long? That was the wonder. Rolling,
lost, illusively free while in fact iron-clad in exigency . . .
he took to drink as a metaphor of his general condition,
renouncing his life-long abstemiousness with the mingled
relief and terror that a latent homosexual of his own age
might have felt in coming out. He gave himself not long
before he would burst apart at the seams anyway, although
what form his ultimate degradation might take he could
only surmise. Perhaps, he had begun to suspect, always
sniffing the air for portents, it might involve sex in some form
or another. A month ago, nothing could have seemed less
probable. He had always thought, a little prudishly, that sex
had never played a very large part in his life, but all of a
sudden it had begun to make its presence felt overwhelmingly—he was passing through a climacteric it seemed. It
was surprising how he was missing even the dry surrogate
he had known; he found that in his present condition he was
not game to develop the plates from the golden picnic day:
they lay where he had left them, his last photographs, in a
corner of the dark room like seeds awaiting germination. He
kept them instinctively for a time of need.

He had never even learnt to masturbate—strange how
even when *right* he was always wrong . . . there seemed to
be some sort of psychological difficulty for him in it. It was
not that he was undersexed, it was surely not *all* in the mind,
no, it had to be a symbol of something deeper. His prostate,
vilely tormented through chronic infection, screamed for
release, staining his underwear. Yet it would have to be a
woman; that was the unwholesome, the most perilous
aspect about it. It would have to be a woman. Even noc-
turnal emission was for him the exception not the rule.
And if a woman, it would have to be a lover—Manwaring
ached—but with an aching not always transparently sexual
—for a lover, mostly because Manwaring's physical body
dangled like a scrotum under a larger, more spiritual body,
an excrescence of his imagination, a hernia of his id brought
on he liked to console himself through maternal strangula-
tion (how he remembered that iron grasp instinct with

starch and talc!)—romantic to absurdity, but somehow justifiable and not altogether ugly, like the muscular torso of a dwarf, if looked at—in the correct manner. But how could he find a lover at his age and in his physical condition? The lover of his dreams, lost girls of the bridle trails . . .

Why am I looking for a wife Danny? Manwaring awoke as from a dream and fearfully refilled his cup. I'll end up with some old virago. You know I'll propose to the first woman who sleeps with me. I have to have a *wife*.

What you must realize, replied Danny, growing formidably cogent with drink, is that a marriage certificate today is only a slip of paper. Most women realize that, in fact, would not *want* to marry you. Let's face it, you've failed once, who's to say you won't fail twice? You're a bad risk, Manwaring. It gets expensive, if nothing else. And what a ridiculous situation—*you* pleading for marriage and children with a woman perfectly prepared to go without.

It wasn't my fault, said Manwaring, that my marriage failed. I didn't walk out of it. And where's this woman you keep talking about? Always referring to this woman . . .

You are right only to a limited extent, continued Danny: We must not apologize for what we are. But we must accept ourselves only to a limited extent. We must be wary of our weaknesses. We must *learn* by our experiences.

Shut up, be quiet, said Manwaring, driven at last beyond endurance. Danny, like one of his priests, saw ever so clearly a path through the forest he himself would never have to tackle. A homily for every occasion, in such consisted his reason. Even the Devil reads me his anathema, thought Manwaring, growing abject. He suddenly wished he could manoeuvre the subject off personalities and onto photography, where all Danny's maxims for safe passage could be seen to fail him miserably. He couldn't even get his foot past the door, not one inch. It was wretched *Manwaring* who had the better eye, but even then he was forever diffident about his work, whereas Danny blew his own trumpet vociferously and at every opportunity and the secret (if it was indeed shared at all) was between the two of them. However—unfortunately—it was life at the moment that presented the difficulties, and there Danny held the whip hand by unanimous general consensus. Manwaring adrift was Manwaring careening with his gunwales inches from the surf . . . it was ballast, that or nothing. Moreover, is was ballast now or never. He would either find ballast or founder; not to sink into merciful oblivion though, that would be too easy, but to bob on, cork-like, a piece of flotsam through a long, long voyage . . . Where? How? Oh Jesus. No one to turn to, no way of formulating the simplest question, as it would no doubt prove to be. And drink was not the answer, it reinforced his already top-heavy superstructure. He needed something that went directly to his vitals and muscles, balls, guts and *legs*, not head. Romance? Religion? He knew what he had to learn. He had to learn to drop his unhealthy craving for perpetuity in all affairs, he had to learn to believe in himself. As he was. But, at the same time, as he was he would not do. Clearly, everything he was *not, that* he had to become. He had to unravel forty years of string and make a straw man out of it. It was a crisis; but who would have thought such waves from such a small and intrinsically uncalamitous pebble, such emanations, looming through his consciousness now like the relentless no-coloured orthogons of the sulfonilamide-induced nightmare? And at an age when most men are nearly soundless and can dream of retirement and gardens? He looked unsteadily at Danny, who looked unsteadily back—or at least, so it seemed . . . So it was. Onwards, half a league. He found himself never any closer to port.

You rush too eagerly towards your own destruction Manwaring. Danny would not desist, had unerring insight into weakness, provoking suspicion in Manwaring as to whether he had always been so strong himself. You're a born bachelor, you made your one mistake, and now it's been forgiven you. Yet already you pine for your former chains. Can you deny it?

Take me to a brothel, replied Manwaring. It is freedom I fear. Who knows what I'll end up doing?

No, said Danny, I would not be guilty of it. And why? Because it is available for free, it is abundant, it is all around us, the least expensive and most rewarding commodity in the world today . . . You married too young to know—it used to be hard to find, I found it so myself once, but believe me, times have changed! *Attitudes* have changed. And old women are not like the middle aged women today, they are less wise, expect more and give less. *Live*, my friend:—and learn again.

It was the persistent voice of the oracle. What, said Manwaring; at *my* age?

Certainly it won't be easy. But I herewith—and here Danny flourished a glass—appoint myself thy guide and protector.

Manwaring felt tears springing into his eyes. It would not trouble old Danny too much if he unloosed the floodgates just a little. Not that tears seemed to follow on from what Danny had just said, for they were not tears of gratitude. Fighting viciously upstream, however, the following ballast-like resolutions were taking form: I will stay chaste and work hard. When Janet is off my hands I will go into a monastery—(he had always felt, deep down, that the right place for him would be a monastery)—where my emotions, redirected, perhaps simply seen in a purer light, perhaps even mistaken for something they may not prove to be—and how happily I would settle for *that*—will probably find a concordant environment for the first time. Near to a garden in a fine climate, preferably awakening at all hours in the morning to spend my days in prayer and rumination, finally making sense of it all with the assistance of arcane texts. Transcribing manuscripts, *penetralia*, perhaps turning out a late-maturing scholar, oh, a surprise for everyone. In the meantime work work work. Only time will tell.

Danny, I'm drunk, said Manwaring, and fell off the sofa. For effect: just a subterfuge to get the man out. He saw Danny, after some solicitous enquiries, walk through the door into the cold night and shut it after him. Already autumn, and only the one red cinder now remaining in his grate. He crawled towards it and fell asleep on the way. He had intended to do some solid thinking but, too tired, fell asleep, sleeping deeply. He knew that Danny was keeping something back, but also felt it didn't matter. Danny had probably cuckolded him. That was just one of the many thoughts he had. All part and parcel of a general conspiracy. But no matter. Danny was welcome anyway, for what are friends for. The cold of the night didn't really matter any more either, didn't trouble him in the least.

The next morning he awoke around ten with his joints constrained as though by a straightjacket. By the time he had embrocated, bathed and loosened up enough to get down into the street it was ten thirty. It had become quite common for him, however, since he had begun to drink, to start work around eleven. Hung over and unshaven, his once immaculate suit shabby and its seams arumple from heavy sleep, his clock stopped, he stepped agonizingly down the seemingly innumerable steps from his flat. He saw, over the length of his descent, a few curious pensioners passing by who stopped and looked up at him. Could this indeed be the man Manwaring, he seemed to hear them say, of whom it is being said that his wife has left him? The Astor Flats were entered via a small false portico behind which a flight of steps rose naked to the elements. They had been one of his wife's principle stumbling blocks. At the level of Katoomba Street he paused to hear the old people conversing in the chatter of falling leaves that blew up the lane past the Cecil from Kingsford Smith Park . . . Manwaring disoriented, dishevelled, as he had been inexorably bound, it now appeared, to finish up. He read satisfaction in the few faces he looked into. Blinking in the relentless sunlight now of new autumn, he made his way across to the Paragon.

Once readjusted to the sepulchral gloom in the cafe, more or less that of his own flat (its curtains now perpetually drawn), he saw, to his surprise, Danny beckoning urgently and somewhat conspiritorially towards him from the furthermost banquette. A figure from a continuum, a cyclorama. The cafe at that hour was near to overflowing with pensioners and tourists taking cups of tea and scones in a bee-like drone of slander.

What is it, said Manwaring, easing himself painfully into

the seat while at the same time attracting the attention of Con. He ordered two coffees.

Look at this, said Danny, producing a magazine from his lap.

Why are you not at work, said Manwaring.

Same to you, said Evans. Because I've been waiting here for you, that's why. I didn't wish to risk waking you after last night. Now look at this.

He opened the magazine, a photographic magazine, the very type of magazine Manwaring had no time for, which had arrived, he went on, in his mail that morning. At long last, as he expressed it. Its chief interest for him lay in that it announced a world wide photographic competition, entries from the Commonwealth and undeveloped countries to constitute a separate section of their own. There was also an open section, presumably for Americans and Europeans.

So what, said Manwaring. There are always competitions.

But this is different, expostulated Danny—bigger, *worldwide*. I thought—at least I *hoped*—you'd be interested too. One of our biggest problems up here is our parochiality, you've always said so yourself. Now there's a portraiture section, and a landscape section suitable for you. I'd hoped we'd both enter in the undeveloped country section.

My Minna Ha Ha Falls, your mayoral party, said Manwaring, resenting the slur on the milieu, though to Danny it was simply a statement of fact like any other.

If you like, yes. But don't laugh, don't look at things that way, don't be like that. Don't refuse to enter competitions. I mean, it's our only chance, our only *hope* . . . I mean, it's lucky in a way I even took out the subscription. I was thinking maybe we could go halves in it.

Manwaring took the magazine and thumbed his way through its unusual glossy print. He found the usual equanimity of his cynicism giving way momently to furious despair and xenophobia. How he *detested* such reminders that he was not, after all, the only photographer in the world! Here came reports of a world outside his in which men spoke freely, knowing what to say, a world by inference richer than his: but was it real? *Could* it be real, that was the crux, could it be *allowed* to be? Could he permit it? Where was the proof of its existence? The necessity that made his virtue was solitude. Parochiality he did not despise, Danny had missed his meaning as usual. Since what could he profit from the company he could get? The consensus was forever in their favour, these foreigners, by more than sheer weight of numbers too he suspected, but how do you compete when you're running what could be for all you know a different race? You learn to think in terms of phase, not time entirely, that's how. So what difference to him what others did? Danny saw it only as an upbraidable reluctance to compete: athlete's nerves. Manwaring's hand went up to his nose, as if in apology, as if to efface this unbushmanlike object and knead it into a more acceptable shape, less foreign, before he spoke.

It'd only be the verdict of the judges Danny—and who's to say they'd be right or wrong? How many photographers are there in the world anyway? I wouldn't buy this journal if I was you, it depresses me. Look at all this equipment they're advertising, for example; I mean I've never seen half of it and I'm supposed to be the local rep. What are your chances? They'll all have better equipment than you, I suppose you realise that. I can't share the subscription either. No money. No inclination, frankly.

All right. But concerning equipment, according to the rules of this competition it shouldn't *matter*, they're supposed to have handicapped to take this sort of thing into account. I had this copy sent me by special delivery.

It's three months old. Manwaring yawned, stretched his arms . . . You'll miss the closing date by the time you get your entry to London, even if you post it today.

Yes, but it may not matter, I'll explain the circumstances. Now: the thing is this (and Manwaring knew what this thing would prove to be)—have you got those plates done for me yet? *You* don't have to enter, but don't think I'm not going to. I'm going to send in several entries, there's no limit. I think—yes I know I'm right in what I'm doing. It's high time we got off our bums up here.

Danny scowled at Manwaring to reinforce the slur, but

Manwaring did not feel impugned. On the contrary he smiled magnanimously at his friend's enthusiasm. Danny thought him fulsome . . .

He is still drunk, but how different he is beginning to look, might have been thinking Danny . . . In his descent to who knows what he takes on a new wryness, a fresh astringency. His jawline stubble and ill-pressed suit lend him a vagabond air not altogether unbecoming in a middle aged Jew down on his luck . . . Something from a dank ghetto, smelling of rags and bones, trans-shipped in error. Manwaring in descent has a strength, a *puissance*, that plateau Manwaring lacked. How well he has taken it all really. And who can tell where he will end up? Who'd have thought his wife meant so much to him, was so *essential* to him? His life has taken of a flavour, now let me see, containing something in it of (that most cherished flavour for spectators) perilous uncertainty.

Do those plates for me Manwaring will you? Today. As a special favour, after all I've been waiting here all morning, I've lost custom—do my plates, I *beg* of you!

All right all right. Manwaring gestured languorously, stifling a yawn, flashing his golden ring like a beam of light, a calliopsis. You might be better off sending them directly to New York.

It depends on shipping movements, but it's true: you could be right. I hadn't thought of it, thanks, I'm grateful to you, I'll follow it up.

By the way—Danny was moving to leave—don't expect to win a prize. Also, it's going to cost you a fortune just to mail all that film.

If you don't enter you can't win Manwaring, it's as simple as that.

And he left.

But his disdain, a turn-about, though not exactly a new order from the previous night, was just that of the competitor for the non-competitor. Infinite but ill-focussed. Now Manwaring understood, momently, a little better, *his* emotions towards Danny in the matter of women. Fresh understanding consoled him like a mountain stream as he drained the two coffees successively into his desiccated throat. Pausing now and again to cough up phlegm. A cold through sleeping on the chilly floor. Now he regretted his fine rashness in having done it. But how soothing to acquire fresh understanding in any area whatsoever. It would soon disappear. Washed up occasionally upon the cambric-clear beach, a branch, a leaf . . . he had only to stoop to pick them up, to toss them onto the heap. Of driftwood and *objets-de-mer* somewhat to his rear. But since none of the early pieces had fitted in with one another harmoniously, he did not think it probable that these later ones would. He saw, he walked on. Forgot, walked clean on. *Physically* though, it must have been stored up somewhere, making excellent sense after its own cryptic fashion. It was enough. To know understanding was being amassed somewhere.

He smiled, paid his bill, walked out. A favonian autumnal breeze blew down Katoomba Street, bearing to him a simulacrum he fancied of Janet's schooltime scent, chalk dust and perspiration, from the convent across the line. Come end of term he planned on moving her out, around end of term would begin the struggle over Janet. Already he was amassing money and fortitude for the struggle, which he foresaw as containing gutter tactics in abundance. Screechings from the gang gang in the direction of Sydney, claiming its young. He would meet the threat though. He had visited a local solicitor, a fellow lodge member (Manwaring had held his term as worshipful master) and made as certain as he could of the legal situation. Everyone knew now. But in deserting the child his wife had made a bad tactical error, possibly, he hoped, fatal. If he were awarded custody of Janet he would be getting all of the fruit with none of the bitter rind of the now deeply regretted marriage that he saw in retrospect had eaten up his young life and prospects. Perhaps he could still make something of himself though, or rather, perhaps he could still create something. But he was at the present in a considerable lull, having taken no photograph in three weeks. Forestalling the inevitable reappraisal which he knew could not now be avoided, be busied himself in performing the merely mechanical duties of his trade, chiefly,

developing prints. He murdered time. His working day had
shrunk to almost half, and when not working he drank or
walked around Katoomba looking for people to talk to on
undistressful subjects. But all this would one day soon have
to stop, it was constipating him.

Through the pharmacy—with an unreciprocated nod
towards one of the girl assistants, though perhaps she had
simply not seen him—up the stairs to his rooftop studio he
made his way. Albert Manwaring, photographer, said the
unpretentious and scarcely legible sign on the door at the
top of the stairs, which he unlocked with a key. He walked
across the open roof of the building to another door giving
access to a small and surprising cupola, invisible from
Katoomba Street, which he unlocked using the same key.
He was now within his workshop. He locked the door behind
him. There were contained within his cupola three rooms—
two dark rooms and a sort of preliminary studio *cum* office
in which, in addition to cardboard cartons and walls full of
his own photography, mainly postcards, he kept outside
work consigned to the pharmacy beneath him to be processed. In the tourist season he casually employed as many
as three local girls and a photographic assistant. But,
although the tourist season had expanded during the time he
had lived in the upper mountains to take in virtually the
entire year, at present there was just himself, he was at work
full time when in the workshop on the developing and
printing side, always somewhat slack at the end of summer
and scarcely enough to busy even him. On a table against
one wall of his studio stood a chipped and discoloured
electric jug. He switched it on, it was always his first morning
act of procrastination, and when it had boiled made for himself two further cups of strong black coffee by pouring the
water directly into a tin fresh with coffee beans, usually a
fresh handful, decanting the resultant solution into his cup.
While drinking, he looked across through the back window
of his studio at the Carrington Hotel, probably the building
he had photographed most. Its immense chimney stack,
dominating the town's approaches, bisected the cloudless
sky from where he stood. It was forever a great comfort. He

went into his dark room, took the plates that Danny had requested him develop—as well as his own golden plates (the latter taken from their corner in a kind of whistling, unthinking, natural ease) and processed them all. Not pausing to eat, interrupting his work only for half-hourly cups of coffee or tea, he followed in silence every stage of the fixing and developing procedure, loving the rubric the more the more he practised it. Staring into the shallow dip-trays of solution he watched the film take shadow form. It was a process he could always marvel at, provided he was left uninterrupted. It never lost mystery for him, not even when defined in chemical terms which he only vaguely understood. For the reason of this love he preferred to work alone, company was not conducive to the mystery, demanding of silence no less than of darkness: least of all the company of casual staff whose unremittant, idle chatter shattered all tranquillity and made processing film into just one more onerous chore. Eventually, he moved into the drying dark room and hung the wet positives onto a line with pegs. Because perhaps of his eyesight, which seemed to discriminate best towards the red end of the spectrum, he moved with a lambent ease in the red-hued blackness of the dark rooms, an ease upon which his casual staff had frequently remarked. He seemed very much at home indeed. And he seemed to carry out this crepuscular disposition, as he did the black, silver oxide impregnated fingertips of his profession (for he scorned gloves) into the world outside. Where the daylight seemed always just that trifle too bright for his eyes.

Looking first at Danny's prints, he saw what he had expected to see, though without any further sense of disappointment in Danny as a man or friend; various dignitaries, a clutch of lower mountain schoolgirls—others, some single portraits—all posed in strongly oblique attitudes, perceptively ill at ease against the usual sylvan backgrounds which now, he had within the last week or so discovered, tended only to bore him. To *bore* him! How long since he would have cut out his *tongue* before making such an admission? Now it seemed as if it had always been the case. He had been scared to admit it, that was all. After all, there

was a strict limit to the variety in the mountain flora, even
allowing it as amongst the most varied on the continent,
and he had photographed it to death. There was not much
more he could do with it probably, hence this sudden change
in attitude, undetectable, like a cancer, until too late. In vain
to try and reinvest surroundings with a mystique he now had
difficulty, and even some embarrassment, in trying to comprehend. Scattered around the studio walls—he made himself another cup of tea, sensing despair for his own future,
which seemed all at once cut off—there hung, and he looked
at them, representative samples from his own practically
innumerable studies over a period of nearly fifteen years—
water falls in abundance, glens, glades, civic investitures,
town halls, courthouses, convict built bridges and bricks,
obelisks unveiled, parks, gardens, larger than average trees,
landslides, rockfalls, military marches, school fetes—with the
feeling that he was looking into a past in which he was now
a complete stranger, a harsh critic, an interloper, an un-
welcome and reluctant intruder. Here, next to his very jug,
for example, stood a picture of Janet peeking like an elf
around a stocky tree fern. He picked it up incredulously.
Beneath it lay a plate of glass curiously defaced, with
Memory Park written all over it in white ink. How apposite.
In a moment of insight he had written his horoscope.
Steeped in the nostalgia that for him followed any emotional
state of sensual perception as the present moment the past,
it had all been done, all this rubbish, in a dream of nostalgia,
a vast nostalgia, a cry, a plea . . . to be heard, to be forgiven
—but unanswered and profitless to pursue and for what. He
looked around, now half beside himself in disbelief. There
a man with an ear trumpet attending the every word of a
clergyman unveiling a memorial. No, no, that had to be one
of Danny's escaped, but Manwaring's eyes were no longer
detainable by bushscapes: here a scoutmaster in comical
Bombay Bloomers—unbelievable! Here a group of young
ladies arched like saplings of birch under a wind in gymnastic
attitudes on the front lawn of a prestigious private school.
His hands went to his ears—no, no, he practically laughed!
The *arch*ness! The *same*ness! How pointless, how impracti-

cal, how entirely out of the mainstream! You don't have to
know where the mainstream flow to know when you're up
some backwater, in stagnation like some ghastly saprophyte.
So little did Manwaring understand the mainstream, he
couldn't decide whether Danny's objurgable prints were good
or bad: perhaps a jaded taste? Curio value? . . . all he could
say was that he, personally, did not like the look of them.
The sum total of his aesthetics to that point. A month ago
they might have seemed all right, but a month ago was a
lifetime ago, a dam had burst since then. Now they affected
him less. But what of *his* future?

Draining his tepid cup he went back into the dark, now
very nervous, to look at his own prints. He put on the red
light and sat on a stool, waiting for his pupils to redilate.
This, he recognized, was the critical moment for him. If he
liked what he saw; then there could no longer subsist any
doubt. It would be confirmed, his suspicion that the camera
was trying to *tell* him something, something that he alone,
cameraless, lacking insight and equilibrium and knowledge,
could never tell himself—that the old game was up, and
hopefully, what the new game would be. What a *cul-de-sac*
his life had suddenly, in the space of a mere month or so,
become, as though through implantation of some malefic
foot or fist across his path. The realization did not dismay
him. He took it in his stride, a little unfairly now, because he
could already see, and knew he was liking what he saw.
He could not go back now.

As his eyes accommodated to the light, the copulating
couple came up nicely. He studied the prints intently, with
a desire to learn from them if he could. There were eight
prints and he had arranged them along the clothes line in
no chronological order, but the sequence they were in,
chosen at random, without looking, pleased him strongly, so
strongly he determined to keep them in it at all costs, fate
now strongly in the fore. He looked at the prints until they
looked back. When they were dry he packed them into a
manilla envelope, carefully marking them in sequence with
white ink. He did not dare to think about them, though it
passed through his mind that he would probably break the

law if he sent such material through the mails. Back in the studio he put all Danny's prints into another manilla envelope and made himself another cup of coffee. It was by now around eight thirty at night. There was a ball on at the Carrington, and as he looked across he could see the couples sauntering around the verandah in their tardy-apish ball clothes. Stupid parochial backwater people. He sat down, not wanting to leave his studio, in love with his isolation though knowing it would soon have to end. His new films had captured *some*thing, but he couldn't really say what. He couldn't be the judge of them himself nor did he wish to be. For the first time in his life he felt casually inclined to submit his work to the judgement of others—confident of their esteem and encomium in direct proportion to their insight—as he was for once genuinely curious as to what the merit of his work might consist in. He had a great *itch* to know what his camera was saying, though he knew he would follow it wherever it led him, he didn't need to know any language for that. Previously, the undoubted charm of his work had remained a mystery, above all to himself, and all at his own insistence. For a start, he detested charm and had never really liked his own work very much, without knowing why. If anyone spoke to him about it, he always turned away. He had declined debate, believing this the only manly course. But now, after all it seemed, there had been something to hide, something unsavoury in his work over and above poor technique, a vacuum of *quiddity*: it certainly seemed freshly possible. Perhaps his dignity had lain, like that of most solitaries, in pretending to disdain, while actually fleeing, comment. Criticism and praise alike had always evinced his mostly silent contempt and resentment, but he felt *differently* now; much more relaxed and talkative. He wanted to know what he had done, how he had done it, and how he could do it again. It hadn't much to do with the bush he thought . . . Maybe it had been the light, maybe not. Certainly not *only* the light probably. With great care he wrote down all he could remember of the technical details of the filming, duration of exposure, camera specifications etc. He then slipped these data, written on a

piece of cartridge paper, into the manilla envelope and
sealed it. He then locked the negatives in a strong box under
the dark room bench, evicting some scenes of Jenolan Caves
House onto the floor to make room. In a curious mood, not
knowing whether to feel buoyant or desperate, but inclining
to the former, perhaps overfull of caffeine, he locked up,
went downstairs and let himself out of the pharmacy. Only
vaguely conscious of his hunger and not wanting to eat much
anyhow, he walked with the two envelopes of prints directly
down to Danny's house near Hinkler Park, a walk that took
him some twenty minutes and during which he merely
looked around him, enjoying the stimulus to his optic nerve.
He stopped only briefly at Danny's, conveyed the prints,
accepted a glass of whisky, announced his own belated and
considered decision to enter the contest, accepted Danny's
felicitations on this, obtained the postal address and excused
himself from further conviviality by suddenly rushing from
the house. Danny, aware of Manwaring's ambivalence towards competitions, stood framed in the doorway of his
home with a glass in his hand and a sympathetic expression
on his face. He fancied Manwaring would head straight for
Hinkler Park and he was not wrong, but he did not follow.
Shutting the door behind him he went straight inside himself, gulping down the whisky in his glass, eager to be done
and to collate and assess his own material afresh. It had
been agreed by the two friends that both manilla envelopes
would have to be in the following morning's mailbag to stand
any chance of meeting the deadline. Danny had also ascertained through his enquiries at the post office that the next
and fastest mail would be trans-Pacific direct to the New
York office. The address he gave Manwaring was accordingly
one in New York. A ship left Sydney in three days time.
For New York.

Manwaring's footsteps forever led him into parks, he had
so little or no control over where he went. Hinkler Park was
very well known and very well liked, and a considerable
favourite, many solitary moments had he spent in it at night
wondering whether to importune Danny over some personal
trifle whether or not to knock on Danny's door; and when

walking with Janet to Echo Point of a weekend the two of
them usually called a halt at Hinkler Park. When she had
been younger he had given her vigorous swings and slippery
dips but at the age of twelve now she would sit composedly
on a swing while he would sit on a nearby bench admiring
her as she trailed her shoes in the dust in that slow and
languid contemplative manner that calmed him so immeas-
urably. In the dark his glasses now aglisten in the ample
streetlighting he sat on a bench after leaving the street and
attempted to collate his thoughts. The huge foreign trees—
he supposed they were elms or oaks—shed leaves in abundance upon his head as a wind had begun to blow crisply
up from down in the valley. He felt cold but did not move.
In another month there would be no more leaves left, only
the massive boles and bare limbs. He tried to imagine a
landscape in which all the trees had similarly lost their
leaves; could he live in such a landscape he wondered,
with no green anywhere for perennial comfort? It seemed
an academic question on several counts, and there were
probably always firs about. His home, just womb—not really
though. He had invented it. Strange how his real childhood
memories had gone—he felt like Janet who had always
lived in the mountains, that was why they and their scrupu-
lous parks were so precious to him. And if he could sneer,
and if he did sneer, then it was because they were now so
much a part of him, so precious to him, they had to share
the responsibility and blame for what he had become. His
earliest recollections went back only a few years, sitting
with his daughter in Hinkler Park. Or Kingsford Smith
Park on a piece of grassy amphitheatre around a perennially
deserted music shell. Or in the little stucco work shells made
for elves at Echo Point Park. Or elsewhere. He had constructed, too late, his first true beginnings in life. Of the
city, the inner city where he and his mother had lived early,
and later of Abbotsford and the upper reaches of the Parramatta River, the house which he had sold to rent an Astor
Flat three thousand feet high—of these things he remembered very little, practically nothing. Nothing had *seemed*
to happen then, no matter what actually had happened, as

much as had happened since. And nothing had really happened since. He had constructed a rebirth, not just a rejuvenescence, in Katoomba, as had Danny, as had Constantine, and several others like them. These men were in fact the essence of the place, they gave it its flavour, strangers and others like them, harbouring curious longings in their minds, loving it with a fervid, unnatural love, and improving it in a way that torpid local people could never understand or admit. Maybe they lived in another Katoomba entirely than the locals, Manwaring often suspected that *their* world was different. Its flavour—they created that, they made it what it was, they gave from each their dream, their subconscious dream of life as they wished it, physically slow, slow-flowing like a stream, spiritually rich, slow but not so slow that there was no end to it. Danny and Manwaring for example, they had no gardens, they looked at the gardens of others and photographed them, stealing them away. Death and pain seemed to grow through Manwaring, but sharply, as they should have done, there was scarcely a bone in his body that did not ache, there was scarcely an organ in his body that functioned properly, but he wasn't sorry, he never went to the doctor, he was glad he lived now with the constant reminder of mortality, of the brevity of life in which each year undercuts the year before it, because it had taught him at last the urgency of moving precisely when the moment came to move. Physically perhaps it might have seemed to the observer that nothing much was going on but inside Manwaring all was in turmoil, feeling like the moment had come to move.

He looked up at the sky the vault of stars through the falling leaves of the elms. As he did so, he felt he died, but the breeze was insistent and it would not let him go, it blew back through him, around him, awoke him, revivified him, opened his eyes and forced him back up the hill. By the way the park looked as he looked back at it he knew he would never see it, the same park, again. Although access would probably never be denied him, the park would remain. The park would remain but he would not, he would never see the park again with the same emotions. His mountain stars were dying inside him, one by one inside him, his trees were losing all their beautiful leaves. In the breeze leaves whispered to him messages—go away. Be gone. A second birthplace was necessarily a hazardous camp, shorter lived and more finite than a first. He thought of his dear black cockatoos, how they tumble from a higher to a lower branch in a pine on wings extended merely to prevent their falling to the ground totally. So slowly do they move their wings. They need, like the albatross, room to move in. Manwaring needed room to move in too, psychic room, he would soon have to reconstruct himself, reinvent himself as he now was in the habit. Any yellow tailed black cockatoo may stay in any one pine tree indefinitely, forever if it wishes and has pine cones left to eat, yet they do not, they are greedy and restless, keep moving on. By so doing they permit the tree to live and propagate. But it is incidental or is it.

For the first time in his life Manwaring began to live for the morning mail, fretting each day the postman's horse passed by him. He had three months, maybe more, of waiting to do, and how the time would not fly.

He had seen them destroying good pine trees by ripping the uppermost branches to pieces in their gulosity for cones, from each of which they usually bit only one morsel. But they were much loved. Leaves fell heavily, dolorously, as he left those nights his parks, drawing in as best he could his own black, malefic-seeming wings of thought, putting a benediction on Hinkler Park and all like it to prosper in his absence. He liked too, he saw, a little bit of the north in his trees, coded in his eyes too deep to outgrow or reconstruct the need for deciduous foliage. Whereas love of the valleys amongst which he had been born he had had to acquire as in a spell. He shutting his eyes for a moment seemed to see a Katoomba of poplars, elms and rhodos, pins of clean-standing red and gold among the native bush too full of dreams and remembrance ever to acknowledge seasons let alone white man. From such a dream a white man personally, reluctantly, but definitely awakes. And now it was all gone forever out of the present, truly a dream, belonging in the past, truly a deception, wearing the past in the air around it, even to look at it was to venture back into the past, it threw his weight back, to move in the present he would have to leave this heavily-weighted scenery and move on into another scene, he remembered Danny or some other man saying in a tired voice how lovers were easy to forget not so acquaintances, who did not penetrate but remained outside forever to threaten forever impossible to assimilate and forget, and he saw the valleys only acquaintances at last. What horror to have had no sanctuary left on the high mountains, what horror to have had no lovers anywhere at any time.

Chapter 4

The letter came five months later, it had nothing to do with
the results of the competition, another of Danny's magazines
had announced those, and their two names were not of
course in the lists; by which they had each chosen to
assume (each in his own private agony had really expected
yet not really expected to see his name and had felt out-
raged . . . echo echo echo . . .) that their entries must
have arrived too late to receive consideration. It was to
Danny's amusement when he discovered that Manwaring
had entered the *Open Portrait* section. He asked to see the
negatives of Manwaring's entries, but Manwaring refused,

claiming the whole thing best forgotten. Indeed, had it not
been for the existence and responsibility of Janet and the
great battle that was raging about her, taking his mind
sometimes off his disappointment in life as whole, eating up
his money, he would certainly have attempted suicide—
some act in one of the valleys, a gesture towards Creation
to cease trifling with him on pain of death, but also; he
had an inkling. He could no longer take a photograph. He
sat most days waiting for his letter, the *deus ex machina*
that would deliver him, how certainly he believed it, his
resources meantime dwindling, his business in that stationary
state which generally precedes death, outside his studio,
both doors fore and aft locked, looking now and again
through dark tinted lenses across at the Carrington, but
mostly staring at the persistently blue sky of a winter so
mild as to terrify him—each day provided a few hot sun-
bathing hours—in which he either sat or lay, generally
drinking whisky, emptying his head of all thoughts and
ambitions, holding back the flywheel that drove him now
at dusk only into useless and humiliating motion in which
he wandered like a robot the newly dead streets from park
to desolate park. Several parties domiciled at the Carrington
complained about him to the manager, mistaking him for a
private detective on a stake out, which made the manager
laugh, and the guests too when they learnt his identity.
Just another mountain man business on the slack it seemed.
But enough work kept coming in to keep him solvent the
miracle was, and the pity was that the letter hadn't come
when the magazine had, two months earlier. When the
letter came, it was spring again, and he had had another
birthday.

The postman was unpunctual and could arrive at any time
in the morning from eight until eleven. On certain mornings,
therefore, Manwaring's agony reshaped itself early, on certain mornings late. He had instructed one of the girls in the
pharmacy to slip his mail—of which there was usually quite
a good deal, owing to potential trade, creditors, solicitors
and an increasing body of customers dissatisfied with his
processing of their film—beneath the door at the top of the
stairs. As soon as he heard the postman's horse, therefore,

he directed his face towards the door at the top of the stairs until such time as he saw his mail emerge from under it. And then, every day for five months, he would redirect himself and his attentions, punishing this mundane correspondence by refusing to open it until late afternoon, and only then because it impeded his passage when he wanted to leave.

One day, early in spring, the postman came late, much later than usual, and the day being warmer than usual, Manwaring was asleep in the sun on his deckchair, clad only in singlet and trousers, his shoes and socks and shirt stacked beside him, when the sound of the postman's horse's hooves—as it was by now the only horse that used the main street regularly—awakened him. The ritual then began. He parted his dry lips cautiously, ungumming the dried saliva, and waited for the searing flow of bile into his mouth. It came. He spat it out. The relentlessly blue sky, always looking not at him, filled his eyes, and he quickly focussed them at the base of the door. Waiting for his morning's mail to debouche forth. After an indeterminate time a girl's footsteps ascended the stairs, and there was a pause. She began to push his mail, letter by letter, under his door. Although she did not mind this, her employer the pharmacist had more than once expressed, on her behalf as he put it, his resentment to Manwaring over this time-wasting punctilio, but Manwaring, who had certain rights and could make while remaining fully within them considerable noise upon the roof of the premises, was quite insistent that this was the very way his morning mail had to be conveyed. The pharmacist had backed down and Manwaring saw that bright day the letters, one after the other, slipping under the door. He did not think of the young girl slipping them, except as the conveyor of his mail, because his ardour had died through frustration and inertia. The less you get the less you want in this respect, likewise conversely. No opportunity had arisen, no woman had approached him, and he had forgotten how, or was too self-conscious, to approach any woman. Anyway, small talk bored him, and he no longer even shaved every morning. Occasionally, he would realize that he needed a shave.

That was all. He realized, but he did not care, that this lack of concern over his appearance was the plainest possible indication to the whole of Katoomba that he was not in the market for sex. He could not even be bothered discussing photography, outside of which he had nothing to say whatever. There were no brothels in the place: he did not care. He was quiescent, the warmer weather, the lighter and more alluring clothing on the pharmacist's assistants notwithstanding. So. He saw the letters thrust—but saw no letter before or after the one. His heart pumped at the sight of this one letter, however—an *airmail envelope*. He had never seen one before. He knew nobody overseas; it had therefore to be the letter he was waiting for. He took the envelope, verified that it was addressed to him—typewritten in fact— and that the stamp bore the great seal of the United States.

He opened the letter and read. Of course it had come by sea. On coarse quality paper, it appeared to be in the form of a roneod brochure, with his name typed after the Dear Mister. Thinking of thousands no doubt similar, his smile froze. But then he noticed the lengthily, hastily, barely legibly pencilled postscript that contained over the page, and he read that first. Then the whole thing, again and again; especially the postscript, so as to be sure it was really there.

> 68 LeGrange Place,
> Jersey City,
> July 5th

Dear Mister Manwaring,

> We are always interested in talent, and we wish to offer you an outlet for your creativity through our recently established photographic agency, which deals only with established trade clientele. If you are interested in trying us, and we can assure you that you will not regret it, please contact us at our above address, stating briefly your speciality and studio requirements, if any.

> Yours sincerely,
> Alvin Gold
> (creative director)

PS. Dear Al; the above is a genuine offer. Pardon the sheet, it was all I could lay my hands on. I recently saw some of your material (I have a friend in the customs), those big old-fashioned plates, I thought it was fine. I always like to see originality, we seem to be running out of it in this country, I don't know about your country, of course that competition was no place for material like yours, but you must have guts and I know you've got talent, I can use you. Al, I'd like to ask you to send me more, I was impressed by your mood and presentation, but we could get into trouble, my friend can't be everywhere, we can't rely on the mails, I'd have to try you out on a personal basis, we have a lot of talented individuals working for us here, I'm sure you'd hit it off with them, and it's the interplay of new ideas (so what's wrong with new wine in old bottles? Your stuff would never have occurred to us), that's what we're interested in. We're not novices over here, we know the market. So if you're ever in New York, or better still—Al, I'm offering you a job straight off, there you go, quick, quick, and if you strike while the iron is hot any visa difficulties I have friends in many places. How about it? Offers like this you won't get every day of the week even over here, I've never been to your country, but I'm prepared to believe, just guessing, that there's not the market over there for your material that you'll find over here. I'm not running a cheap joint here Al, I'm building up and I don't care how long it takes, a group of genuinely creative photographers, a whole new concept—people from all over the world, the most unlikely places. Sexuality is universal. I wish I could offer to pay your fare but my travel agent tells me it's unbelievable and, anyway, your paying your own fare would be a sign of your good faith. I'm not saying you won't stick Al, because I know you'll recognize a good thing when you see it. So let me have your answer, I wish I could leave the offer standing, but I just can't, you'd be surprised the talent around today, it's been coming to my notice from everywhere in the world, the most unlikely places, thanks to my friend in the customs, and I can't employ everyone

as much as I'd like to. I'm getting a good team together,
I've picked a few people to write to at random, and you're
one of the chosen few. Congratulations. But as you know
Al, we're catering to a forever jaded taste in our field,
and we can't have too many new ideas men like yourself,
men who can arrive on a new yet viable approach. I
think nostalgia will sell. So let's have that verdict return
mail.

Best wishes,
Al

(how is it all us good guys get christened Al? I knew you'd
like that one)

At random . . . Manwaring eventually put down the letter
and looked across towards the Carrington. The tone of the
letter seemed contrived. Surely people did not really speak
that way, or choose their employees at random. And Jersey
City. Where was that? What did it matter anyway, this
was it. It *had* to be it. Strange how intuition adumbrates
our future in advance. Enough to destroy a man's faith in
causation. To be a part of a creative community, to be
invited to join; never mind what appeared to be a misinter-
pretation of his goals and abilities, he felt he could rise, or
sink where necessary, to any occasion now. A toehold was
all he had asked of the world, and the world, through Al
Gold, had offered him a toehold. Now, the present, in which
his talents had been recognized. The prophet in his own
country. He thought, as he looked across at his own country
—represented by the monstrous Carrington and the tedious
blue beyonder—I will show you, you philistines, that your
lifelong siege has been repelled in my favour at last. It was
to him as if a veil had been lifted from his surrounds. His
ulcer straightway began to heal, he could feel it healing.
His pituitary and adrenal cortex sluggishly rebegan about
their business. He took a fresh bottle of whisky from the
cupboard and drank, drank and drank. Toasting himself, his
own almost unbelievable faith in himself over a lifetime,
and his good fortune. Or rather, the circumstances that
benevolent fates had conspired for him, testing his mettle

a little, as was only fair and always the case as any biography attested, to see if he was man enough to hold out. He had been. He had held out and now his siege was broken. The past five months joined noiselessly the forty-five preceding years. He was at long last what he had always wanted to be; a tourist. He could walk now through any park in any place in the manner of the average man, seeing only trees and not phantoms and rebukes. He sloughed off ten and more skins of diffidence and dejection, thawing in an avalanche occasioned by the newly benign sun; beckoning him to follow it—across the seas to sunny Jersey City, where his body would be denied the opportunity to further rust, gnawed at by its own idle acids. It would be work work and more work. How he hungered for it. He could sell the business to Danny, sell the lot. Vend the momento mori and all its contents. He foresaw only one snag; Janet.

The situation where Janet was concerned, notwithstanding protracted litigation on the part of both his wife and himself over almost a year, remained unclear and unsatisfactory. His wife refused him a divorce, and threatened him with lurid counterpetitions—though on what grounds he could only surmise—in the event of his attempting to force one on the grounds of desertion. It had been ruled by a court that Janet should remain for the indefinite future at the convent where her father had access to her of a weekend, it being, in the opinion of the court, in her own best interests to do so. He had been successful in obtaining an injunction from another Catholic judge restraining his wife from removing Janet from the convent altogether. On the other hand, he had been assured by all the legal authorities he had consulted that he had, at present, under the state divorce law, no grounds for divorce. So go ahead, they advised him with winks, play the rogue, get drunk, take women back to your flat: because your wife will never give you that divorce. Instead, he found himself, in respect of women at least (and the more he drank the less he cared for them), a model of propriety. Five years time, he could petition on the grounds of separation. Until then, the status quo, by court order. Every month his wife came and took Janet back to Bondi for the weekend. Sometimes Janet went off of her own accord. The existence of this hitherto unsuspected maternal nexus initially distressed him terribly. But of course, he had no right to feel so, as he did not want Janet to go through life without a mother's love—although, in her position, he would have welcomed the opportunity—it was her reciprocation of this attenuated regard that so puzzled him. On holidays too Janet went down to Bondi, as she said, for the beach. In the end he decided it was best she get a surfeit of her mother if possible, he began to encourage her in her trips to Sydney, offered money, in the hope that she would eventually see in her mother what he now saw; a twenty-nine carat bitch. But there were no signs of such a chill. Indeed, if any chill had begun, it was between Janet and himself. She refused to join him in his attacks on her mother, a loyalty he deplored. She had also recently begun to upbraid him in all seriousness over his appearance and the admittedly filthy condition of his flat. However, he felt that she still loved him slightly the more of the two of them, partly because of her age, and would also welcome, mostly because of her age, a new life with him alone. The problem lay in the illegality of removing her from the convent, let alone the country. To think that it was illegal for him to take his own daughter with him wherever he went! The courts had denied him natural justice; he took it as a personal challenge to circumvent their rulings. For Janet to accompany him to Jersey City would require his wife's permission, how laughable. How utterly out of the question. He could of course leave Janet behind, with all the other detritus of his life, but this course seemed neither fair nor just; because Janet, in a way he did not fully comprehend, belonged inalienably more to the future than to the past. She might need the wider scope of Jersey City for her own development, she was a talented girl. In any event, standing there on the rooftop, a man reborn in hope, he was nevertheless a man with a problem. But a problem at least practical in that it could admit of a practical solution. Unlike most of his perennial problems. He had to get Janet out of the convent and into Jersey City under an immigrant visa.

He had to elope with his own daughter. Needless to say, he dared not speak to anyone in Katoomba on the subject . . . no knowing who could be secretly conveying his informations back to his wife in Sydney, he trusted none of them. But at least he now had a friend he could trust implicitly, moreover, a man of considerable influence.

He went into the cupola and composed a note. *Dear Al,* he began, deciding on the informality after a moment's hesitation; *many thanks indeed for your generous offer. Needless to say, I intend to take it up, there is indeed very little market for my material here.* (As he wrote this, in a hand somewhat unsteady through drink and excitement, he could not help but glance up at his innumerable postcards, for which there had grown, in fact, over the years, an insatiable demand. They alone sustained him. In his daily mail there were always requests for his cards, some from as far away as Toowoomba and Port Augusta—and not infrequently letters from his employers exhorting him to endeavour to capitalize on this demand by seeking further outlets. But this, through silence and inaction, he declined to do. He made prints only. He sought no further outlets. Stocks were low, negatives were wearing thin, there were rumours of discontent in the tourists seeking an extended range. He did not care. He dearly hoped to see his last cards sold before he left, when he would personally strip the studio walls and add them to a final pyre of negatives and inauthentic existence)—*However, there is in fact likely to be some difficulty over visas. The facts are these Al: I am separated from my wife, and my only child, a girl now almost thirteen, from whom I am inseparable and from whom I could not bear to be parted on a permanent basis, will require my wife's permission to leave the country (Australia). Needless to say, this will not be forthcoming. I could fake her signature I suppose, but I would like your advice on how I ought to go about this matter. I don't ever want to come back here, so maybe you could arrange some false entry papers for Janet and myself? I hope I'm worth the trouble. I'll leave it up to you. Also, how are schools over there in Jersey City? I suppose there will be no difficulty in finding a suitable school for Janet to attend? Yours, with deep-felt thanks, Al Manwaring.*

No, no, thought Manwaring on rereading, and rewrote, *with thanks, Albert Manwaring.* He posted the letter, returning with candour the inquisitive gaze of the post mistress. Letters to foreign parts, ultimate symptom of social decay. Now, he thought at last, waiting time can be *used.* He went back to his flat, shaved for the first time in nearly a week, and in a gesture of affirmation towards the cosmos, put on his best suit and treated himself to a dinner at the Paragon. Periodically, he dazedly removed his airmail envelope and reread its contents. Had it been only that morning? Only that very morning? And what sort of a man was this Gold? Hungry now for a woman to impress himself upon, he made after his meal for the lounge bar at the Carrington, where he sat smoking a cheroot. He attempted conversation with various obviously married women.

Rebuff after rebuff, he withdrew himself to the verandah and withdrew the airmail envelope, brandishing it high like the talisman it was, it pushed him back up, up to where he belonged, to where no rebuff could be taken seriously, above sexuality, beyond self-esteem: back into the mainstream, well attired, clean shaven, which is, after all, where every man's responsibility towards his outside world must end.

Chapter 5

The last view Manwaring ever took of Katoomba consisted in Danny farewelling him from the platform, the beginnings of a winter morning almost twelve months later, a cloud up from the valleys reassuringly exuding from street level the odious mountain moisture osculant between mist and drizzle—Danny's pipe, his infernal pipe, and the smoke from it, trailing as the train drew out of the platform. A last vision of his friend's wet, fresh camel hair coat, bright with beads of moisture. And, of course, the Carrington's smoke stack. Beside Manwaring on the train sat Janet, under the impression that she was on a visit to her mother. Manwaring had

even, despite his trepidation at this facinorous lie, hinted at
parental reconciliation. He bore with him a portmanteau of
his own few remaining clothes—most of which in a frenzy
of abnegation he had recently donated to the local Vincent
de Paul Society—and Janet carried a satchel and her violin
in a case. Manwaring was determined to enter his quite
secret new life bearing as few trappings of his old as
possible. Janet and a few good clothes only. The violin made
him uneasy, but there was nothing he could do about that.
He intended to disembark (having ascertained that Jersey
City, right across the Hudson, was really part of New York
City to all intents and purposes) as indigent as any European refugee. He had told no one of the tickets and passports in his wallet, they were a matter solely between a
shipping agent and himself at this time. He had had to tell
lies, many lies, as in lies had lain his only way. He had had
to bribe a Sydney woman to sign Janet's passport, had had
to teach her to forge his wife's signature before a justice of
the peace. He too had had to lie under oath. He had paid
this woman to lie under oath. He had had to tell lies to
Janet and Danny in particular. Strangely, perhaps on
account of the guilt that all this lying inevitably engendered,
his warmth towards the two of them had fallen off since the
news of his good fortune. But he had expected all sorts of
emotional vagaries to result from the mild obsession that he
had enjoyed over this first real success in his life, and he
hoped that normality might eventually reassert itself. On
the other side. He would write to Danny from the United
States, explain everything and offer apologies, plead for-
giveness and understanding. To Danny, who had bought
out his workshop and business, he had spoken only of
nebulous plans for a similar business undertaking in Sydney.
Danny, believing him implicitly with a naïvety that Manwaring found disconcerting, even a little pathetic (but why
should he have not believed him?), had seemed genuinely
sorry to see his friend go. Frankly, he was surprised at Manwaring's freshly acquired self-confidence. He came to the
station to see them both off, taking probably not much
account of the gesture, expecting Manwaring soon back

among his beloved mountains, probably seeing it a lovers'
tiff, no more. Both Janet and he therefore probably wondered why Manwaring's valediction was so prolonged, so
sententious even for him . . . after all, Sydney lay only
sixty-five miles away. Heartless friend and father though he
was proving himself, Manwaring knew in his heart that his
talent *had* to come first, even allowing for his advanced
age and limited life expectancy. Janet might be more, might
be less talented than he, maybe a rural backwater upbringing could suit her best, but he could not risk such a sacrifice.
And others were now, after a fashion, relying on him.
Others far away. Others far different. Al Gold had written
him several more letters outlining proposals. Business, it
seemed, was booming. And always, *always*—that being the
American way—there remained room for expansion—not
like in some other countries. Deviousness came easily to
Manwaring, he was distressed to find that he wore his
manifold deceptions like a coat of many colours quite
comfortably, enjoying the challenge of his own duplicity.
He cried at the station though, and embraced Danny fiercely,
to the acute embarrassment of Janet; had they looked a
little more closely, however, they would have seen that his
tears were different to the tears they remembered in him.
There, there father, came a murmur from his daughter as
she ushered him into their compartment. In a blur of alien
fog-enshrouded timber and shacks they descended to the
port of Sydney. Where the sky was miraculously clearer.
Embarkation time ten pm. That very night, oh my god,
thought Manwaring, all our papers are in order, passports,
courtesy of my friends, all in order. Americans can arrange
anything. They were to sail, in strictest stealth, via Wellington, Papeete, Colon or Balboa depending on traffic through
the Panama, thence direct to New York in a Greek passenger liner. Janet was either going to have to be shanghaied
aboard, or alternatively, the afternoon could be directed
towards explanation. Manwaring favoured the former, did
not wish, was not *game*, to broach the latter, better to
explain all that after the event. Present the child with a
fait accompli and rely on her trust in him. He could hardly

convey a screaming, protesting girl aboard ship and keep her locked in her cabin for five weeks in the hope of attracting no notice. In his pocket, therefore—he even had the unfeelingness to fumble with it on the train, brushing against Janet's arm as he did while looking out the window—was a phial of strong sleeping draughts, purchased without the mandatory prescription from the pharmacy as a last reluctant favour, several of which he somehow or other hoped to insinuate into Janet prior to embarkation. Yes, it might arouse suspicion to carry her up the gangplank unconscious, but she was only a young girl, ill but not contagiously so, perhaps the after effects of vaccination he could explain if questioned; and their papers were all in order. He felt he had only just managed to keep intact his web of deceit, really quite a masterful coup. It would take Janet's mother more than five weeks to think of them leaving the country, of that he was confident enough. No one had ever left the country before. How difficult it had been, for example, to convince Janet of the desirability of her smallpox vaccination. She had stood her ground initially, but eventually succumbed at his insistence, based upon, he had claimed, recent medical evidence brought to his attention that smallpox vaccination prior to the menache—she said she already menstruated—or just subsequent to it then, was attended by side effects so minimal by comparison with those later in life as to render criminal the waiving of her current golden opportunity. He offered to be vaccinated along with her, just to show it didn't hurt. As a result, she spent two days off school in a fever. He took her to his flat, and stayed home to fret over her, and to feed her broth, fussing as his mother had fussed over him. So deep was his desire for her to accompany him, so confident was he that she would see, in the long run, the justification for the admittedly devious means he had been forced to employ: that at no time did he feel other than a mildly conventional guilt. But there was no doubt about it, even that guilt had taken its toll of him. His ulcer, if that was what it was, and not a terminal gastric cancer, raged afresh. When they left the train at Central he made directly for the milk bar and ordered a milkshake for himself and, as an afterthought, another for Janet. She stood, looking around her. It was early in a school holiday and many children were about. So sweet, as she sucked at her straw, here eyes straying under the gaze of her father in her only coat. Her last Australian clothes, but she didn't know that. How pitifully inadequate their two ports plus one violin case looked. Naked into the world!

Take this, he said suddenly, producing a sleeping draught from his pocket.

What for? Wide eyed in mock wonder she looked up at him, a little actress at any time.

It will soothe your nerves. Actually, already himself acutely nervous, he regretted the prematurity of this gesture, though no doubt a gradual sedation would achieve its ends as efficiently as a fulminant and perhaps forced overdose later.

There's nothing wrong with my nerves, Daddy. I think you're the one with nerves.

She touched his arm, compelling him to look at her. He almost took the draught himself. A shame to be placed in this situation of abducting one's own daughter. And to think she fancied they were shortly to visit her mother in Bondi. In actuality she would soon, since boarding began at two pm, as soon as he could contrive it, be laying on a bunk in a B deck cabin for two that had cost him half the price of his business or near enough, heavily sedated, bound for Jersey City. The quicker he skipped this country the better he began to think, freshly aware at the milkbar with its hordes of clamouring patrons of its calamitous early influence upon him. Yes, it had been a near thing, nearest thing you ever saw . . . Waves of remembrance, like nausea, he was bringing up snatches, daguerrotypes of maternally dominated childhood. He looked around, fearful of being cornered, driven back, time or space would be equally loathsome, by some figure of authority. The Masonic send-offs, the toasts . . . to his success in new ventures . . . 'The Fish' that night it all failed . . . mountain birds there would be in startled flight, ignorant, wide-eyed, unapproachable . . . defeat, endlessly driven back through a chain of forbears into improbable feats of pioneering. Strange inappropriate lands . . . born in Abbotsford, Sydney suburb, Australia . . . it's a small world but not that small. Ha—the pioneering lay in the retreat these days, and the more intrepid ran the faster . . . and similar dolorous thoughts to these. He did not like to think of the trans-Tasman conversations that would transpire between his daughter and himself. He hoped the cabins were hermetically insular with respect to sound. Stabilized, the agent had assured him. Stabilized against all contingencies.

In fact, he had left this particular period of time, from the leaving of their train to the sailing of their ship, as a complete blank in his master plan. Not through oversight: he had told himself he would have to play it by ear. And now the time had arrived. And now he had turned stone deaf in terror. His terror showed. He was aware that he had assumed a ghastly grin. His daughter was looking at this grin as she stroked his arm. Fortunately, she could be relied upon to misinterpret all his physical symptoms of distress. He felt her hand tightening on his arm. How she admired him for initiating this *rapprochement*, she said. Flush of words, above all, of innocence. Every second that ticked away on the giant hands of the railway clock above them added yet another second of resentment to come. He saw, all too clearly, affrighted, appalled now at the inevitable repercussions, her bitterness. She would never forgive. For that was her nature. But she would not *see* until too late, and her tenderness now would be seen by her later as what it already was to him, unreal, unreal as the chicanery that had evinced it. It was unreal, it did not exist, this touching of his arm in tenderness.

Don't worry father, she said. I know how you must be feeling. But mother will be ever so pleased to see you. She's told me often how she wishes we could all be back together.

His daughter always spoke as though she were reading a part in a school play written by a nun with no knowledge of human nature. It disgusted him.

He drained his milkshake and ordered another. Double

malt, set it up. Playing for time. But there was a limit to the amount of milk even a dyspeptic could consume. It was by then twelve o'clock.

Would you like to go for a walk? He gulped some antacid, all at once terrified at the finality of what he had arranged. The venture forth, each generation. Headed for some European port, he might have felt relaxed. But you can never go back. Never. There is a cosmic rule which says the flywheel flies always foward. The pawl is within us.

She was beginning to look at him a little suspiciously with the passing minutes, perhaps it had been over the mark to offer her a sleeping draught so early. But then he had always used those near and dear to him as reflective surfaces off which to bounce his own torment. And he was a great procrastinator. Another milkshake for myself and a Mickey Finn for my daughter here. This approach was hopeless.

Can't we go straight out to Bondi? I'd love to ring mother and let her know we're on our way.

But at once he had their bags in his hands and was moving for the station exit. Still in his heavy coat in the milder weather. Constant motion was the only answer. I'd like to show you around Sydney a little first Janet, we spend so little of our time together. I have not told your mother to expect us. It was to be a surprise.

Oh. Then at least we will leave our bags and coats here in a locker. As they passed through the locker room.

No, we will not be returning here, it will be inconvenient for us. We will have to catch a Bondi tram. Yes, a great surprise.

Can we go to the Domain.

By all means. And from there we can take in the State Art Gallery, where there are pictures of bushrangers that I know will interest you, and we can go through the Botanical Gardens, see all the plants. Your mother, as you may be aware, does not care for the outdoors, or to any great extent for the indoors for that matter. In view of this, perhaps, on our way over we should seize this especial day, take in all that we can, glance over the Mitchell Library, so many books you would not credit. On such a lovely sunny day as this it would be criminal not to walk unendingly.

And by then, thought Manwaring, we will be down by the docks. Perhaps as a finale to this junket, an inspection of an ocean-going liner.

Excuse me, he said, at the Railway Square tramstop where they stood waiting for a downtown tram. He disappeared into a subterranean men's toilet, leaving Janet at the tramstop by an ornate drinking fountain, to guard their baggage. Struck with a thought. There were many advantages, he had come to realize, in travelling light. In the privacy of a penny cubicle he withdrew his pouch of documents from the interior of his coat—and yes, as he had suspected, acting through that pervasive sixth sense which had already saved him from so many follies, or perhaps merely overcautious, he had not thrown out his complimentary visitors' boarding passes to the SS *Melena*. They were there, just like in appearance two pink passports from the Katoomba Savoy. An idea had suggested itself to him. A curruscation of strategy. They could board as visitors, thereby obviating all possible difficulties over getting Janet aboard, the only really critical phase of the entire operation, then, in the cabin, with his eyes closed and a prayer for the future on his lips, he could drug her or hit her once over the head or some such thing, leaving her in the cabin, which if necessary he could bribe a steward to lock or unlock, then, hiding her under her bunk or stuffing her into a cupboard, deship himself, pass through formal boarding procedures with their baggage and violin, and meet all problems with Janet on the open seas, subsequently, as they arose. Best, as far as the ship's company went, to plead ignorance and stupidity. But the child was sick, purser, and I did not wish to risk, as you would understand if you had a bone of sympathy in your body or a child of your own back in Piraeus, the strain for her of passing through the tedious embarkation and customs procedures . . . anyhow, as you have seen for yourself, her papers are all in order. They would not heave to or turn the ship about on account of Janet. He had been told that their ship, somewhat of a rusting hulk in company with the rest of its fleet, circumnavigated the globe non-stop except for occasional days in port taking on passengers and supplies, hadn't seen a drydock in years. Nothing short of a maritime catastrophe would be permitted to impede its pellmell run round the globe—Sydney, Tahiti, Panama, New York, Southhampton, Piraeus, Suez, Calcutta, Fremantle, Sydney, on the other hand the agent had assured him the cuisine was superb. Guaranteed to constipate an Olympic athlete.

And so, re-emerging and having satisfied nature, Manwaring acted without further ado as his daughter's cicerone to his green and familiar Sydney, his own dubiosity at the course the day had taken evaporating in his nostalgia for this final, painless duty, his mind and body obviously desperate for a few hours respite, an unadulterated and pure pleasure in the winter day and the all but empty Domain, the scattered figs, all never to be seen again or thought of, the paths, even the cameo city. Fig strewn. And the mock buildings, the library with its cavernous and portentous air as though no one should shout out in it for fear of dislodging the colony's naked dust and cobwebs and musty mock scholarship, more than one century old and undisturbed. He asked to be let see some photography in the Dixon, but permission was denied him by the custodian. He trod venomously all around and over Australia on the tiled foyer mosaic, thinking how little he cared for or admired Bass and Flinders and their confreres and schoolboy exploits. It was a pubescent dream, all this a dream, this colony, a dream of the accursed British, another fluttering of their dusty, blood-encrusted gonfalon. Should have had the good sense to have waged our own war of independence, but too late, at this point in time, for that. The bloodless coup is a stamp without ink. Within the library he took down a Who's Who and pointed out a few entries of interest to Janet. The local cardinal for one. She seemed genuinely interested. They had already been to see 'Bailed Up' with the log across the road in the state gallery. Janet, showing gratifying discernment, had preferred some dingy Turner or Corot in an ornate frame. He had looked around for an American painting but had not been able to find one.

And then into the Gardens, his treasured Gardens, a touch of civilization, if not quite the Versailles of his entitlement. He gave in gladly to the afternoon's recrudescent nature worship. With the shipping off the Kirribilli dolphins and occasionally in transit towards or from the heads, the city had a feigned, cosmopolitan air about it. He looked down to see what he could see of his feigned, cosmopolitan self against the green turf. His head rose up as from a lovebed of edelweiss to a chord by Wagner. He was content. In particular, he was content to be leaving this country forever. The sudden sight of, for example, grotesque Bondi, with its great sprawl of red roofing could induce, if suddenly flashed before him and even out of all this calm, fatal trauma. Already he was growing more refined, in preparation for the New World, which was also the Old World; in fact, the Real World. Farm Cove, James Ruse, see here the First Fleet, cargo unloading to Yorkshire accents, much bustle; and in the background of the cyclorama, Aboriginals, standing in dumb incomprehension, already feeling the shafts falling from their spears . . . and behold, the result. Never let a Yorkshireman smoke your pipe or discover your island, Janet.

They sat on the grass near the pandanus and looked at the harbour. He described, as though Janet were blind, its movements lovingly. What a lovely harbour, said Manwaring, in genuine appreciation. The door to his oubliette. How would you fancy sailing out that harbour some day Janet? I'd love it, she replied, but carrying no conviction. Her tone was weary, and she was responding only because afraid to face his petulance alone. Then he was up, up, grabbing the bags and the violin case, pulling at her, speaking of a surprise in store, a long-promised treat. It was now four. The SS *Melena* was docked in Sydney Cove, not ten minutes walk away. Past the stands of bamboo in front of the gubernatorial residence, the Queen's representative on this claimed soil, frowning dense-headed visage between starched epaulettes. Manwaring spoke freely of China and the high mountains of the Himalaya Range where pandas browsed in what properly speaking had to be described as bamboo *plain*. Bamboo being a grass, he pointed out, largest of the grass family, what wonders the world holds. Would you not like to see the world, my daughter, or a bit of it?

No, said Janet, I want to see my mother. There were signs, familiar to Manwaring, that she would soon break down and cry. After all, she was only young. She knew all was not well, the sixth sense, the unveiled or at least partially veiled only third eye, was hereditary. She was no fool this girl, the gardens, the history, did not impress her, she had had enough of the entire prevarication. Manwaring, setting down their baggage one last time, near the rocks before the final gate, wearily produced his trump cards. He wished so heartily that he could sit on the rocks and look across at the harbour, costive earnest expression like a person in one of Danny's photographs, while Janet played on their last day and mutual behalf a threnody for what they were leaving, on her violin. But this was not possible.

Look, he said, what I have managed to get hold of. Two tickets to see that ship over there. He pointed at it. Its exterior was indeed unprepossessing.

She looked at him, at his face strained with dissimulation, as though she had seen right through every miserable such love-stifling gesture he had ever tried to make at her. His dissimulated enthusiasm froze on his face. She pitied him for needing her enthusiasm. She was a woman, reacting to him in the inappropriate manner that other women had. It could be dangerous.

However, being only thirteen years old, she got up as bidden and went with him out the Garden gate. They walked past the tramshed on Bennelong Point. Manwaring became wry, and told his disinterested daughter how Bennelong had been taken to London, more or less as a freak on display, but had not enjoyed much happiness or success there. Like Darwin's Jeremy Button before or had it been after him. Something fresh and interesting for each and every London season from our intrepid mutton-chopped explorers of the Royal Society. Stale odours of talc and starch and farts in diverticulous bustles to be dispelled in a presence strewn with ill-at-ease savages in evening dress,

still nevertheless exuding an aroma of rank nature percept-
ible to each nostril, played at by a string quartet and
expected to enjoy it. Manwaring felt for the reassurance of
his own nose, his own real passport.

But she was not interested and seemed to miss his point,
as implicit, he had begun to hope, as any implicit point
could ever be. That grafts did not always take. That round
pegs could not always be fitted with success into square
holes. Where, by the way, had been his mountain Aboriginals? Had they lurked behind the ferns and gums he had
been in the very process of devivifying? No, but their sullen
spirits were everywhere even in the city, came patiently
from between the bars in the fence of the governor's ill-
merited mansion, came out of the bamboo. Spirits of the
Hawkesbury Sandstone waiting for their chance of a second
Dreamtime. And as far as he was concerned, they could have
it. They mocked in not mocking. You are welcome Bennelong, thought Manwaring, to accept my apologies over these
unseemingly depredations. It is clear civilization has no
business here, and never had. I, had I been the fop Banks,
should have personally declared the whole continent a
faunal reserve.

They walked, fallen into each their silence, across the
Quay, over the now subterranean Tank Stream, to the berth
of the SS *Melena*. It all went so smoothly, to the last detail.
In the cabin, which was providentially unlocked, he offered
her two sleeping draughts. She took them, without hesitat-
ing, without resisting. He said they would make her feel
less tired. She did not attempt to explain to him that they
were sleeping draughts. When he went through customs, he
explained that his daughter was already aboard asleep in
her bunk, carried there by a visitor; exhausted through
travel. He had been unable to prevent it. An assistant purser
went with him to see her, and was satisfied. Their papers
were duly stamped. Perhaps because Manwaring had given
up all hope of ultimate escape he carried out this final,
dangerous, irrevocable assignment on foreign soil as casually
as though perdition lay both ahead and behind and all round
him and any deeds of his no longer mattered, no longer

could protect him. As he ascended the visitors' gangplank, Janet's hand in his, their luggage in a locker awaiting his pick up later, he looked down into the water once. The Pacific Ocean. He was soon to see how almost unbelievably blue it was off the continental shelf, as blue as the Caribbean was green and greasy, and the Atlantic in its turn slate-grey. He supposed he should have been happy at this trend, but thinking back on it later, he was not. Perhaps Australia, in tenderness, was only a large South Pacific island properly considered and Banks and Flinders to the contrary, perhaps, after all, he told himself after leaving New Zealand and then Tahiti, only a large island, a sympathetic land, a grotesque giant South Pacific island in which men could relax, and once did relax, and should again relax. He could not forget the island as easily as he had hoped. He left it with a sense of deep failure. He thought continually of Australia, it troubled him. He recalled in vain the unhappy lives the Aboriginals had seemed to the missionaries to lead, terrified to venture beyond the coals of their fires at night, every day embarking with stone age weaponry upon a fresh attempt to wrest enough food for subsistence. Perhaps that was the correct way to live. After all, what did missionaries know. It is only when in the bush with a purpose that this dreadful nostalgia I have suffered from disappears, saw Manwaring, as though for the first time plainly, in transit. With visions before his eyes, asleep and awake, of his ghastly Blue Mountains postcards. Although the reflection was by no means new to him, it seemed fresh each time. In dreams it came, and in wakening, like flowing blood. He had had no real purpose there—had not been looking for food. Any food of his came from the bushland which the white man, his stock, had laid waste. Oh, the shame. Driving out the spirits, hence the emptiness of the hinterland veldt. Oh, how many times on that voyage he attempted to understand the experiment— of its having been a failed experiment, of that, there could no longer be held any doubt; and at different times, he thought he saw afresh why—although it was quite probably the same vision, again and again.

One day out of Papeete there occurred, for him, a particularly painful incident. Painful and illuminating. Not of itself, but in what it led him to consider. The ship stopped to pick up two drifting fishermen, who had sent up their only flare in the late afternoon from a clear blue sea into a clear blue sky. Half the ship had seen the flare, and shortly afterwards the pulsing of the ship's engines ceased, leaving a dreadful calm. The engine of their launch had broken down they said later, and the French Navy having searched for them for half a day had given them up for lost. At this time, they claimed, they had been no more than five miles off Moorea. Now they were nearly a hundred. They were two Tahitians, dressed, most inappropriately as it seemed to Manwaring, in tourist tee shirts with coconuts printed on them. As though sent forth as preliminary advertising. Apparently they had been out of fresh water for two days. They were taken aboard and, despite their dehydration, drank themselves into great drunkenness in the Castaway Lounge that night, the toast of the ship, at the captain's request. Manwaring, visiting the toilet at four am as was his habit, found one of them semi-comatose on the floor, still retching violently. Through what he supposed was coincidence, of the entire ship, they were given to sleep in that night the cabin next to his, which happened to be empty. It had been Manwaring's fortune to walk by these two men in the narrow corridor at six pm, dressed in his suit on his way to dinner, as they stood, fresh from their ordeal, a few minutes after having been dismissed by the captain, outside the door of the empty cabin while the steward fumbled for a key. They smiled politely. They held their fishing rods, which was all they had been permitted to bring aboard. Their launch they had been most reluctantly compelled to abandon, as the captain of the *Melena* insisted it would be swamped in the wake of the ship, he could not slow down, his schedule being so rigid, and now, thanks to them, delayed. How many cameras Manwaring saw trained upon these hapless shipwrecked mariners as they were helped aboard. And yet he was on deck with the rest of the voyeurs; cameraless perhaps, but on deck just the same. To witness their salvation. It was difficult to credit that another day or two and these men would have been dead of thirst, yet that same night they could get drunk, retch out their guts and no doubt copulate, judging from the number of women obviously desirous for their sexual autograph that evening in the Castaway Bar. Manwaring the photographer, alone it seemed to him of all the B deck passengers, did not photograph them as their launch inched nearer and nearer to the drifting ship. He at least did not want their autograph. At the sight shortly afterwards of their launch, however, empty, now legal salvage, disappearing slowly in the wake, he had to fight an overwhelming desire to leap overboard with perhaps a week's viaticum and fresh water and, praying for a favourable current, stake his claim on the mercy of the high seas. After all, these men's forbears had made it to New Zealand. Nothing stayed him except—that his fate was sealed. Too old. But more than just age, something else: he thought he knew now, thanks to life in the high mountains, better than to attempt to interfere any more with the natural world. He would buy forever now his fish from the fish shops of New York. Physical beauty was an artifact, not seen by man in his primordial and intended predatory condition, and art cannot justify itself. It is an interloping. He comforted himself, thinking of the wasted life behind him, that the proper study of his camera was man. As the empty launch, his for the claiming, drifted away on a mild, cerulean sea, one hundred miles from paradise. Had it not been said of Gauguin in these parts that when he entered paradise he took his European brain along? That most accursed of liabilities out of doors.

How terrifyingly small the world seemed. In next to no time at all they were passing through the Panama Canal. Manwaring had been tempted to stay right back in folksy Wellington, with all its tasteful wooden housing and freshly incredible greenery, but his fate was sealed; he had sealed it himself by staying aboard ship. During their Tasman crossing Janet had repeatedly said that they would have to get off in Wellington, that they had no option but to. Yet, some strange force stronger than either of their consciences sent their feet scurrying back down to the dock after a day's tourist wandering through Wellington, to be farewelled as the ship sailed out into the night by a group of wistful Maoris singing their strange songs. By this stage even, three days from Sydney, Janet's hand had found its way back into that of her father. The maelstrom circumvented. Her mansuetude, however, troubled Manwaring; churlishly perhaps under the circumstances, he would have preferred to have seen in her less perfidy. There was more or less in Janet than he had reckoned on. She had forgiven him, it seemed, on the surface—the surface had taken over. There was much truant in her, much adventuress, more than he had dared to hope. She was excited, as any young girl might be, at the prospect of a fresh life. And this, thanks to his blood within her, she could not help but allow to outweigh all her more proper, more responsible considerations. Which is not to deny that they existed, and even at times proved troublesome to her, both during the voyage and what lay for them at its other end.

TWO

Chapter 6

Janet, who later changed her name in the course of her profession to Jean, which carried over into her private life until eventually only her father called her Janet any more, even her son always called her Jean, married twice; in fact it was as though the very name Janet was an embarrassment to her, the first man, father of her only son, an entertainer on the stage from the age of about eleven or so and known in those early days as Wee Georgie Harris, whom she divorced on grounds of adultery after he came to her while she was pregnant during a lull in World War Two, what made it all the more sad was that she had been trying to conceive for the entire seven years of their marriage, something improbable about her womb made it unlikely that she would ever conceive apparently, but she did, just the once, but when he came home on leave she, in her naïve pleasure and excitement, found him appalled at the thought of the situation, struck a nasty underbelly blow by fate, the complications, the alimony, because he already had a girl in the armed forces pregnant as it turned out, and had decided to marry *her*. Thus, by making both boys legitimate, proving himself a thorough gentleman. So at his pleading she divorced him, then too proud to take the alimony the court awarded her she went back to Jersey City to live with her father, as much as she hated the idea of that, Jersey City as much as her father, he was intolerably sentimental by this stage, practically in his dotage to all appearances, used to cry whenever he saw the boy (whom they decided to call Danny) and thought over the circumstances of his birth—but determined, nevertheless, in the old tradition, to see him through, to give him every advantage and the best of educations, for he had brains, that much was apparent from an early age. She was by this stage, in fact they were both, they were all three of them therefore, US citizens. While with George—they had met because he, a big name already by his early twenties, but somewhat a miscellaneous talent in the smallish world of radio, now producing, now writing execrable scripts but suitable to a tee for what they were intended, barnstorming the country, now in front of the microphone with a guitar and a double entendre, and she, billed often enough to her horror but eventual reluctance only as the 'Aussie Girl'— though anything less Aussielike than her father by that stage would have been hard to imagine—mainly an announcer and singer of popular songs, had found themselves together on several one night stands, the type of shows that were very big in small communities around that time, the thirties, before television took the country over, in the days when live entertainment was still alive: he was already engaged to another girl somewhat of a soubrette apparently somewhere at the back of the stage, but the novelty of encountering a *virgin* was too much for him, like most men at

heart he cherished the thought of a *virgin* for a wife but
had given up all hope of finding one in the circles wherein
he moved; he just had to marry her. He had to do it. She
loved him, to begin with. Perhaps always loved him, for
nothing retains a woman's affections so much as sensual
weakness in her ex-husband, it's a vice difficult not to forgive, especially when accompanied by a warm, generous,
confiding personality and George to give him his due had
that. She was a virgin all right, so naïve, couldn't even get
the gist of half his double entendres, her father predictably
had protected her from any knowledge of his own business
to an abnormal degree, to the degree that when ultimately
she found out that his occupation was filming, then later
producing, pornographic studio sessions and blue movies,
she never forgave him for it. Actually, she did forgive him,
for how could she not? You think you can handle that sort
of material all your days then come home without your
hands smelling? Well *you* never cottoned on . . . They had
dreadful arguments after she'd found out, but had to take
one another for what they were, in mutual and self-imposed
exile from all that had been clean and relatively unsullied.
Even at the age of thirteen Janet had been fully responsible
for her defection, her apostasy, right back there on the
Wellington docks, and they both were aware of this. It took
all force from her arguments. Of course, her father knew
he hadn't a leg to stand on rationally speaking, but since he
never spoke rationally this didn't matter, somehow he had
come to believe that it (their anabasis) had all been for the
best, all for the best of us after all he would reiterate—and
they now included the poor innocent brat Danny—in that
filthy city, rotten with fuel fumes from the Jersey turnpike
and riddled with Mafia racketeers, and he part and parcel
of it all by his own volition. Are you *mad!* she would say to
him when in his self-justificatory moods. But she had to
smile, for his success certainly represented an achievement
in its way: after all, everything he had done photographi-
cally in Australia had turned out to be at least twenty years
behind the times. Yet somehow he saw, or at least persisted
in saying he saw, some obscure amoral justification for his

squalid existence, and it was this self-righteousness that upset her, although it might just have been a result of the shock that had come on finding he had spent his life painfully uncovering knowledge that turned out to be common knowledge to the world at large, it couldn't be denied he seemed fulfilled, what went into the family makeup was too complicated and horrible and terrible to dwell upon for too long, so they both decided to do the best they could with Danny, the cleanest slate they could lay their hands on, hoping that he would escape (presumably through mutation or exclusively double recessive phenotype) what they had fallen into, colleagues in sin as they had been on the run from the relative purity of the antipodean high mountains into the world's whorehouse and entertainment capital because unable to withstand boredom, hoping against hope that the sins of the fathers, now with the additional nasty admixture of George Harris who fucked and ran as a lifelong barnstorm from rural town to rural town like a charlatan with a platform of nostrums across the entire Great Lakes area mostly, Illinois and Michigan especially, would not seep too deep into young Danny and mar him beyond redemption, who would be protected from the flesh as even Manwaring had not been able to protect Janet, it was thus imperative that Janet, who was not a filthy girl and had never even sucked her old man's penis despite seven years of his almost nightly entreaties for her to do so—so he never really got his way with her she thought often in later life with satisfaction—you can only lead a horse to water—just an *ingenue*, a talented girl, and out in the country where they come clean and straight, Des Moines, places like that, well even Youngstown it was surprising really the hearts of gold lurking under the filthiest and gruffest of exteriors— they recognized purity in front of them when they saw it, the 'Aussie Girl' was a great favourite with them, they knew a girl who wouldn't suck a cock when they saw one and they admired her for that, and it was noticeable that after he was divorced by the 'Aussie Girl' George Harris' career never attained the heights to which he had reasonably aspired, so many years in the business, incipient openings (save for er, what shall they be called: they open wider all the time in that way they have until nightmares come of not being able to quench their yawns) suddenly closed all round, but it took him two more marriages to work out why, films, for example, where he would have been a natural, all the bravado in the world about him, maybe not so much a star as type cast in the picaro cameo role, for he was a handsome brute, they just never came his way. And when the 'Aussie Girl' wanted to go back to being just plain Janet again, it couldn't be, not even in Jersey City, they had radios, she was accustomed to the smiles of the Mafia men from limousines, she had that unfortunate knack of bringing out all that was best and protective in the worst of men, also, she later found when she married a second time, contrariwise of educing that which was pettiest and worst in the best and kindest of men, and probably for the same reasons, taking Danny with her at the age of six from their apartment on the banks of the even then putrid Hudson River, she remained, as a concession, 'Jean' to everybody.

She'd known, and her father had stressed, that her second marriage had to be a little more sapient than her first, not self-indulgent, an act of sacrifice if needs be, to a stayer, a man of some substance in the community—and preferably not the Jersey City community, they had all levels of degrees of respectability there—a respectable man who had the means to give Danny what he would need to become—well, frankly, a doctor, a doctor would be fine, the very thing. Manwaring had become so Jewish since living and working amongst real Jews for fifteen years that all he wanted for a grandson or a son or a son-in-law was a doctor. All the other men in the business too, even Al Gold's son was a surgeon, felt the same way. In fact, Janet often used to think to herself, she used to think a lot late at nights, a solitary thinker and stayer awake particularly after her divorce, that more doctors come out of the filth and slime of the community than seems even tolerably compatible with the utter falsity of the doctrine of sin and its immediate wages of guilt. Here were men making dirty movies, though denying anything wrong with that of course—never once was Janet allowed to see any of her father's work—she didn't particularly want to frankly, probably would have burst out laughing and hurt his feelings—though when she brought it up, to his perpetually acute distress, he *insisted* he adopted a morally neutral tone over the whole deal—it was at least certain he was impotent—as do the pimps, the pushers, the bootleggers, the purveyors of all vice and filth and sin everywhere, Janet could scarcely help but consider—but so long as they dedicated their offspring to community aid, they somehow in their own minds nullify their own nefarious existences and die happy, even if by a burst of machine gun fire face first into a plate of cannelloni, as was not all that uncommon, they had that one last happy moment, their books were square. So Danny it was for the Manwarings, Danny it had to be. The big hope. Albert and Janet, therefore, after George had disappeared over the horizon in a cloud of big talk, fetid spermatazoa and unpaid alimony, decided to start redeeming the family line, so many blots on the scutcheon already it looked like a pair of drawers hung out overnight from the clothes line of their Jersey City brownstone. And now Harris had added his genes to the porridge what in God's name would not be dragged in. Jean, the 'Aussie Girl'; but no longer a performer even though nowhere near thirty years of age and an income guaranteed, especially now George had inflamed public sympathy, a shrewder business woman would have capitalized, after all, what public was it took Shirley Temple to their hearts, but she just naturally rose above this venal impulse to stay in the game, for now she saw the game for what it was, game in which genitalia and sloppy gushing hearts do all the real talking, behind the scenes, and anyway, she wanted Danny to have the unbringing that's known as the 'stable environment', it especially appeals to show business personalities who cannot possibly provide it—though think of how many grade A undesirables come from this so called stable environment, it's a familial expiation, that's what it is and generally to the detriment of its charges . . . and not a succession of hotel rooms at night and pictures of him, a puzzled little boy, in the women's pages of the local daily, yes, I take my son along everywhere I play, he does his schoolwork by correspondence, sleeps in the trunk if needs be, we are inseparable. Jean, the 'Aussie Girl' was as devoted a mother and Albert as devoted a grandfather as any boy could possibly wish for, but each had learnt a little over the years, enough to realize that the devotion of this wounded basically sensual mother and this wounded tender-hearted, guilt-ridden grandfather were about as undesirable a combination for the stable environment as would be possible to invent, so she began looking round for a husband, no hurry. Look: let it take you ten years, said Manwaring, her co-conspirator, but for God's sake find a respectable doctor, marry, for the love of Christ, a doctor, and there'll be some hope for all three of us yet. He had taken to wearing phylacteries. She, an excommunicant since her divorce, still wore a crucifix. In such an environment—to bring in money 'Jean' took a job in the program office of RCA, point blank refusing despite popular outrage to go ever again on the air or appear in public—Danny spent the first six years of his life playing with all the Jewish kids in the neighbourhood, fed with gusto by their mothers, a community concern, who knew all about him, maybe the happiest days of his life. But no boy brought up in Jewish Jersey City can go out into the world without a burden of guilt on his back like the Old Man of the Sea, however hard his parent tries to protect him from it. He may not be aware of it until quite late, but it's there. The guilt of generations is breathed in with the air in places like that, and if you're not deaf, dumb, blind and stupid—and young Danny was perspicacious and very bright—heterozygous vigour—certain anomalies in the lives of those around you start to strike you very young. By the time his mother took him off to live with his new father he knew what his grandfather's business was, for example. And understood it, and what it catered for. That's not to say he didn't look down his nose at it, though. Nice and aquiline, his nose.

When Danny was six years old his mother remarried, a doctor in Ann Arbor, Jewish honorary at the hospital, a urologist to Manwaring's great delight—family functions

became for him an opportunity to corner his son-in-law
(everything he could have wished for in a son-in-law at
last) and detail his urinogenital problems, eventually Jake
in good humour ectomized his prostate and that seemed to
ease his situation, to quieten him down a bit—shortly afterwards however in an outburst of vituperation he renounced
his occupation and adopted land in a philippic of self abuse
against the sins of the world to whomsoever would listen
to him, at least six weeks of this, he even made a special trip
to Ann Arbor just to berate himself in the company of his
family, all the while Jake listening agreeing where necessary
—and eventually became a religious fanatic, just as he had
always hoped he would. And such perfect timing, just about
more or less the time when he would have retired from the
business anyway, which tended to obtund the sword of his
self-righteousness and renunciation just a little. Being simple
of mind he found it difficult to understand the intricacies
and subtleties of the Cabala and the Jewish mystagogues of
his neighbourhood were all intellectuals with vocabularies
and accents he couldn't understand one word in ten, but he
found what he was looking for in the Bhagavad Gita, he
thought he understood it with no difficulty, and there were
prescriptions in it for men like himself—the Vedanta were
beginning to attract the progressive elements within the
Jersey City neighbourhood even in those days, early times,
he ripped off his phylacteries, took the Gita to his heart,
forsook all his worldly goods, and eventually announced a
decision to retire to the Ramakrishna Ashram in Hollywood,
where the West Coast climate would also be good for his
old age. And this he did, as there was nothing really left
for him in Jersey City after Janet and Danny had gone to
Michigan, it had always been an empty shell really. So it
turned out his life ran the course he had once prophesied
for it back among the high mountains.

Janet and Danny and Jake and Jake's daughter Sylvia
once or twice politely visited him in his retreat, being on
the West Coast for Jake to attend a medical convention in
Los Angeles, although he was beyond caring whether he
had any visitors or not or whether he lived or died another

day for that matter, amongst eucalypts ironically enough he strolled out in a saffron robe without a hint of self consciousness, he had found contentment it seemed, he saw right through them all four of them how they secretly envied him his cosmic equanimity, but useless to proselytize. He did not adhere to all the tenets of his faith, just those which it suited him to. Jersey City, once he left it, became just a memory, a dream and not such a pleasant one, except possibly but by no means certainly for Danny, first generation USA, because, as Janet had learnt looking back over her own life and trying to make some sense of it, all adult experience is just a plexus, a web woven round a few early things, say, Hinkler Park, a favourite tree with a swing hanging from it when a child, houses, the way the sky used to look from the swing, a few sensual impressions, and when that web is torn or irreparably damaged as by translocation, then that life can know no deep pleasures.

Which is not to deny Ann Arbor is a pleasant enough town, in fact a town as like any other town in the USA as any town can be, a good community, and Jake, who had a daughter Sylvia of his own from a former marriage (about which nothing much was ever said—it's amazing the troubles even a scholar can land himself in, Manwaring used to remark out of his great respect, prior to his enlightenment, for scholars), a good husband, a paradigm, so tolerant of everyone's foibles, strong and calm and agonizingly wise and learned, stability . . . Janet needed him and the community of which he was a part and an expression, though learned to hate him as well, not deep inside, quite close to the surface really, but of course he saw all that, took it in his stride . . . or could it have been merely the strangeness, the perpetual *strangeness* of her surroundings (it could have been of course that she would have stayed a lifelong stranger in Katoomba, there are people like that, complete, absolute strangers once outside the womb), the people of the academic community she found were, *au fond*, mean and shrewd and bitchy and calculating just as in show business, not even in the rarified air of scholarship are these, the most fundamental of human traits apparently, lost. Or perhaps it was just that second marriages ought to be outlawed, no one knows their motives any more or has a clue about anyone else's, lives are so full of unknowns and grim determination and bitter secrets and sudden hurts that the partner could not possibly have foreseen . . . Anyhow, Jake kept himself very busy what with his practice and perpetual worry and concern over his patients all part of the business of being a doctor for which he received no emolument, taught as a professor at the University of Michigan Medical Center, she didn't often go in to see him, it wasn't her world, surely you don't need all that disinfectant Jake for that little bit of blood and guts . . . in short, was the very pillar of the community that she had picked him for when she'd first met him through a mutual friend at a place in the Catskills, that she'd known she and her boy needed so badly. But things didn't turn out quite as expected, or rather, as expected, things didn't turn out quite as expected if that makes any sense . . . she felt more than a little resentment, for example, that her whole life had become just a plinth for her son. After all, everyone should be equal, and when was *her* chance coming? She wasn't old. She didn't feel old. Others aged around her, but she didn't get old, never felt grown up. She was always astounded to read press reports of 'women' of her age, what a way to describe them. But if there now existed stability, she had it with Jake. Janet, or as she was always called now 'Jean' had moved well and truly outside her old radio circle of acquaintances, not much hurt or embarrassment was tossed up through old acquaintances, thankfully for Danny's sake George never did amount to much and she fell into an *external* anonymity as merely a wife and mother that she'd never before known, but it didn't feel internally a bit different.

Jake's house—his surname and hers now was ugly but uncompromising and somehow she felt inevitable Gruzman but Danny stayed Harris—was neither grand nor plush, just comfortable and unostentatious (but if she felt like cavilling, she'd say to the nobody there to listen it was ostentatious in its very lack of ostentation, how just like old Jake—but one must plant a firm foot on such spirals, especially in a second marriage where there's not much structure in a winding stair), made out of American dark timber, both inside and out, on a fairly lonely road though in a good neighbourhood on the Detroit side of town—he used every winter to take Danny with him on holiday, just the two of them would go on hunting and canoeing trips up to Lake Superior, for weeks together in the early winter or late fall. She wondered what they said to one another during those solitary weeks together, to tell the truth she was jealous, she could have taken ten lovers, she was still very attractive, but she didn't really want one, Jake was the kind he would never let on if he did know: except when in a rare temper he was the gentlest, the most polite of men, not a little like Manwaring in general appearance, from a distance at least (paternal and absent mindedly youthful, as though he had forgotten to grow old) but more hair up his nostrils and on his chest and wore spectacles, probably through vanity, only when reading (where'd your father get a name like Manwaring anyway he'd asked her once—that's not a Jewish name, and to be sure, it wasn't either. She'd asked her father once herself and, after a minute or so of silence he'd answered that either it was an Anglicization or else he'd been adopted—and then he'd burst out laughing), out of the back windows of her kitchen she'd watch the expanse of grey snow clouds and the barren yard and copses when they'd leave her, alone as they put it with Sylvia, who was at Bryn Mawr and never came home when she could avoid it without seeming extremely rude; especially when just her stepmother was there—Jean suspected she went often to see her real mother—though once again, there was nothing really, nothing you could put your finger on, *wrong* in their relationship—it was just not right from beginning to end, that's all—so was alone most early winters to all intents, it was strange how these intellectuals loved to dress up in furs and get out into the woods and feel that ice cracking underneath their canoes in the beginning of winter—and even her father now in a saffron robe was just an intellectual minus intellect—did they imagine it made them real men or something perhaps? So puerile. But at least it gave her the opportunity to readjust the thermostat, Jake liked the house to be hot, when he came out of the cold it had to be into the *heat*, frequently a gradient of over seventy degrees between the inside and the outside of the house, surely not in the best of medical traditions . . . no, the sadness was to witness the sadness of the air they assumed as they made to depart and departed, as though conscripted, helpless but to obey, an obligation for men to get out of doors under inclement circumstances coerced into rolling in the snow and ice so that they could know they were still men, hunters, could still feel, coded into their programs as if in cautious afterthought by their demiurge, well if it saved them for just two weeks of the year from the utter but unfingerable once again, *lifelessness* that surrounded them in every other particular; well and good. Jake wore such an impenetrable mask for a face—Jean knew he was medically, socially, any arena, every way, one hundred percent solid sterling citizen, right for Danny, but knew he hated it as much as she hated it, but couldn't speak about it, for to start speaking would mean for him never to stop. Maybe he confided only in men. His every most genuine gesture had a way of appearing contrived, deliberated, practised during a former existence. She reminded him of an alien learning to imitate a human being. The manual: Make the occasional mistake, otherwise you will arouse suspicion . . . Yet it was really not a condition to joke over, how much closer Danny and he had grown than Danny and she, he could look at her on any cold, fingery afternoon in winter, look right through her with those X-ray eyes of his, neutrino beams from deepest space, while at the same time in a harmless domestic gesture stamp snow, the appearance of which, melting on the forever unfamiliar wood of the forever unfamiliar floor of her forever unfamiliar house, mesmerized her—put his arm around Danny, her Danny, and she'd handed him over. Out of the window those snow clouds, those barren trees—she avoided the sight when downtown shopping of any negro in winter clothes, it brought into too sharp a perspective her own situation, imagined or otherwise—made her think of warm beds with George, wishing at times she could have pleased him more, but knowing really it would have made no difference, men like that can never be satisfied. Which is a very unfair observation to make about any human being. Even in Jake's eyes that were never completely lidded over when he slept—a stranger sharing her bed, eventually single beds, single rooms, always a stranger, no mutual dreams, no other than purely physical osculation—came hints somehow she used to feel, projecting, that he was not pleased either, she would have been disappointed if he was, he was unlike the others, did not, had never *expected* to be pleased this side or the other of the grave, had seen the world at first sight with painful clarity, and was bearing stoically and with as little display of stoicism as he could display a life he found each fresh day freshly unendurable. But endured, not knowing what else to do. And which she, supposedly his wife but never feeling it, could not ease. No cauterizing, no ordeal, no success, no pleasure, no trial, no vain hope of an afterlife with houris and harps—or even rebirth, no belief in anyone wiser than himself—his ineffable smile at the sight of her father in his saffron robe, disguised as polite greeting for example—death in life. She did not want Danny to grow up like that, well she didn't think he would anyway, he didn't have that sort of blood in him— could see it in Sylvia though, poor Sylvia, Jake took over Danny leaving Sylvia presumably to Jean, Sylvia, of course, sharp as a tack, must have realized this, they had absolutely nothing in common. She was another in whose veins ran a clammy ichor, no one should envy these Jews thought Jean. Strained attempts at conversation during days they some- times spent shopping in Philadelphia while Jake attended a urological convention at Temple U . . . her stepdaughter, long of hair, and deep of limb and breast and mind, but from the date of her birth a cosmic write off—and so pain- fully *aware* of it, and so painfully *uncomplaining* about it, that was the hard thing to see—her daughter, whose flesh she had never touched, whose mind she would never under- stand—condemned herself to a kind a perpetual adolescence, she found her daughter too old and wise—deracinated, she found herself increasingly stranded in her memory, of all places, in a day that resounded through her dreams, that one day she'd spent with her father in Wellington, that one day of her life that seemed real to her, fully vivid. She'd listened to murmurs, the voices of Danny and Jake arranging some trip together, or discussing Danny's boringly excellent grades; as in a dream, and her dreams were her life. The twang of her daughter's voice, who, if she had been able to touch her, probably would have opened out, maybe dangerously for them both, like a flower . . . suffering, the irony of it was, more from *her* own faultless father than Jean had ever suffered from hers, who had jumped her through hoops all her life. The joke was, that with all his talk of sufferings, Manwaring had never really suffered at all. As long as you can talk, you don't know what real suffering means. It means not being able to talk about your suffering. Life had been a game for him—and of how many misanthropes on the surface can this not be said?—what, for example, if he had had no applecarts to overturn? No systems to rail against? No enemies to quarrel with? Jake and Sylvia would have smiled at all this. Manwaring, who had no morals, no brains, no abilities worth mentioning in his new environment, had nevertheless triumphed, because, in his simplicity, he had unfolded his wings at the end and floated *like a bird*. What on *earth* had been the nature of those people back in the high mountains through continual self comparison with which he had arrived upon his estimate of *complexity*! The mind baulked. Although it had been her home as a girl, and she had been happy enough in it. She remembered, when she remembered it, the mountain birds, her father's photographs, and a girl at the convent who had done her business in the toilet like a sheep, countless droppings, had eaten like a sheep, had exercised and breathed like a sheep. What had become of her—but it was not a real question, one knew with certainty that she would be wiping the snivelling noses of about half a dozen brats in the same mountain town she'd been born in. A real question would be; where is my *own* mother now? If she could only touch Sylvia, a letter might arrive one day in the mail from her own mother; but she could never touch Sylvia. One trip the men went on they left her a book, as though in apology and hopefully, partial explanation. It was called *A Week on the Concord and Merrimack Rivers*. She read it but it did not edify her. Perhaps it was meant to show they canoed on a stream of words, not water. Where was George, who had used words in a totally different sense, more earthy, and somehow, though less articulately she supposed, infinitely more successfully, he had once told her in confidence, after lovemaking he was full of little confidences, talked all night, never-endingly, about himself, he was at least honest enough not to pretend any interest in anyone but himself, why he was forever uneasy in the company of men, it is because I know that they are all jealous of me he had said, secretly all jealous of me. Sailing into Wellington that night she had stood on the deck and seen strange land for the first time, the serene snow capped peaks of the north island, grey seabirds and their large brown young flying beneath the ship's rail for mile after mile.

Chapter 7

Jean's first and last lover as distinct from husband was one
of Jake's students, an Anglo-Saxon youth from somewhere
up in Massachusetts, probably Boston, very vigorous and
slightly coarse in his manner, not really her type although it
would never really have occurred to her to think of any
man along such lines as being her type or not her type, she
would never have had the courage and it would never really
have occurred for her to approach any man, she wasn't all
that interested in sex or intrigue, too old for all the stuff
not so much physically as mentally worn out, wearied of
men, not in the mildest way would she initiate or acknow-

ledge any approach, and they came now and again of course, because she had come to hate sexuality and all the harm it does to people, poisoning life at its very well-head as her father was fond of saying, and anyway, she only met men socially when she acted as hostess for Jake's occasional departmental get togethers at their home, joyless affairs with everyone too scared to drink much through fear of talking on other than the safest of safe ground, through fear of letting go in front of colleagues, through fear and mistrust, but on the surface—smiles and conviviality. Jake at such times was seen in his element with little wry smiles and sad grins during every conversation. With utter irrationality he always tried to get Sylvia to come up, there were the inevitable long distance phone calls beforehand and his silence to endure after Sylvia's polite refusals; either he was trying to humiliate her by this, pretending to be trying to marry her off to the occasional unmarried visiting luminary, generally confirmed homosexual—his monstrous callousness towards his daughter could only indicate, Jean had decided, that he hated Sylvia, perhaps it was Sylvia's misfortune to resemble her mother in some way obnoxious to him—or else because he felt Jean was not up to much as a hostess, but that would have been unlikely, as she was usually a very good, very cool hostess, just right for the atmosphere at Jake's parties. In all probability he had begun to suffer acute jealousy over Jean's innocent yet strangely voluptuous beauty—she always regretted her beauty, personally, in herself, of course her attention had been drawn to it many times by many men, but she scorned good looks in others, and saw her own beauty only as a curse to make men greedy and lustful and loathsome and inhuman, especially now she was no longer a personality but just an urban housewife, how the little lights came up in their eyes, horrible to see— all right, she had to admit she attracted the odd sober, scared man into light, maybe even mildly flirtatious conversation, but it was only a way for her to reduce tedium, of course it may have been that she still had some of the old air of purity about her, some women never lose their virginity, which is after all a state of mind and not just a

matter of a punctured hymen—Jake being fifteen years her
senior with the best intentions in the world was not up to
much in bed. So he was probably more than a little concerned over his potency, and so when in the company of
younger men he would probably try to subdue this concern,
so even was his keel even a feather in the wrong place . . .
having Sylvia up would help but she never came to remind
him of the former glory that had been his, this was what
Jean had concluded: understandably, when a young, agree-
ably blond and strongly muscular Anglo Saxon youth—in
build reminding her of George her ex-husband and Danny
her son, both thorough-going mesomorphs—even though the
youth, actually a man, was married with two small children
even though still in his early twenties—understandably
when he arrived unannounced at her back door one early
winter day when Danny and Jake had gone off for two
weeks camping the previous day it would have given Jake a
fit of apoplexy, but the youth mistook her smile at this
thought for a cordial greeting instead and came right on in,
pulling off a big jacket with tartan plaid like a lumberjack
wears, hanging it on Jake's hook. It had to happen one day,
and this was the day, for no particular reason. It was perfectly obvious what he had come there for, but perhaps he
imagined it wasn't, he had some story of course of wanting
to see Jake simulating surprise when told with a smile that
Jake was away. He did avoid (for he was by no means the
first male visitor who had visited her in hope), with singular
and rare good taste those, to her, revolting sexual mannerisms most men adopt when on the make, steeped in significance and deep asides and understanding, even managed a
fair performance of being interested in Jean as a human
being, avoiding all hint of sexual differentiation between
them, a pair of drones having a quiet tête-a-tete was all it
was . . . prepared, it seemed, to bide his time. After all, he'd
probably worked out he had two whole weeks to establish
himself and while she deplored his arrogance she had to
admire his determination to be patient, which was always
the best policy. But that alone would not have been enough.
How weak she was though, that day, for no particular

reason, how she disappointed herself, for how quickly her veneer of sophistication fell away, though all sophistication is but a veneer . . . how desperate she was to talk, she realized, he had figured her quite rightly that day, she was glad of company. Within two minutes her outer defences were stripped clean away. But she hadn't given any indication which could have led him to expect this—so what did he *really* want? Why had he chosen her for his insult? If they are not after your body, she thought, then they are after your mind and your reminiscences and all three if it can be comfortably managed the greedy little creatures, though she realized that take away from a life body mind and reminiscences it doesn't leave very much to love. Although it was just this little, indefinable but much brooded over bit that she felt *true* lovers *would* love, if they still existed. As in days presumably of yore. Over cigarettes and coffee therefore in the characteristically bookstrewn and untidy ashtray filled Gruzman lounge room she looked out of the window that day, and saw the bleak winter sky and heard herself puking it all up, all her loneliness, to this arrogant bastard for no good reason, her private history, though she had to admire his nerve in parking his battered pickup squarely in their drive blocking all chance of a getaway if he decided for example to rape her . . . would she really even want to get away she wondered . . . how pathetic she had become. No one ever called, she had no good female friends, like George, she had always aroused coolness and resentment in her own sex and had no intimates, just waiting to die perhaps or for Danny to be properly born; although unlike George, she did not ascribe it to their jealousy. She did not know what it was due to. All we seek is a hearing, she thought, of this time-worn material puked up once again. In exchange for a fuck he extends me his ear. But of course that way, with never a good thought for a member of the opposite sex, there lies no possibility of personal growth, there lies no possibility even of a simulacrum of love ever again. And she felt constricted.

She therefore sought to stamp out her ever-welling cynicism, just for that one day and more or less as an experiment, lending her own shoulder to breach the parapet, so all this man had actually to do was to sit quietly and listen to her. Wanting ever so much to *like* him, she extinguished cigarette after cigarette while he waited patiently like a bird of prey, smelling her weakness, listening to her speak, looking ingenuously into her eyes taking care that she noted how he refrained from touching her or even casting his eyes over her body in that brazen way another man might have been tempted to adopt. And so, by behaving in the way *he* thought the potential seducer would not behave, behaving, if he could only have known it and as she would have been glad to have told him if he had wanted advice, in the way all potential seducers invariably do behave, beyond a certain IQ that is or of at least a certain minimal experience. He most probably was not even listening to a single word she was saying, but was gentleman enough to respect the necessary preliminaries. And oh how necessary these preliminaries are to a married woman she realized. For some reason that day, from the time of his knock at the door, she was conscious of herself conducting preliminaries. The intended inamorata must be given time and scope to create of herself a sympathetic picture before she permits herself the sensual luxury of becoming a fallen woman. Looking at him again, she wondered what he really wanted. Not only sex, she eventually ruled in his favour, overruling cynicism, even staunching regret, because it would have been most convenient and certainly safest to have dealt on that occasion with one of those men who think they just want sex, who lay their penis on your prie-dieu and invite you to take it or leave it, but quickly, as they have no time to waste, a million women to proposition while their prostate's still intact—but here was a man with time, a rare man, a man with a little graciousness—or had she been so long out of the mainstream she had missed a recent trend? Or was she growing so old and weak she was easy prey? She liked though the thought of a man who had time to waste; one thing her two husbands shared in common neither of them ever had any time to waste. The trouble lay only in that she didn't want sex. How would she be able to tell this young man this, he would be bound to be bitterly disappointed. Sex, of and in itself, disgusted her, in and through sex she had seen people she had liked become less themselves, not more, as they had thought. Sex, she could tell him, if you can only see through it, stifles your individuality because all ejaculations are the same, right down to their duration on the stop watch, you ask Jake, the hand of Nature moves in and at that ecstatic moment rotates the old barrel wheel handle, grinds out yet another paean. But he would not want to listen if he was like other men. We should conspire against this duality that makes us forever one another's prey instead of which we pretend it is all we have to live for. Her father, she thought in this connection of her father, that great enemy of duality in all its forms. Make him a mesomorph though, give him back his youth and a fresh prostate and she wondered how long it would take him to rid himself of his saffron robe. She smoked and smoked, allowing the smoke to drift from her lips and nose as from a censer, deliberately provocative, hoping something would develop, speaking about her father and, impulsively, of certain aspects she remembered of her girlhood in Australia. It was certainly not what her muscular *vis-a-vis* had expected. But then it happened; the epiphany she had seemed to await for how many years. As she spoke of her childhood, he began to show genuine interest, he was unable to conceal an interest in *Australia*, what a strange country, he said, what a strange childhood, and became lost for a moment, genuinely, objectively lost to her, there was not the slightest doubt, she thought as he cracked with one hand the knuckles of the other and looked down, that it had cast a shadow, if just for one second, perhaps no more than that, her childhood, her birthplace, upon his overwhelming preoccupation with her as a woman. She saw this and seized upon it, focusing her whole attention on him, seeing him now as less than a stranger. Perhaps anything might have done it, it was nothing in him, it was something in her, but it was enough. It was what she had awaited. She thought, I am unblocked. And was. All at once and with the proper feelings of romance and mystery her heart began to beat faster, she felt her bladder and bowels constricting and trembling her vaginal walls beginning to moisten and her nipples sending wave after pulsating wave throughout her breasts. Something like that. As though inhabiting another's body she stood up and let her hair down, ever so slowly. Holding the bobby pins in her teeth as she took them one by one from her black hair. The interloper sat now with a numbed expression, unable to decide what he'd done wrong. She had confused and upset him, destroyed his timetable, things were no longer going according to plan, he registered the wretched plight of any man his preplanned schedule taken away. Had he played his cards wrong? Yes, certainly with Jake he had played his cards wrong. Jake did not like him as a person and as a man and thought him not much good at his work. About that Jean didn't know, Jake had confided in her, and she trusted implicitly his judgement in such matters, she had no option but to. If the boy came here with mixed motives, she thought as she withdrew the last pin to flaunt her mane of hair at him, one of them has certainly been revenge. So what. She no longer cared. This was to be her day. He had passed what had turned out to be a difficult, fiendish and imprevisible little initiation ceremony of which she and he both could have known nothing beforehand. He was human and she was human. He cared a little, and so he could come into her inner sanctum if that was what he took it for. He was to be pitied if he was not good at his work, because he didn't look the type who wouldn't care about that, and so he could suckle at her breasts. It would be nice to be in bed with a gentile again. As though hearing another's voice she said, let's not waste any more time, not a minute longer, come on.

The effect upon him of having had his presumptive initiative usurped was predictably devastating. She was prepared to believe he had lost even his erection. She smiled. Where's all that self confidence now, she thought, perhaps even whispered, as she watched him hunting round for his cigarettes, anything to do with his hands. He now prevaricated. He was now wondering whether it was not a case of the poor old user being used, a feminine gambit he had probably heard of but never thought he'd encounter. She saw passing over and again his face that old familiar linotype women learn to read: what have I here, a woman of the bloody world? She imagined him depicting himself soon to be kicked out of the bed hearing downstairs a strident voice from the bedroom declaiming not much of a cocksman buster, even old Jake can do better than that three times in rapid succession and I refer to his twenty one gun salute . . . Can the grapevine have failed me? How come I never heard about all this on the grapevine? Good. It was the mark of the sensitive individual fear of impotence and the grapevine. About the grapevine and herself, she did not care. She had him at her mercy. He followed her into a bedroom, she climbing and walking in an exaggerated lope. That's Jake's bed, she said to him when they came to it, feeling a little light in the head and heart, Jake sleeps there. Do you want to get into it? He looked very afraid, perhaps not as experienced as she and he both had thought. She stripped to the waist, but never allowed his eyes to move from hers in punishment for his being such a bold boy as to have come there in the beginning, in command initially, but then relaxing entirely so as to let things slide over to him, they embraced and he fondled and licked her mouth and her ears and her breasts, very hungry, but a little afraid of the ejaculatio praecox. To disgrace himself in her eyes. She enjoyed him as she had never enjoyed poor Jake, and as they looked in one another's eyes there seemed a hint in them of mutual respect, perhaps even incipient love, he was young enough still to be capable of love. And if he was unhappy at work and at home, why then, so much the worse for him and so much the better for her. How nice it was going to be presently to feel that strong, foreign young body pulsing out all its failure and probably nascent inkling that owing to corrupt worldly values it was going to be considered to house a mediocrity, a crumb bum as Jake liked to call them, through not being sick enough, tough enough or mean enough. Overwhelmed by a sexual appetency she would not a day earlier have believed herself capable of, somehow it had arisen within her and in no way in response to him, she felt a desire to devour the contents of this little sturdy house of flesh and circuitry that her husband would see only as so much plumbing, partly to spite her husband in his purblindness but also as if it was all she wanted from the entire cosmos at that time, the universe somehow condensed into a few droplets of precious semen to be withdrawn and not to be spilt from this stranger, but at such times there can be no strangers can there, we are all intimates in this galaxy at least, all the force pleasure and misery —the sight of a man more man than most men prepared to voluntarily reduce himself to sheer animal and all for one's own sake, it has to be beautiful and the ultimate gesture of faith. Misplaced faith maybe, but she felt she could love this man for the gesture alone. Oh, the immense *relief* of it all for her, the tendering of the *love* of this stranger.

Stand up, she said, take off all your clothes. He did so trembling, even removed his socks, sure sign of unbending intent. You've made babies with these, she said, taking his genitals in her hands, good, I'm glad, I'm proud for your young wife, I hate virgins. And how they had then laughed, happy uncomplex laughter it seemed to her, rolling around in the bed wrestling all over Jake's pillow that day, at one point they had a fight like a pair of dogs over the pillowcase with their teeth snarling at one another, until she had made her breasts slowly undulate, having noted early in the game that this distracted him to a degree . . . she was already, before anything much had happened, afraid for his wife and children, afraid for herself, because when a young man seeks out an older woman with an unblemished reputation with all the young girls there are around the campuses it can only mean something dangerous and at the same time something admirable in him, ie he's tired just as she was of all the crap, can no longer pretend to be interested in word games that no longer interest him, after tail not so much as, well, perhaps, let's hope, love. Leaving her own slacks on, she bent over his penis (that's what they call it in the medical texts) and watched the rolling of his eyes as she beckoned him on with her lips into a helpless temporal grave. Attempting to understand what he was thinking, but eventually concluding that he was no longer thinking at all, she swallowed the acrid universe like a pill, a thing she had never done before but instinctively expert, soothing him afterwards, for he had begun to cry, cry like a baby.

Why?

She pulled his head down between her breasts and let him redeem his wounded masculinity as soon as he was able, surrendering to him her slacks, which in his anxiety he tore, and in the time that was hardly time that followed afterwards they saw only one another's desperate eyes, anxious now only to be mutually adored. To touch, to touch. But even in her ecstasy she was thinking the things that all the other men in her life had taught her to think, it's just a fuck like any other fuck when all's said and done, tried so often and always found so lacking because it has to be this way, every woman and every man the same in this, this primeval glissando, cunningly coded this dissimulation, there *is* a way to touch—but we weren't taught it. It isn't in us. This, why this is just a confidence trick to make us all look ridiculous down here and keep the show rolling on for reasons unknown . . .

In a world of fucking we have made love he said to her afterwards, although he was now obviously bored, sated, wanting to be up and about and to be clean and single and feel the winter air on his dry and shrunken prick, oh she knew these signs, to be free . . . smiling at the felicity of the phrase. That's what they say to all the girls, yet back among the boys on the grapevine fucking it will stay. If they could only hear the words on one another's lips at night they might fear one another less. But she smiled, finding no answer in her. In the crystallinity of relief after this masturbation, she felt her cynicism returning quite naturally. What could she have expected of him anyway? She would have liked to have talked, but he only wanted to leave. Don't think that because you can get up now and run you will escape the suffering you have stolen. They were each content because they had each found themselves, individually speaking, capable of more generosity than they had imagined they contained. They projected things on one another, and

smiled. We look into one another's eyes only to see our own
proud reflections there. As in the mirrors that some men
need. And what is more, it does us no harm to indulge ourselves this way, on the contrary, it enlarges us, to relearn old
truths freshly is no disgrace. If only Manwaring could have
seen that in the line of his work. Great clarity of the mind
after intercourse. She had nothing to offer him, absolutely
nothing. You have a gift she said to this stranger, a great
gift. You will be a traveller. He didn't understand, though
how delightedly he laughed, possibly because it sounded
like a valediction of some sort, she was being ungenerous
again, she had used him for her own purposes and how long
since she had heard such fresh laughter? It was worth all the
opprobrium it would bring her, because something in his
manner told her he would be a great talker as well. But she
didn't really care. Too languid to seal his lips forever. As he
dressed, she watched his self satisfaction, he might even
have enjoyed her, he could even have been thinking I'll file
for divorce tomorrow and go back into general practice for
her, stuff this town and all the people in it—but hoping no
doubt deep in the heart of him that it would not quite come
to this. And confident that she didn't want it to: after all,
that's the beauty of the relationship with the married
woman, the ultimatum that never comes, her or me, who's it
to be . . . single girls are so greedy. He played for a little
while with her breasts as though it constituted bad manners
not to, then excused himself and drove away. He never
came back. There could have been reasons why, but she did
not want to think about them. He could have come back,
but never did. The others that followed timidly in his tracks
got instead the treatment they so richly deserved. Heard
about it on the grapevine.

If there is a trend in the family, Jean used to think, then
it is towards intellect, bodily strength and healthiness of
attitude. Thank God. It seemed hard to cavil at this. She
thought of her father, emotion personified but eyeless. His
reaction to every situation had been purely instinctive, and
he could be a monk now only because of his emotional
nature which could find satisfaction in the daylong contem-

plation of even a leaf she was prepared to believe, whereas under the same circumstances anyone else would have gone mad with boredom. He had often said to her that his reason for leaving Australia had been on account of boredom there, but he described her boredom, not his. Not so much present as incipient, however. Nascent. The mountain environment, as he put it, had offered insufficient scope to a child of her, already then obvious if to him mystifying, potential. But then again her mother had been nobody's fool. He himself could have stayed there forever in perfect contentment and tranquility, but in the best interests of his child, and against the specific instructions of a court (which was why she must never go back) he had removed her to Radio City. She had him to thank for what she had become. And he seemed genuinely anxious that she thank him. The way he looked at her.

She supposed he was right. By virtue of each generation's deliberate choice to dilute their bloodline through miscegenation with people as unlike themselves as they could find, changing continents where necessary to do so, the odious, sensual, over intuitive, over-emotional Manwaring bloodline appeared to be on the way out. There could soon perhaps be a genuine champagne celebration, maybe Danny's child. What she, for instance, had not personally achieved by way of nature with George Harris—and thinking back on it she understood now a little better her father's horror at her initial choice, if choice it had been, which had gone far deeper than mere horror or disapproval, and which she at the time had failed to comprehend—though she understood it well now thinking ahead of her own reaction should Danny walk in one day with a gravid chorus girl or bluestocking—learn to avoid these extremes as they take generations to work out—she had managed to provide by way of nurture with Jake, the realignment. If you cannot breed them, then you must achieve a graft of some description. Danny appeared to have virtually no emotions whatsoever. It could be that in his case the pendulum had swung too far. But then it would be up to him to rectify this situation in his own marriage. Hopefully, he would not go overboard about it. But it would be his lookout if he did. It was not her responsibility. Each generation must take stock of itself. It could not, for example, have been envisaged by Jean that Jake and Danny would become such firm favourites the one with the other.

As for herself, she supposed she was someplace in the middle. Still too much of that dank, sinful, odious, ghetto blood. But she was not like her father—she *reproved* herself over her blood. She knew the doctrine of original sin and had heard as far back as the convent, with a sinking heart, of the doctrine of predestination. Which she instinctively believed, as the concept of the beneficent Creator she could never entertain. She entered the church, but God probably never even knew she existed. Didn't see her there. Not in the books. So by massive efforts of self control which no one understood or appreciated—including her father, who had no conception of self control and wouldn't have approved of it if he had—she had stayed pretty much for a Manwaring on the straight and narrow. Which she hated, but it was an obligation she felt towards Danny. That's why she deserted her profession. After all, the Lord's Prayer says lead us not into temptation, not help us overcome it. Once you *see* it as temptation, as Christ so wisely remarked, makes no difference whether you give in or not, if you *wanted* to, you *did*, as far as I'm concerned. And I'm going to punish you for it. That's why you've got to get it out of your bloodline: that's why it makes sound sense *only* when approached in the correct manner, ie, as a means of diluting a crumb bum blood line. But this doing it with unbelievers and without even making children; why that's ridiculous and degrading, the most unnatural affront I think I've ever received . . . To all intents and purposes, therefore, you might as well give in. Like Manwaring, now he *always* gave in.

Save one. One intent and purpose. Social dignity. Family standing. Manwaring despised this, had gone three thousand miles out of his way to become a pornographic film maker and disgrace the family standing. But his family was only the one daughter—and she didn't really matter as he no doubt realized, representing as she did some sort of half-way house, a *tertium quid* between her father and her son. Two extremes, as unlike one another as chalk and cheese. Couldn't even confabulate concerning the weather with one another. She ended up both *avoiding* temptation—which was honest of her and over which she prided herself—like abandoning her profession early and the George Harris people that dominate that profession—and she forewent opportunities, over which she could hear her father Man-waring half crying out Coward: Gutless Wonder! And look, the score of transgressions goes up irregardless. But she didn't heed, she wasn't listening. Looking to the future. For the sake of her son, that he should never know his mother was a potential nymphomaniac, religious fanatic, alcoholic, drug addict and all the rest, she forewent opportunities. Of course, in any life there is bound to be the occasional lapse down into reality. Reality—a sort of Limbo really. What the people call real moral lapse, having never read their bibles close enough. She had questions she would have liked to have asked though. Why had her father set her down right in the middle of Radio City? Was it just so as to see if she was up to the stresses there? Was it just to see if she could survive? Was it to see if she would sink or swim? Just plain old dispensation?

Tell me God, which is sinking and which is swimming, so I'll know. This was the essence of all her prayer. Cut off from both the world of emotion (which in its purest form is very squalid when seen through the eye of the intellect) and the world of the intellect (which in its purest form is very barren when seen through the eye of the emotion), she stood dazed. Bedazzled, turning like a slowing top in a collapsing gyre. Behind her, pure emotion she thought, ahead pure American intellect. She stood, seeing herself as no doubt a monstrosity to them both. Her father, filled in his later days with never ending talk of the cosmos—of which, she was convinced, he knew nothing—her son, who couldn't speak to her at all, and from whom she hid in the house, lest one day to find that Jake had made him too perspicacious to even *like* her any more. She felt his embrace

always somewhat less than warm. Was he afraid of her? Did
he detest her and didn't want her to know? Jake had taught
him to spare the feelings of the weak? Don't worry, she
should have liked to have reassured him in some round
about fashion, it's not contagious my darling son. I tried to
get rid of it for you as much as I could. She was glad about
Jake, had Jake not been available or someone like Jake she
might have overloaded her son like so many single mothers
do with guilt and affection and thwarted, sensual motherly
love with the best intentions in the world albeit, perhaps
even turning him into a frustrated faggot. So it was as well
she had married Jake after all, Jake with whom she was so
unhappy. She might have been different herself if she only
had had a mother. As far back as the Manwarings could
remember, only the one parent. Now wait a minute, could
this . . . perhaps . . . *explain*? . . . A very stern mother, if
Manwaring's verdict was accepted. A stern and horrible
woman of great severity. But she (Jean) remembered
pleasant days, only pleasant days when visiting Bondi with
walks just the two of them along the beach, streets where
every goddam garden had its frangipani tree . . . a mother
who had seemed friendly and loving, but as though all the
time *waiting* . . . waiting perhaps for the day she could
tell her daughter what the old man was like, assuming she
didn't already know, apologize for his prepotency and explain how this dreadful error had come about in the first
instance. Like sidling up to a corgi cattle dog cross, look, I
don't know how I could have let this thing happen, first
thing I remember there he was somehow worked his way
between my legs . . . But she had waited too long. The same
mother she had eventually to remind herself who had signed
her off into a convent like a teratological case because she
couldn't be bothered looking after her, or perhaps seeing
her father over the years coming out in her in vicious
quotidian little ways, too terrible to behold over any lengthier
a period. Who hadn't bothered instigating so much as an
enquiry into her disappearance. Her disappearance from the
convent.

She remembered the convent well. Mass in Ann Arbor

just wasn't the same as back home in old Mount Saint Mary. Mount Saint Mary, why I wouldn't want to be guilty of it. Mountain schoolgirl humour. But nothing in Ann Arbor to compare with this. Nothing in America the same. Looked at from one viewpoint it was a better land, from another a worse land, but no one could deny it was not the same land. Early she learnt to shut up about this, growing to appreciate that Americans do not like to hear their peerless country compared unfavourably with any other. Just an infant in a diaper, Manwaring used to say, sitting back in his Jersey City brownstone feet up over a bottle of Jim Beam: just a baby in a diaper, his country he was referring to. Never any conviction in his voice when speaking of his old country though. He never understood it. So with no mother and no father to speak of, no friend and no lover, just an American son, an American husband, an American step-daughter and no religion really because the church was in the wrong country, she began to cause the other members of her family more than just passing concern. I worry about her, they'd say to one another when she wasn't in the room, yes, I'm definitely deeply concerned. She did not doubt that Jake had heard of, and of course forgiven, her little breach of etiquette in screwing his student. Jean, he would say, My God how I worry over you . . . you're going to end up a grade A schizophrenic you know that? You see, Jake *too* was no fool. She was the only fool in Ann Arbor Michigan. What I want Jake, is a few foolish friends . . . *Read*, take up pottery, take lovers if you have to . . . I'm a man of the world . . . but for Christ's sake be happy, all I want is to see you happy. Out of his own unspeakable misery he had this immense desire for happiness in his wife, at any personal cost, he did not care. Anything, he did not care. But she denied him even that.

When you offer me books, pots and lovers Jake, you do us both an injustice. Firstly, you turn yourself into even more of a gutless cur than you are normally, and secondly, you spoil for me all these books, pots and presumptive lovers. As a matter of fact, I don't want your books, pots and lovers. I don't know what I want, and neither do you. So

why don't you just shut up? I just know I hate this country
and what it turns people into. Take yourself for example, a
reasonable specimen of a mid-European Jew who should
always have a tear in his eye and a matzo ball in his belly.
Take everyone you've ever introduced me to, you unbeliever.
Know what I'd like to do? I'd like to buy an automatic rifle
on your credit card and come into your hospital and show
you some *real* blood and guts for a change. Real blood Jake,
that's what comes out of your body when someone shoots
you.

I've seen plenty of that Jean.

No you haven't, I can tell.

If you're so sick of the place Jean, why don't you get out
of the country, go back to where you came from? If you
think it'll make you any happier, please do it. But let me
caution you before you spend all that money of mine; you'd
be a malcontent anywhere. You just so happened to grow up
here, and it suits your purposes to blame your sorry lot on
the USA. Well anywhere else would have been exactly the
same for you, believe me.

I don't believe you. Anyway, I was born here Jake, born
and bred in this briar patch to all intents and purposes. But
you don't have to worry any more, because I'm going to get
a job, I'll teach you.

At last—some sensible talk. He was relieved until he found
out what the job was.

She managed to get herself a job as some sort of factotum
or menial in a school for mentally retarded children. Her
pay was negligible, her tasks the most menial imaginable;
the changing of soiled trousers and skirts, the sweeping out
of the staff rooms, preparation of cut lunches, washing up,
running errands for the teachers etc. Apparently she's seen
the job advertised in a local paper and felt that God (and
that's Christ's old man not Jehovah as she pointed out to
Jake, who thought an atheist and broadminded enough to
marry a Catholic—probably went out of his way in fact to
find one—still had an exposed nerve somewhere in the
religious area which Jean used frequently to probe after
during the course of arguments)—God wanted her to do it.

But that's negro work, expostulated Jake. Wait a minute,
what I meant was; and whilst I've nothing against negroes
—now here Jean was laughing and Jake flushing because
she'd caught him out he with his small l liberalism as it
seemed to her . . . a little unfairly perhaps as a matter of
fact some of his best friends were negroes and they weren't
easy to find in the circles in which he moved—but it was at
least a comfort to his wife to know so many were anxious
to befriend the dark people, they would never want for
friends in spirit Jean thought. She often pretended to herself
she was herself passing as white, it helped her live with
the facts of her existence. Or at least enabled her to lay the
blame. Nothing against negroes but I'm not exactly red hot
over the prospect of any wife of mine working as a menial.
You just did this to get at me didn't you. Fancy, going to
such lengths.

No, Jean kept unaccountably laughing at him (Danny
could hear quite a lot from his room), no, you don't understand at all.

Well then, it's an obscene expiation of *guilt*, that's what it is.

Now you're getting warm. Guilt, that's your speciality.

The old ploy of the transferred epithet. Jean well understood that the chilly cerebration of Jake and his ilk owed
itself in large part to an overreaction away from their gushing, over-emotional parent. Jake still had a mother in
Philadelphia, Goldie Gruzman, of whom he was acutely
embarrassed, perhaps partly because of the name, and in fact
the initial attraction between Jake and Jean had lain in their
mutual and at the time (in the Catskills) comical great
embarrassment over their parent. However, instead of
matching Manwaring up with Goldie, which would have
been the sensible thing to do she being a respectable if very
old widow and a great cook and would probably have suited
Manwaring very well at the time, scolded no doubt a lot
of the increeping religious bullshit out of him; they had
married one another. Their parents, initially a joke, became
in time an embarrassment, pulled out as taunts in fights.
To get away from Goldie, Jake had gone to live in an
emotional North Pole. You're just jealous you're not capable

of it, Jean. Where Goldie could not grasp at him. Only Jean, who with her obsessively illogical behaviour had probably begun to remind him of his mother, was able to upset his frigid equanimity. And so she had taken, no doubt in order solely to humiliate him, a job as a menial to a group of teratological children whom he personally would have aborted or done away with shortly after birth, or as soon as their condition became apparent. How he detested in Catholicism its illogical concern for the human detritus that was already cluttering the world up for the rest of humanity! He even took in several anti-Catholic tracts, finding to his surprise that they amused Jean, who read them avidly.

As far as his attitude towards negroes went, he was certainly very embarrassed for these people in their plight and would have done anything for them short of actual physical association. Danny had cause to remember from his room how at one of his more memorable *soirées* he brought along in all innocence a visiting colleague, young Polack from Buffalo who had mortified Jake's liberal Jewish colleagues along with Jake—(and in so doing delighted Jean)—by loudly confessing himself a rabid nigger-hating bigot. He also drank too much, behaviour which also endeared him to Jean, who even attempted to match him drink for drink until driven back from the bar by Jake's obvious displeasure and jealousy: because like most men, Jake feared most of all the unknown; the negroes, wasps and suchlike; and it was always men like the Polack that he suspected most and suffered his greatest silent torment over, absolutely incapable of understanding that Jean would have nothing to do with her spiritual equals, being far too nervous and ill at ease in her foreign environment, but liked instead, was *forced* in fact, to seek out elsewhere the innocent—a trait she deplored in herself, queen of the spiritual kids—sad to see anyone so gifted so unsure of herself, unable to adjust to a strange milieu, even Jake admitted this—though it was to his ultimate advantage of course.

This admission, made so candidly in deathly silence and general embarrassment and shifting feet, the Polack then attempted to defend on a purely scientific basis, citing IQ tests (suppressed, as he put it, by the authorities, being political dynamite) showing the negro to be the mental inferior of the white man, and pointing out that, on a strictly Darwinian basis, it would not be too surprising to find that a people descended from successful slaves (those least successful in a strictly Darwinian sense taken to include the most spirited and intelligent as well as the stupidest)— which also implied progenitors from Africa stupid enough to be caught—would be less intelligent than the average white man: whereas (smiling at Jean over the whisky bottle glad to feel her warm radiant sympathy for his stand, though of course it was not for his stand, which she found in fact as odious and detestable as did her husband, but for his courage in daring to take such a stand in a roomful of small liberals) take the Jews, for instance—contrasting Jews to white men looking round he noted with feigned surprise that they were all Jews in the room with the exception of himself and the student from Boston and maybe Jean; but went on undisconcerted, too drunk even to care—well, bred in urban ghettos for generations, living for centuries off your wits, I am not surprised to find you all above average IQ. On the other hand—he gulped down his final whisky as if signalling an end to the discussion—brains aren't everything.

Jake had chided, half smiling quietly in the utter silence, it's not true you know. The Polack had laughed unbelievably loudly, looked across at Jean, slapped his thigh. The party, now out of hand, came to a rapid and premature close. Afterwards, Jean and Jake had a violent argument, Jean by then quite drunk and foul-mouthed as she always got when drunk, and Jake very jealous of her attentions to the loathsome Polack, or anyway, what he mistook as her attentions . . . and how can you fight clean after all when the woman you've married turns out to admire a dirty-minded bigot? What do you see to admire in that shit, he shouted in language uncharacteristic of him: I wouldn't be surprised if you two got it off together behind my back! Yes, you'd think that she shouted back, that's the very thing you *would* think, but I am not *all* tits and cunt you know! Ever occur to you that I might even have a brain and sympathies that aren't under hormonal control? Goddam quacks, think you know it all. . . . Jesus Christ Jake, you give me the shits when you go on like this . . . (How lucky, Danny used to think, the house was in an area of sparse residential density, well-spaced houses out of earshot of one another—or could it be that such language is not unheard of in less professional circles?) . . . I like the guy because he has the courage of his *convictions*. Now you heard him say how when he was a kid the blacks moved into the neighbourhood and his father lost his job . . . Ok—and you think *I* was born with a silver spoon in my goddam mouth? You think there weren't blacks in South Philadelphia? . . . Oh, I know Jake, I know about it all: but Jews are *different* . . . Jews are different—Jews are *not* different! Jesus Christ woman! How sick I am of hearing that remark! What's the difference between a Jew and a goddam Polack for Christ's sake? Catholicism, that's what: enough to make one a bigot and the other not I'm telling you Jean. Anyway, that guy's work, if you only knew . . . If you're about to tell me he's no good at his work, save your breath Jake, I'll kill you, so help me God I will kill you Jake! You and your bloody work! Perk on your work! Don't you infect my Danny with your puritanical ethics or I'm warning you, I'll kill you, I'll put a leglock on your filthy head some night . . .

Suffice it to say that when Jean took a job in expiation of her many guilts and sadnesses her husband Jake was less than overjoyed about it. He had fought, struggled all his life; and now this. His wife by choice a menial. It was quite true that his parents had been penniless immigrants—but; as Jean liked to point out, where is the successful Jewish doctor whose parents were *not* penniless immigrants? Jake, you old two-faced son-of-a-bitch—you can have no *conception* of what it's like to be a negro—If ever I should catch you with a negro Jean . . . You'd scream and he'd beat your fucking brains out for you . . .

Danny generally heard this sad filthy and degrading talk in snatches from his room. When he was little he'd tell his mother in the morning, relating what he'd heard or what he'd thought he'd heard and she'd just say, ssh, my honey bun, a nightmare. When he was older, an adolescent, he'd confront Jake with the facts and Jake would stare and stare at him as though compelled to decide anew whether they were spiritual flesh and blood, always deciding eventually that they were, two men with more in common than the two women of the house. Up some creek onto Lake Superior fishing, Danny by now an adolescent and cramming it in for MIT, Jake would tell him all about it. Talk to him about his mother Jean as though she was some wicked stepmother he had lumbered his deeply beloved boy with after a weekend of unaccountable sexual madness. A young and silly lady. And he spoke to Danny as though Danny was he himself, only younger, and could expect as a matter of course to face the problems he had faced later in his own life. The same problems that had plagued his life would soon face his son, of that he seemed absolutely convinced.

The water would be still and grey and the sky grey too. Sometimes it would be snowing. There would be very few fish. Danny would listen intently. He had a great respect for his stepfather. A strong man, well groomed, dark even though in his late fifties, mildly paranoid, surmounted by an incongruous hunting cap. It's not a good idea, he'd say to Danny, for a scholar—and you'll be a scholar, a better one than me if I'm not mistaken—how do I put this to you, you know I love your mother but I want to give you *advice*, you understand me? Scholars—I don't like the word, let's just say men of intellect—shouldn't marry women like your mother unless they're prepared to let the woman have her *head*. You know what I mean? By head? A young and spirited filly? Get what I mean? I don't have to spell everything out I hope? You know what I'm getting at? Hell, it's no crime . . . I'm not narrow minded, and I'm not making accusations, now don't go getting me wrong, we've been quite happy, I've got no evidence, nothing. It's just—and he would generally heave a genuine, despondent sigh—a young, attractive, spirited woman—and not all that er, hot up top, you know? Of course, it just means she's a bit more honest than the rest, doesn't pretend to understand things no woman understands. Women have no love of *concepts*,

Danny. You'll learn this as you grow older. It's one of the most mystifying things in the world to me—your own mother, your own daughter, your own wife: you're a complete mystery to them all, you know that? *Concepts,* you know what I mean, the things that make the world go round for guys like us. I'm not saying we're lucky, we just have to take ourselves as we are, for we are what we are. And they are what they are. And what I'm trying to say is; it's a mistake if you're not prepared to make a *complete* doormat out of yourself—and I guess I come into that category, and I hope you do too—to marry a woman like Jean unless you've got the time for her.

He would say this, his gravamen, very fast. There would then be a short silence.

By time I mean approximately twenty-four hours a day. Much less time than that and they get dissatisfied, oh, nothing you can put your finger on, they start to systematically destroy your peace of mind with their behaviour. First, they're always arguing with you. They don't mean what they say, half the time they don't know what they're talking about—but they can't help it. They can't help themselves. You're to blame, you see—for everything. You don't spend enough time with them. It's your fault their pie crust collapses or their kiln explodes. Fact is, twenty-four hours a day wouldn't be enough. I won't go on, not wanting to offend you. One thing can lead to another. As man to man Danny, as scholar to scholar; don't be a doormat like I would be if I lay down a little flatter: if you find a highly attractive, high-spirited, highly sexed, highly intelligent young woman—and Christ they're everywhere—you know what I mean when I say intelligent, I mean *interested* in things, alive, not what we would understand by intelligence —the sort of woman you would crave to marry—I beg you: don't marry her. And also Danny—if you'll pardon the crudity, try not to fuck her either, because with the best will in the world guys like us are not hard-hearted enough for our own good. That soft Jewish centre, you know? It's still somewhere inside us, we'll carry it through our lives like the brand from a concentration camp. Well it rears its

ugly head as they say, at such moments. I'm speaking of
love, Danny. Jews love love. They can't screw a certain type
of woman without they fall head over heels in love with her
—I ask you to look at your mother and me. I ask you to look
and learn. Did I say we're happy? I exaggerated. Well at
least I got you in that little exchange. But take my advice
Danny. Believe me, twice bitten you'd think thrice shy, but
if your mother left I know what'd happen to me, even at
my age. If I didn't cut my own balls out I'd make the same
stupid mistake again. And again and again. And honestly, I
just haven't the *time* for them Danny, with the best will in
the world I haven't got the *time*. I can't give them what they
want—the more you give them, you know, the more they
want. But the converse is not also true. I don't want to turn
you into a cynic before your time Danny, but for God's
sake, see if you can't be the first man in the world to learn
from another's mistakes. I'd be really proud if you did, you
know. I'm not asking you to be a celibate—jack off, it's
safest. One time all the scholars lived in monasteries—like
your old grandfather, now he's no scholar, but I've always
admired that man and do you know why? Because he never
married a second time. What self control! How I envy him!
In many ways, he could be a lesson to us both.

Then they would continue with their fishing, which would
actually have proceeded uninterrupted throughout the
monologue. And Danny would think of what his father had
said, and think of what his grandfather and mother would
say in defence if they knew how to speak to him, but mostly
he would think about his fishing, because at that stage of
his life to tell the truth that was what interested him most.
To tell the truth he didn't feel all that terribly Jewish and
hung up at all, and he wondered not a little where in God's
name all these guilts that bore down with such heavy bur-
dens his mother and his father and his mother's father and
his father's mother and his stepsister, and which he only
improperly understood, came from.

Chapter 8

Things around the house quietened down considerably after Jean got her job, and Jake learnt to live with the fact of it. It fulfils a need in her, he had confided to Danny, it's not enough she uses me as a doormat, she has to be a doormat too, but not for me you understand. Something about Saint Teresa it may have been licking up the phlegm of the lepers. I tell you Danny, it's a danger sign—we'll have to watch her, she'll end up with symptoms like her old man so help me God. I've heard of guilt, but this is ridiculous. You want to thank your lucky stars you had who you had for a father. Now Jake did not like to remind himself that Danny was less than his natural son, and when he drew attention to Danny's being the natural son of George Harris it was only ever for Danny's reassurance. He seemed anxious that Danny should always be aware that even Goldie Gruzman he had escaped. What a coup, what a feat. Level-headed intelligent Jake for an old man yet no Goldie Gruzman for a grandma.

In fact Jean seemed aware of the need to maintain her precarious mental equipoise. Notwithstanding her duties as a menial—she would never discuss these at home and compensated as best she could by grooming herself especially nicely for Jake's benefit, he eventually mellowed about the whole thing, he was a very fair man intrinsically, after all he didn't try to stop her from taking the job, it must have been, Danny used to think, that he had a fair sized masochistic streak in him, he seemed to *want* to be hurt by the woman he had married, despite protests over every little hurtful incident. For himself, he never apparently played around with women, although he was always very handsome and distinguished in appearance. As in fact. For, as he said to Danny, with my marital record who needs it. He also lacked the time. No, the hurt had to come from Jean.

She was by then in her early forties, though didn't look much out of her early thirties, she took to reading books and wearing reading glasses. With a perpetual cigarette in her languid yet strangely disciplined hand she would stay up at night reading books till all hours. What sort of books is she reading Danny, Jake would want to know. Danny would wander obediently out from his own highly sophisticated studies and glance at the titles his mother was reading. Pascal. Baudelaire. Shaw. He reported them back. Oh, I get it, heavy literature. Well well. Jake would tap his forehead and his face lit up cynically smiling—of course Jean would only ever blow smoke in Jake's face if he tried to see for himself. But he appreciated that it was for her a way of keeping together her sanity. Hang on honey he would sometimes pat her on the shoulder as he passed and wink at Danny, but she ignored him. It was best. She hated him, making no secret of the fact anymore. This delighted Jake.

He boasted of the fact to colleagues while she stood solitary
and sultry at the other end of the bar like an ad from Vogue.
How they would all have loved to screw her, but they
couldn't. She wasn't available and they knew it. As if daring
her to leave he would taunt her, going a little further each
time, knowing of course she would never leave. Everyone
knew she had nowhere to go and no self confidence in a
strange land. Everyone except Jake, that is. Perhaps he
thought she stayed because she loved him so. Danny used
to try to explain her position to Jake, the better to understand it himself, but Jake couldn't be bothered listening for
very long. Didn't seem very sympathetic either. Too long
the Jews have had the whole world for their home Danny
for me to sympathize with this nostalgia of hers over Australia. If she's a real Jew—and one look at old Manwaring
convinces me of it, irrespective of her mother—then it
shouldn't matter to her where she lives. The world's her
oyster, if she only but knew it. But she doesn't know it, Dad.
Yeah well I've tried to tell her son, what more can I do. She
won't listen. Waste no sympathy on her, believe me, it's a
mental situation of her own creation. Like her Catholicism.
The only Jewish thing about her is she can't live with herself.

In the year before he left for MIT Danny began to try to
approach his mother and understand her better. She was so
lovely, so proud, so complex he thought. So unapproachable
too. He discovered she couldn't treat him as a man. He was
something Jake had stolen as a baby. She was vaguely
pleased he was going to be a scholar, that's if their colloquies
on the subject were any guide. Glad he had plenty of money
behind him and so on; all thanks to her of course, but her
attentions were elsewhere. On herself, pretty much. Danny
began to feel a little resentment about this. Her carefully
modulated smoking and drinking as though sparing herself
for something ahead that would demand her full physical
fitness—her sense of being forever on the brink of *something*
—herself. As though she would some day soon sprout wings
or turn into a sibyl or a poetess or something; God only
knew. The air of the whole household waiting—the air of
never ending *expectancy* in the household . . . Danny used

to feel that a natural way for them to have passed their evenings would have been to hunt throughout the house looking under all cushions and beds—for that *something*. This air of strain and sempiternal tension took its toll on Danny. Danny looked forward eventually to going off to MIT, though wondered how Jake and Jean would get on without him. Alone together. And as the time approached, it seemed to be causing a little concern to Jake at well. He started talking to Danny about Australia. Did he think she might like to go back for a holiday? Was that the problem did he think?

He didn't know. She had made of her whole life a problem. A trip overseas was not going to cure that, could quite easily exacerbate matters. When Christmas that year came round, and Sylvia as she always did came home for Christmas, they stood around their Christmas tree—Jean having gone to midnight mass, somehow or other having managed to wheedle her way back into her church, probably had to confess living with Jake as a mortal sin every confession—but her good works as a menial no doubt tipped the scale, they discovered that the subnormal school was run by nuns—to find that Jake had bought for Jean, in addition to some other more lavish gifts, maybe that year a new car, a new fur coat—a volume of Australian bush ballads he'd managed to get Sylvia to dig up for him. And as Jean undid the wrapping Jake beamed and winked at Danny and Sylvia both. But her look of disbelief when she opened it. Like one who has received a great shock she looked up at Jake and gently, half rising, kissed him on the cheek. Then she practically in a daze wandered off into her room, shutting gently the door behind her. Concerned, they all eventually went in, not wanting to see Christmas spoiled over such a trifle—Christmas which in deference to Jean had eventually displaced Thanksgiving as the time for the family to be together —to find her in tears, staring out the window at the snow. Sitting on her bed in tears. Her shoulders seemed so frail as she sat there, she seemed so young and vulnerable, the more so for being so smartly dressed and bejewelled and perfumed, that Jake put his arm on one of her shoulders and Danny his arm on her other, and even Sylvia took her hand. They all loved her, she was apparently enduring a life situation none of them could have tolerated. Perhaps they instinctively realized it. Couldn't properly understand it, but they knew real tears when they saw them. They all hugged her in turn as she wept uncontrollably. There there, said Jake, we'll take a holiday won't we, we'll go see the old country, spend a few days in Hawaii on the way, how about that huh Jean? He rubbed his hands in friendly anticipation. Jake back of Bourke. A Jew at home anywhere in the cosmos. After dinner he read aloud to them—Danny sat quietly having found that he of the three had the least to say or offer his mother—such verse as 'Clancy of the Overflow' and 'The Sick Stockrider'. The children listened less than entranced while Jean smoked and appeared restless. Jake seemed to derive the most enjoyment from his reading in his round, broad, Philadelphian accent. Ridiculously incongruous and completely out of tone with the subject matter, Danny and Sylvia exchanged wan smiles. From time to time though Jake looked up in boyish disbelief over some phrase or other that had taken his fancy. Afterwards he sat back, nestled the yielding Jean under one arm and Sylvia under the other, on the sofa. But in his eyes was the Outback. Those were the days huh Danny.

Danny shrugged, sipped his port. His resemblance, personality-wise, to Sylvia had grown, even to Jake, astounding. Next to Jake he was closest to Sylvia. In fact, his father used to think, he alone of us can probably understand her silences, her beauty that repels suitors instead of encouraging them, that neutral, pristine look upon her face. They used to play their guitars together without speaking in Danny's room, they hardly ever spoke. It didn't seem necessary for them. Neither of them were terribly verbal. Though Sylvia worked in a bookshop in Philadelphia. Presumably they did have emotions. She didn't seem very interested in men, she lived on her own in a house in Cheltenham, read a lot though. Jean and she used to talk about books when she came home now. How about that, Jake used to say to Danny when

Sylvia was home, the two men doing the washing up in aprons so as to give the girls a bit of a break—they're talking in there to one another. They can finally talk. Danny—you don't know what this *means* to me. Danny had a fair idea. Jake seemed to imagine he had created around himself, after so much trying, a family at last. No one had the heart to disillusion him concerning this. It seemed for him so important to think he had a warm family around him at last. Growing old, emotion rearing its ugly head. He might also have been nervous at the thought of Danny so soon leaving, Sylvia so irrevocably lost. Not really a terribly successful pater familias, everyone alienated one way or another, the two women having each in their own way submitted to cruel and inexorable fate, Danny still largely an unknown quantity. Perhaps liable to go off the rails, perhaps not having sufficient reason for staying on them. Needing the right environment. If he lacks anything, Jake would say to Jean, he spoke a lot to her of Danny in those last months because not unnaturally it was a neutral subject that interested them both, it's motivation. He's got brains aplenty, but he doesn't seem to have too much push. Too happy a home life said Jean smiling, yeah exactly said Jake—before realizing. Ok, it's ok said Jean who had not really intended to offend, he's been very happy with you, you've been whatever else you've been an excellent father for my son. Yeah well, when I'm not around to push him I don't know how he'll fare. His momentum will carry him through school, but after that well I just don't know. I guess we'll have to wait and see.

I guess we will, said Jean.

Sylvia, just before Danny left home, about a week before-hand in fact, came home unexpectedly over the weekend and told them all, deliberately waiting until they were all together in the lounge room, that she expected Jake to arrange an abortion for her. Her sense of irony was such that her gesture in waiting to tell them all at the same time was a major coup. No hint of her motivation. Maybe a hint of an ineffable smile. Were they shocked? No, too sophisti-cated for that. Were they pleased? Hard to say. At least it showed them she was not a total lesbian. Were they disappointed? Her act reverberated throughout the room—echo echo echo . . . the still ashtray littered bookstrewn room.

I can't arrange an abortion for you just like that, said Jake. Why don't you keep the baby? Don't you know who the father is?

Yes, said Sylvia. He's a negro. A big, black, muscular buck negro.

Jake, realizing this to be nothing other than a concerted attack upon himself, but helpless to confront it, looked across desperately at his son Danny for support. His eyes at that moment. Danny, as indignant as he had ever felt in his entire life, stood up and said—you're sluts. You're sluts the pair of you. Jake, shaking his head in disbelief and with tears in his eyes, saw Danny at that moment upstage Sylvia so far as he was concerned for all time. Indeed, the smiles on the faces of the women had frozen. All action had frozen. So it seemed the usurping had been total. And now we know where we stand. Someone had eventually said it, it could have been any one out of the four. The pseudo-family disintegrated in a cloud of realization at that point. Sylvia, you fix your own abortion—and get out of this house. Jean, I think I'll leave early for school. I want time to look around Boston a little first.

Of course things were eventually smoothed over on the surface, though no longer was Jake able to pretend he had built around himself the family of his dreams. He tidied up all loose ends though, and particularly the problem of his and Jean's coexistence after Danny's departure, by dying of a myocardial infarction a bare two weeks after Danny left home. In that oh so efficient medical manner of his he contrived to die the perfect death. The three survivors all smoked cigarettes over his funeral, all cried genuine tears, more for the state of suffering humanity on the part of the women, more for the loss of his one and only friend on the part of Danny. Goldie missed the funeral, having fouled up her travel arrangements, nearly ninety years of age anyway, what could they have expected. The maenads Sylvia and Jean, temporarily smooth and enticing as lovers, quite naturally invited Danny back to the family house; but he didn't

want to go near that house again. They were already drunk
and he was scared of what they might do to him if they
got him in that house again alone. He did not want even to
consider it. Silly of him perhaps, but he felt enough guilt
already. Who was it sprang from whose head fully grown
and armed? He went directly from the funeral to the bus
station. Having acquired over that day a new perspective of
life. He wanted his trip back to Boston to take him as long
as possible. As long as any sea voyage from one hemisphere
to another. He tried to think on the trip, looking out the
window, but he couldn't. Couldn't think. He began to
stumble. He stumbled through to a *summa cum laude* from
MIT without lifting his head once from a book. Too scared
to lift his head for fear of what he might see if he did.
Plenty of drive, you could say, at that point in his life. Hearing various voices too in the night, mostly reproachful.
Knowing now with certainty, though at an essentially subconscious level—how else account for his later vagaries?—
that there were ghosts and spirits with his name written on
them as for all the other Manwarings. Voices from the stage
and coming muffled from under writing quilts on the floor
as well. Enjoying themselves thoroughly, every last one of
them. Not like him. Upon graduating he left immediately
for Berkeley to line up for his doctorate. Like one who on
some lonesome road doth walk in fear and dread.

THREE

Chapter 9

Over breakfast Sylvia asked him did he have his bags all packed ready and he said yes, I guess so. So why don't we have our coffee outside on the porch. They often did this, in any weather. They went together outside onto the porch, it was about nine thirty am, and though it was the day after Christmas (they'd spent Christmas alone together, by choice), well below freezing, it was nice for as long as you could stand it to feel the winter air and to see the haw of one's breath. The street they lived in was a very quiet street, very conservative street, not far from Burholme Park, the park being the estate of a former Philadelphia lawyer with a branch of the local library and a little museum in it. It made for the quiet life to live in a Republican neighbourhood in Cheltenham, outside the city limits, Sylvia had lived there since leaving Bryn Mawr. On the lawn up the street one householder had gone so far as to build out of packed snow posies like in a floral clock which read, Welcome Home from Vietnam my son David Schneider! Every day Danny walked to work at the Institute across the park. Sylvia took the train to and from the city. They had no car. That Roosevelt Boulevarde Sylvia used to say, oh man, experimental expressway number one. Danny had driven his old pickup back with him from the West Coast but the last time it broke down he left it to its fate in a street in Tioga. Shopping was the only problem, but as they weren't short on money (thanks largely to Sylvia) they took cabs. They stayed home most nights when Danny wasn't working or Sylvia taking a class up at the School of Arts, except for an occasional weekend in New York. Over the way their neighbour raised Old Glory in a reverential manner, then stood a moment in silent respect before going back indoors. Danny and Sylvia exchanged wan smiles at this, sipping coffee. Almost every one of the uniformly old, gabled two storey homes in their street had Old Glory on display somewhere out front, either from a flagpole or a standard from an upper storey. Except them. I have to draw the line somewhere, Sylvia had explained. Their own house was a whitewashed colonial rented from Homer Hoffman Realty. A beautiful house inside, with a large crab apple in a small but overgrown yard. On finishing up at Berkeley Danny had chosen to do post-doctoral work at the Institute, mostly so as he could live with Sylvia as she was about the only person he really knew who was left in the world. Once school was out he felt with a chill that he could postpone his life no longer: but he didn't really have too many ideas on what he would do. He was still really postponing, but he knew his day of judgement was drawing near.

Already, what with the slump in the sciences all over the country, he was growing concerned over his job prospects. It was becoming very hard for a young biochemist to get into a good faculty, and his work hadn't gone all as well as he might have liked. He didn't really have the number of publications that he should have had, considering the time he'd put in. It didn't really seem to him altogether his fault, he'd followed up a few ideas that had gone nowhere: and yet he understood well enough that picking winners is a big part of the game. Frankly, winners and losers looked pretty much alike to him. However, by manoeuvring himself into a fairly small corner, he was in a small way a small authority on one particular approach to one particular technique. That's the way you do it, if you can't expand, contract. For a surprisingly long time the same illusion will be created—movement, in and of itself acknowledged good. Until eventually you contract into a point. But he didn't kid himself the work he'd done was going to be enough to get him onto a good faculty. Most of all, he seemed to lack the ability, or for that matter the desire, to suck up to the big boys; even his own supervisors, nice enough men in their way they had all been too. It did not augur well. In some way be did not quite understand he resented everything they taught him, and no doubt this had not passed unnoticed. Nothing passes unnoticed, for that is the way of the sciences. His tendency to work with the minimum rather than the maximum possible accuracy had also earned him he feared a reputation as a sloppy worker. However no one disputed his capacity for rationalizing any result. When jobs are tight though, the first to be passed over he had heard are the unfriendly, those with personality problems. He wanted nothing to do with his colleagues outside of the lab, and no doubt this, in their eyes, constituted a personality problem of the gravest possible magnitude. And yet oddly enough he did not strike himself as an introvert. Probably everyone has these hang-ups, he used to try to console himself, the others are just more expert at concealing them, it's nothing peculiar to myself. But he could not always bring himself to believe it. Such a straight, uncomplicated looking person. There was a fundamental difference between the others and himself, and it went deeper than he being him and they them. He did not like to dwell on this distinction however, whatever it consisted in, at a conscious level. It was true that one of the reasons, although not the only reason and certainly not the chief reason, he had been so anxious to join Sylvia was so as to catch up on what was happening around the place outside the lab. Perchance as insurance.

Ironically enough, although he'd spent so many years on the Berkeley campus, from the vicinity of which much of the new spirit as Sylvia understood it had emanated, the whole Bay area, he'd not become too involved with campus activities, which during his stay there had necessitated the closing of the labs for prolonged periods on at least three occasions, and which had annoyed him no end resulting as they had in a delay in the submission of his thesis. Frankly, he'd said to Sylvia, those guys gave me the shits. I never could sympathize with them too much. They're all as anti-intellectual as hell, so what are they doing on a campus in the first place? Goddam SDS. You wouldn't like it if some bastard threw a bomb into your bookshop would you? Well they did that to a lab near where I was one day. Poor goddam friend of mine who had just spent six weeks on an enzyme prep had to start all over again. Sylvia had laughed. Nonetheless, Berkeley had made him restless.

One of the reasons he'd moved in with Sylvia was so she could bring him home all the books he ought to read. He had the idea that if he only read enough he'd get the picture eventually. She worked in a pretty progressive bookshop, handled a great deal of underground material. They'd even been busted once or twice, but that was in the early days. Those days were over. The permissive society is here Danny, Sylvia had said, so be sure and get your permit. Though to him she did not seem all that progressive. Far from it. She seemed, for example, surprised that one thing he'd picked up at Berkeley was the habit of smoking marihuana. He was an habitual user of marihuana. That's nothing Sylvia, he told her, even the jocks smoke it nowadays. This remark all the more striking from him as he looked so much like a jock himself. But he wasn't a jock, he wasn't anything at all. In the Bay area I understand the Seventh Day Adventists have introduced it into their religious observances. He tendered to her pharmacological evidence of its relative innocuousness when compared to alcohol, so as to be sure she would not misconstrue his motives in smoking it. After all, he had a logical reason for taking the stuff. It wasn't like he was some head or anything like that. Not exactly a Merry Prankster. He read the books, he smoked the grass, but somehow, Sylvia used to think, not quite in the spirit in which they were intended. His main love outside of science appeared to be art.

His taste was execrable. He would keep dragging her up to New York weekends where his particular goal would always prove to be, approached by no matter how devious a route, the Rousseaus in the Museum of Modern Art. Now look at these Sylvia, he'd say to her, that's what I call painting. Afterwards they'd take in something off Broadway. But he always found the avant-garde theatre boring. Not enough in it to stimulate me mentally, he'd say, I can only take so much of that obscenity and Vietnam gush. Being a biochemist, he'd failed his medical himself. Christ, he'd say after putting down something like Watermelon Sugar; give me Hemingway any day. Sylvia would despair of him. Oh dear Danny, I don't know why I bother with you, I really don't. We'll have to get you out of that Institute I can see before we can reconstruct a human being. I'd love to see you kicked out of science. But only for your own sake, you understand. Why don't you publish some deliberate lies?

I've published enough undeliberate lies Sylvia, and who knew the difference? Anyway, what am I supposed to do for a living? Sweep streets?

Others have done it.

Others can have it. Even the spades won't sweep the streets anymore—you should see the streets down near Penn . . .

Don't call them spades Danny. You know I don't like that.

Oh yeah, I'm sorry.

At twenty-six Danny felt aeons older, or else somehow irrevocably out of phase with Sylvia his sister, who was somewhere, he believed, in her mid to early thirties. Still unmarried, probably neither of them would ever marry, life seemed, with the best will in the world, to have passed them by. They might even end up staying together, one could never be certain the other was not planning this, the Sitwells of Cheltenham Sylvia called them. But Danny could not complain. It now seemed to him in retrospect that he had been a deliberate shirker. Finally out of school (though he noticed that he was described on his NIH Fellowship notification as a postdoctoral student—take up a faculty position at age fifty eventually) he looked back and saw that he had actually, without even being aware of it, become a man while in there nose to the bench. No one around to notify him. Just follow your nose had been his one pitiful philosophy. Just keep following your nose and ambling along and you're bound to end up somewhere, might look up some day to discover yourself a Nobel Laureate. But once out of school, in such an atmosphere as the Institute where East Coast Jews intent upon Nobel Prizes and other secrets of the universe literally ran from bench to desk and back again, it was at once apparent that a big lead had been opened up between those who had hitherto ambled along and those who had run at a hare's pace with eyes skinned. In school, this had not been at all apparent. How unfair. Danny realized that the gap was already too great to close. So things did not appear to Danny at age twenty-six terribly satisfactory in any respect. He sipped that morning his coffee with gloved hands. Sylvia loved him to wear gloves—sometimes at what could have been described as the most inappropriate of times.

Understand you'll be seeing the Legion marching again this afternoon if the weather holds out he remarked, trying to soften for her the departure he had committed himself to later that day; another rally down in the park. They seem to be making a regular thing of it. Christ almightly, they keep trying to sell me those little badges of theirs when I'm walking to school. By God, they get out early on the winter streets. Ladies' auxiliary or whatever they call themselves.

You mean you get out late. You know you're a disgrace to the whole tone of this neighbourhood? Danny usually worked nights and often didn't leave for work mornings until well after ten. Hey, why don't you take me with you this afternoon?

She smiled at him. They usually avoided one another's eyes. Their love too deep and strange. The only beautiful thing they had. She'd asked timidly and smiled timidly, but he knew she genuinely wanted to come. She could get the time off, and he hadn't even asked her.

Oh honey, there'd be nowhere for you to stay—we're all in the student dorms, you know . . . Ever since they had begun sleeping together they were both totally out of their depth. Just looking at one another could send shivers up their spines. And at their age—incredible. Their secret made them very proud of themselves. Especially in a neighbourhood that would have tarred and feathered them. Of course, it wasn't really incest, no consanguinity whatsoever, but it felt like incest, it was as deep and mysterious and fulfilling as only incest can be. Probably would spoil them henceforth for sex with strangers. It was nice to keep everything within the family, no strangers could ever hope to plumb such depths in one another. Fancy marriage to some total stranger. And after twenty five, everyone's a stranger. You don't know where they've been.

She pulled a suitably wry face at him, and hugged her knees with cold. Looking at her, so beautiful, he realized, not for the first time, that he could never have hoped to lay a woman as beautiful as her if she hadn't been his sister and neurotic about strangers. Other women seemed not very interested in him. Even on the horny and almost unbelievably promiscuous Berkeley campus where private, one partner sex as he understood it had long been considered bourgeois and *passé* he had been unable to score. One early rebuff (brooding over it often though in later years he eventually realized that it could easily have been construed otherwise and probably *would* have been by some suaver individual than himself) and that was enough for him, he wasn't going to stand for that sort of stuff, he pulled his head in for all time he had then resolved; jacked off. It's hard to think you're really clever and handsome and women *still* don't care for you. It doesn't bear thinking about really. It makes you feel women see you as some sort of glossy replica of what a man ought to be. And you don't know what a man ought to be. So the arrangement with Sylvia suited him—and for some reason he couldn't begin to comprehend Sylvia too—far more perfectly and profoundly than any conventional shack up with some stranger could have.

It was great to think of being in California again tomorrow. He was flying out to LA that evening for the Enzyme Mechanism Conference at UC Santa Barbara. Part of his grant allowed him expenses for such things. What a ridiculous time to hold a conference though. On first coming to Philadelphia he had been unable to tolerate the fresh cold. He still didn't enjoy it, or rather, he still noticed it, whereas someone like Sylvia didn't. He didn't like it at all. It didn't seem natural men should voluntarily live in such weather. Especially when other, milder weather was still relatively easy of access in all parts of the globe. Something happened to the human being Sylvia when he moved into the colder climate. Look at your Scandinavians, forever on the point of committing suicide. And who could blame them. I can never understand how it is that warmer climates don't produce totally different cultures . . . And I don't just mean to compare Frisco with New York. Perhaps they're so happy in the best climate, they just shut up altogether, a continent we've never even heard of, an Atlantis a Mount Analogue of the truly wise, the truly silent.

He'd originally hoped to take a postdoc in Europe, hoping Sylvia would go too, Oxford or Cambridge, very nice on the American dollar, but the changed employment situation made it unwise to fuck around too long. You always have to take another postdoc back home while job hunting. Jesus Sylvia, I don't know how the negroes can stand living in a place like this in winter in all their unheated tenements. And they're all from down in the warm South, they're just up here for the welfare aren't they? . . . Remember never to call a spade a spade in front of Sylvia again . . . one of her more sensitive areas. It did not do to think back. Or forward. Live in the present. She was now permanently sterile apparently. Poor kid. Oh well honey he'd console her, I'll end up impotent myself, so we'll make a good pair in our old age. And think of the money we save on condoms . . . Sylvia had a magnificent laugh, very few had been privileged to hear it, a magnificent body, a magnificent mind too he felt convinced, one day he hoped to understand them all. But according to her he was making only the slowest of slow progress, just barely progressing. So why did she waste her time on him? He didn't like to look a gift horse in the mouth. A black gift horse, teeth white—with her mouth wide open an inch from his eye in orgasm he would stare into that beautifully sculptured cavity. Sterilized my poor sister for life, lecherous black brutes, depriving me of my ultimate fantasy in so doing . . . however, acting no doubt under instructions.

Although not scheduled to fly out until seven pm East Coast time he had to leave the house shortly after lunch because of the train service on Sundays being so abysmally infrequent. Three trains all day. He left Sylvia with a fraternal kiss to her forehead and walked the half mile to Cheltenham Station in the beginnings of a snow storm, planning to take the two pm out of Fox Chase which meant it would arrive in Cheltenham around two ten. He liked the feel of snow on his naked face and head, he would never wear a hat of any description—it was the only manly thing to do, leave Sylvia at home in their centrally heated house while he ventured forth. In his suitcase a few light clothes and some slides for the talk he was scheduled to give on the Wednesday, the last day of the three day convention. How he hated such conventions, never a big convention man. To his regret, some controversial data to put it mildly which he had repeated and repeated. Ever add a column of figures time and time again to get the same answer every time and still you have no faith in the result? But he had to believe his data, though no one at the Institute did, or liked his interpretation of it very much for that matter— and on the Wednesday it would be his lot to present it before the heavies whom, he suspected, would greet it with at best reserved scepticism and at worst withering scorn, depending upon the tone of the whole affair, depending upon whether by then they had the sufficient taste of blood in their mouths. The conference was strictly by invitation only. Had it not been that his preceptor at the Institute was one of the national conveners he would never have been invited. It was an honour he supposed. Several of his fellow Institute postdocs, also desperate for jobs and also honoured enough to have gotten the nod, were looking forward to it avidly he knew. However, he saw it as less an opportunity to suck up jobwise to the heavies (he knew he would eschew the heavies, he always did so, either through jealousy or more likely he liked to think some quite fundamental temperamental incompatibility, perhaps his preceptor had invited him only in order to give him one last chance in that stifling atmosphere to prove himself before committing himself to the considered decision over the grapevine Harris is definitely not your boy for any faculty appointment)— than as a junket to see his beloved West Coast again at no personal expense. Why so beloved, he often wondered. Had it been only the climate? To his colleagues, the travelling to and fro represented a mere inconvenience, something to be endured with fortitude. To Danny it was the whole point and purpose of the exercise. Such an attitude he had developed, no wonder he chose to keep to himself. Afraid his colleagues might see right into him some day. Gang up. Just before you strike at me with that scalpel gang, he would say to them at the very end—what did you see in me anyway? As a matter of purely personal curiosity, you understand, to be used if necessary in some future existence. Confound them all with his pluck, innate faith in the law of karma and the transmigration of souls. Most unscientific. At this stage it was expressing itself only as a vague spiritual malaise, no more, a dissatisfaction with his researches, no more than this.

Cheltenham had a contrivedly quaint (to him) deliberately Old World air—although he realized it was all perfectly authentic—not a little reminiscent of New England. He didn't care for such environments to the extent Sylvia did. Such environments were paying homage to a past he didn't share. Philadelphia, for example—home of Benjamin

Franklin, that worthy, purveyor of prudence as the highest, wildest virtue. Emerson. Whatever happened to the Transcendentalists? Now there were Yankees one could warm to. *Each must stand on his glass tripod, if he would keep his electricity.* The first book he could remember was Walden, given him by his father. The leaves were falling. Memories of his dead father in a canoe. His own antithesis on that afternoon in Benjamin Franklin. Lightning has been known to strike many times the same residence gentlemen, my fellow citizens, may I therefore humbly present before you . . . but he was a scientist too. Best remember that, at least until after Wednesday. Not a single storey home in the entire Cheltenham residential area. At the station, which comprised only a platform a foot or so off the ground in the shadow of a decrepit, boarded up shack that had formerly served as a ticket office, indicative of the financial state of the railroad company that it could no longer afford to staff its ticket offices, he stood, quite alone, the only venturer forth by rail out of Cheltenham that Boxing Day it would seem, fifteen minutes to wait for his train. One of the joys he knew best, the sudden appearance of a train from a seemingly immemorially deserted track. Looking across the tracks, for Cheltenham overlooked a junction, standing now wet with melted snow, he watched the snow flurries. After a short time of this, just as he had expected, he was seized with an immense nostalgia for his sister Sylvia, who was to him what Cheltenham was, and the woods with not a leaf intact, and the snow, and even the Institute. Leave the mind blank, and Sylvia was sure to stealthily enter. To lay against naked Sylvia, deep and warm of breast and thigh, was the proper way, the only respectable and prudent way, to spend Sunday afternoon, eyes together fixed upon the snow-spattered bedroom window in wonder. Through which no nearby householder could see in. The memory of Sylvia, that smell of toast and hay in her armpits, her moist yet unfecund belly, stirred him into an erection. He felt the most profound regret that Sylvia had seen fit to begin menstruating Christmas Eve. Such a Jewess. For what is worse than setting out upon a long journey with an erection

By the time his train (two filthy and reluctant carriages

arrived, his erection had gone, and he was dismayed to find
that partly because of the snow and partly on account of
the windows in the carriages were never washed he could
scarcely see a foot either side of the track. This really did
not matter all that much from a superficial point of view,
as he knew very well what was there: Saturday mornings
he often went into work with Sylvia when he wasn't working, just to browse in her book store and be near her, later
they'd lunch somewhere . . . it was just that it seemed a
poor omen for his journey. Night flights were bad enough,
but he had to make some concessions to Sylvia. And now he
couldn't even see his way through suburban Philadelphia.
He might end up seeing nothing. Below us now the lights
of Kansas City, below us now the lights of Las Vegas. But
he knew what was out there only too well. Ugly, barren
copses of trees in the first instance, with all the papers and
trash accumulated throughout the year on display amongst
their stumps. Somewhere around Wayne Junction, where
they crossed Germantown Avenue, negro Philadelphia
proper began. A demarcation line of perhaps one city block
in some areas. And pushing ever outwards, ever outwards.
He had never, not even in New Haven, not even in Newark,
not even in Manhattan, not even in his home town Jersey
City—though admittedly he'd never seen Washington or
Baltimore—seen anything as horrid and as hopeless as this
inner suburban Philadelphia. Although it was probably just
that he was better acquainted with it. Talk about the sins
of the fathers will visit.

Nicetown, a trip down Germantown Avenue any working
day of the week saw a sea of negroes, surly motherfucking
bastards lounging round on street corners, stroking flick
knives, meditating the evening's crimes, freezing to death in
synthetic fibres and cotton from the old cotton fields back
home in midwinter, vending seditious anti-American literature, not a job or an ambition amongst them, the only way
up and out on the end of a syringe or a drumstick or a
boxing glove, everyman, Philly Joe, Mahommed Ali. NIH
advertising on the station hoardings—the dangers of downs
and ups. Who in a place like this needs a down? And looking

across it all proud William Penn from City Hall, by decree no building to be taller than he, goddam awfullest city in the USA. Your first prize one week your second prize two weeks in Philadelphia. Called in to see Philadelphia once it was closed for the week-end—Medical Centre of the universe. Spring Garden Street. What cynic thought up these names? He got out at the Reading terminal and pushed his way through all the lazy spades lounging around, probably travelled all day up and down the elevators for something to do, down into the street. Every spade the spade that had screwed his sister and everywhere spades. And she'd enjoyed it. An atavistic grudge, no more. Lazy goddam sons of bitches, he thought, push me out into the suburbs just so as to support your filthy drug habits, send the city treasury bankrupt with your indolence, wouldn't work in an iron lung, and now as a result I have to live in a polarized Republican neighbourhood with the American Legion haranguing me all weekend through loudspeakers on the declining moral fibre of the nation. Git back, go on, down south, tote that bale, leave all white women alone. Near to the glass doors of the station exit a negro girl sat on a folding stool knitting with miraculous speed and precision brightly coloured caps and scarves which an accomplice attempted to force upon passers by.

A white drunk staggered from a doorway in pursuit of a bumper, sad, all-seeing eyes that had seen the city in better days. Recollections of flowers and blue skies over Spring Garden Street, little white girls safe to stoop down tie up their shoelaces in any public underpass. All the stores of course were open in Avarice City USA. He walked with a sinking heart past the whimpy shops, also shops selling trashy, meretriciously packaged items of apparel, synthetic sweaters the sleeves of which guaranteed to sag six inches in their first week of wear; through City Square to the hotel from which he would take a limousine to the airport. And near to the hotel on an exposed corner—the Krishna worshippers, worshipping Krishna, essentially a West Coast cult and entirely out of context in this city of William Penn, uncaring concerning the elements, shuffling sandalled feet blue with cold and freezing their asses in saffron robes to the refrain of conch and finger cymbal, chanting their incantations. Cerebral looking neurasthenics mostly who would no doubt feel the cold considerably. Their eyes closed, their heads shaven, some incongruously in spectacles, a few girls, a bearded and stoned hippie type shuffling alongside, feeling the cold, maybe cold turkey in his case. All eyes closed. I am this one, I am that one—a large poster of Krishna in the window of Sylvia's bookshop, dark eyes handsome Dravidian. They provided the only colour in a city as grey as its denizens were black. As the cities and the skies become greyer, my brothers, so the people will become blacker and more feral. Then at last the white man will leave our shores . . . Once in the limousine though, he could not put them out of his mind. In their discipline and severity he felt a multifarious rebuke that pricked all aspects of his being. Cosmic, it seemed to him, on a cosmic scale. The sound of their conch, washed up primordially, he imagined to himself, upon some Goan shore, echoed through his ears. Would he explain enzymes in such cold with such ardour? Not on your life, because in ten years time what he said would stand revealed as so much outmoded crap. Recollections of mortal embarrassment whenever worthies such as Emerson or Schopenhauer had permitted themselves a scientific aside. Present the passer by with your wave equation for the human being, your ultimate goal, only to see him pass by unmoved. You run after him, obtruding your wave equation, thinking perhaps he did not understand. He presses a charge of nuisance, and properly so. Think about in the cell—what have you offered him but a piece of paper nothing to his purpose? And yet the sound of a chant and a conch, something altogether different. Something more of eternity in it. He should look his grandfather up. The sound of a chant and a conch. His grandfather had heard that sound. That sound of a chant and a conch. His grandfather also a traveller. His bona fide father a great traveller too. Merely keeping up a tradition on this enzymological junket. His grandfather whose fault it was that he was where he was today Shit City USA.

Passing the mountains of abandoned motor vehicles ready for the crusher en route to the airport he thought he recognized his own pickup truck. Let he who is without fault fuck off out of it and leave the casting of stones to the rest of us here, we're more experienced. The truck in which he had driven up and down, up and down, Oregon to the Mexican border the West Coast how many times. On the lookout for what. Just travelling to no purpose. What was it the noble Yankee Emerson had advised his fellow Yankees concerning their insidious propensity for travelling to Europe on the slightest of pretexts to gape and lose their innocence forever? Stay home, my fellow countrymen, act the stalwart, do the job, be the man, monuments such as you delight in gazing upon were not constructed by wanderers such as yourselves. Well, that lesson at least they seemed to have learnt. The flow had been in the main reversed. Or at least equalized. And there were now plenty of home monuments, such monuments. Refineries as far as the eye could delimit. Don't look at me, I threw my pickup away. And when you want to lose your innocence nowadays, this is your venue of choice.

At the airport he watched, to pass away the time, the international flights landing. College kids returning from European Christmas holidays on the sniff of an oil rag (one hundred US dollars Liechtenstein Airlines DC3 return junket) to be greeted in all cases by their doting parents with open arms and wallets. Same parents who a generation earlier had spent their life savings on a one way ticket from Oppression. Hard now to conceive of anything more oppressive than these refugees from Oppression. Hit the gas on the freeway, don't look down on the superhighway, because down there is a black man from every brownstone and he is looking up and he is shaking his fist and he is poking his tongue out and he is saying—Motherfuckers! You brought me here! You made me what I am today! Only it's not true, it's ridiculous, I had no part in it, au contraire, I am first generation, you are fifth generation down there USA. Danny saw himself as at least as much at home as his black neighbours, ie, completely at sea. How about we link arms just the two of us black neighbour, split down South? I mean *really* south this time man? I drop you off in New Guinea, you head for the highlands with a tear of gratitude towards me in your eye and a smile on your face looking already for your first Bird of Paradise rip out all its tail feathers. I just keep on moseying down to the old South Pole, that is unless something should crop up in the interim to take my mind off myself . . .

At six pm he stepped aboard the placenta of his United flight. Suffering for some reason from nervous tenesmus, irritable colon syndrome, overwhelming but fruitless desire to piss and shit himself. Cold weather. Joy. Excitement. The sound of a chant and a conch. Apprehension. Fear. Terror. Wanderlust. Cultural shock on passing from Cheltenham to the airport for only the second time, hadn't been back in the east long enough, that much at least was apparent. The sound though of a conch and a chant, recognizable voice of the West Coast calling him back from across the Great Divide.

Sitting next to him in the aisle seat during the flight was a fat Philadelphian whose manner indicated that he would not be averse to conversation. On his way back from the john he would smile engagingly at Danny, who always pretended not to notice. The man watched the movie, which Danny also watched, though without paying for the soundtrack in the case of Danny. Danny found a movie more illuminating without its soundtrack. It left play for interpretation. Danny felt incredible restlessness. He asked the stewardess for a map and looked for about half an hour at the whole of the United States on the map. This was shortly after take off. He found the states that most appealed to him on the map were Wyoming, North Dakota and Montana. He had never been to these states. He had never been to so many states. He had a great desire to visit Butte in particular. Even Oregon, some place out in the wilds of Washington State; anywhere but Pennsylvania. He hated all that Dutch countryside, Newhope, places like that, cobbled streets crammed with charter buses. He seriously wondered if Thursday would see him flying back there. From time to time he looked out of the window down out of the plane, but the cloud cover was so thick there were only a few undifferentiated pools of light now and again indicating some urban centre, and he could never be sure which urban centre was which. Snow through to the Rockies according to the pilot. After the movie had finished—a western with Lee Marvin in massive pantomime throughout—he pulled out the latest JBC and began desultorily skimming through it. The fat Philadelphian at the sight of this could no longer contain himself. See you're reading some sort of scientific periodical there, he said. They were over Nevada by then, and the cloud had cleared. My son's a scientist, a physicist —strained pride in his voice anxious for approbation having raised to his credit a scientist. Incredulously, Danny heard himself making the following callous remark:

Can it man, will you? Some other time. I want to get on with my reading.

Danny looking askance shortly afterwards saw the man lift his knees and depart for some empty seat further back in the plane. He hadn't enjoyed the rebuke. On the other hand, he probably felt guilty for having interrupted a scientist. If he had a scientist son he would know that one must never interrupt a reading scientist. Akin to disturbing a copulating bear. Probably great ambivalence mixed in with his hurt feelings as he retired to the furthermost section of the plane.

Danny made attempts to read various papers in the journal, but found them all incomprehensible. He realized he was not even concentrating. He was not in the best frame of mind for a scientific convention. He had slumped from his earlier manic phase into a depression in which he was capable of registration only. Outside and all around him the dark US night. Protected from it, however, by the fruits of science. Settle in Baja California for preference, some fishing village, bask in the sun, smoke grass all day and night. Grow incredibly wise down there.

He'd run out of steam.

Every man has a time like this, there's just no mistaking it in retrospect, though at the time nothing very special, time when he understands, generally through physical processes of nausea and anxiety, often at the most inconvenient and unexpected of times, his path has ended in an impasse. There is a wall before him he cannot surmount. He does not choose to surmount the wall, but bursts right through it (it is paper thin) onto another, more agreeable path. Alternatively, the wall is seen to be unbreachable. He is merely faster at getting to it than the others (his coevals), less expert at climbing walls, more perspicacious—it doesn't really matter. He will entertain all these possibilities incessantly in the future, they are with him now for all time impossible to subdue or disentangle, frequently simultaneously in the beginning but one eventually dominates. Should it tend to be the one that promotes the greatest sense of failure in the individual, you will observe the individual in later life much given to modes of escape from cogitation—drink, drugs and women. Should it tend to be the one that promotes the greatest sense of achievement, the individual is a self-deluding fool. Shit, thought Danny, all those years and I never realized. I need a new guru. A Bay mystagogue.

His feelings were in fact still vacillating. He didn't see yet that he would never regain his former attitude towards life. After all, he'd had periods of discontent before, who has not; but this was different—a climacteric had it been less extended. You can start bleeding to death for example from a peptic ulcer haemorrhage and not even know it. Slight weakness, that's all you feel, not unlike the old micturition syncope you're so familiar with. You're still in there laughing, knocking back your JB on the rocks, you're dying and you don't even know it. It may take you several years. So it is when your tide starts going out. At first, you don't even know it. Why look, it has left a big conch in its path. You pick it up and blow it. On the other hand, he held on his lap a reputable periodical, *Journal of Biological Chemistry*. On the other, he was looking out a window hermetically sealed into a starry desert, and not too far away were communities of people for whom the existence of that starry desert and the possibility of contemplation in such a desert, were all that mattered. California, rat-house of the universe. More sects on the rolls than you could point a fescue at.

But if there's one thing travel in the USA impresses upon the traveller, it's that one little person amongst all these millions matters not one jot. Look around. You just slip down out of sight, no one's going to miss you. Round about half the population under the table at this point in time ssshing one another, don't let the others in on this secret underground. Sylvia would do anything with him anyway. Jean gone, no one knew where she'd gone to. Jake dead, maybe turning slowly in his grave at this point, clawing ethereal claws at the tombstone to get out and speak a few words of advice in the manner of the ghost from Hamlet. But, and perhaps through no accident, there still existed someone who *could* be spoken to. After a fashion—Danny remembered prior attempts uneasily. Old man Manwaring out in Hollywood in world of starry meditation through the smog under eucalypts (*E. globulus* Californian Blue Gum I believe they call it) in a saffron robe. A creed for the simple minded, frankly Danny didn't feel too comfortable with Hindus. It was to his discredit, however. Conch and chant revealed as his grandfather's admonition plain and straightforward carried in the wind, Krishna to Arjuna—change your vacillatory ways, seize for all time or drop that casual plexus, you'll drop another caste, fall down into another continent, so help us both. The plane pulled them down into the odious LA photochemical smog. Danny put away his JBC and looked around for the man he had insulted. He wished to apologize. He couldn't see the man, and the fasten your seat belt sign was now on. Back on the West Coast now. Fuck all Philadelphian fat men now. Too late now. He adjusted his watch. Realized he was tired, too much drink and listening to the Brandenburgs with Sylvia the previous night. Christmas night.

Sylvia.

He was booked in on the last Golden West twin otter into Santa Barbara. Why not just drop out now, escape to Hollywood, merge there with the other drop outs? He was just a late developer that was all. Knock three times on the monastery lintel: wasn't that what Siddhartha would have done under similar circumstances? Instead he boarded

when came the time to board it his Golden West flight like
the dutiful son of science he no longer was. Only maybe he
didn't know it yet. Flying low over the channel all the oil
rigs. Too much kelp on the beaches, aftermath of the great
rig disaster. But is was only a matter of time now. To what?
Dangerous red blood beginning to pulse out from every
haemopoeitic centre—Harris and Manwaring written on
every pulsating erythrocyte. Superimposed Gruzman centres
dying like stars over the last Nevada night. Dangerous West
Coast air instinct with salt spray from his forbear's great
ocean the Pacific. In total temper with the times. Blood will
out. Forbears he suddenly shed all resentment towards,
sure if he'd have been Harris he'd have deserted every
pregnant woman about the place. Would speak to the man
cordially now if he could be unearthed—but why create
embarrassment all round? Screw them and leave them, that
is your red-blooded policy of choice. Hit and run. Generation beneath him on the hit and run generally speaking.
Industry at a standstill in ten years time. Monasteries and
deserts full to overcrowding, women with babes in arms
claiming maintenance beating on the doors and lintels disturbing the monastic peace and quiet. Saint Francis ecce
homo. Having confounded them when young with your
promiscuity, confound them still further when old by enter-
ing the monastery. Screech to a sudden, grinding halt sit
and look at the sky. Two bob each way, as they say. Hard
somehow to capitalize on previous karma. But as it's all
forgiven in the end, better by far to have sins and not merely
unfulfilled lusts to repent. Better by far than being merely
some horrible, switched off, cerebral Philadelphian pseudo-
Jewish pedagogue with no hope in this life or the next.

Out to Santa Barbara airport and no one was home. It was
all but closed up, janitor mopping the floors. Waiting for
the last flight of the evening, his. Got a cab driver to take
him over to the campus a mere stone's throw away. Stupid
rube took him to the wrong dorms, any fool could see they
were deserted. But the cab had gone before he had the time
to turn around and notice. Huge buildings. All doors fore
and aft locked. It was warm, warm and balmy and humid

being the wet season, no such thing as winter in Ca., and he was dressed for a Philadelphian snow storm. Circadian rhythms distressed by the time change, sea change, disorientated . . . Let them stay that way forever.

He did not know where the right dorm was or where to start looking for it. Such huge campuses. Maybe all the scientists had gone to bed early in readiness for the next day slides under their pillows? Unlikely the doors would be locked even under such improbable circumstances. There is an insomniac in every group of scientists. He lay down under a Pacific bush out front of the spurious dorm, it was deserted, tried to sleep with his suitcase for a pillow, Santa Barbara campus landscape pebbles for a bed, he could never get to sleep that way. Too much balmy Pacific air and starlight. Never go back to the east. The conference was delayed, cancelled, a mere excuse to get him to visit his grandfather. Learn the truth at last concerning his presence on this continent. Leaving his suitcase, he started wandering around the various halls of residence. He could hear the sea. A negro cop on patrol caught him in headlights full beam, drew a gun, demanded an explanation as to what he was doing there. No way out of it now. They went back and got his suitcase and he was driven to the right dorm, the cop very anxious to be of assistance once having ascertained that he was a visiting scientist from the East Coast, the cop being, as he expressed himself, 'a great believer in science'. A student on duty at the dorm assigned him a room. He went to it. Found it was a two man room, his roommate already asleep in an adjoining room. He shut the door. Looked around. Good, a switched on student room. Posters all over the walls. Judging from the evidence, a social scientist. Soft science trying to become a hard science, should save itself the trouble. Scavanged around in search of a roach, not liking to carry the weed across state lines, but in vain as no one could be so crass as to leave a roach in any room where a scientist of the hard variety might stumble upon it, whip out an instant analysis kit and make a direct call to the gubernatorial residence. On the bookshelf, amongst sociological texts, the unexpurgated Justine by De Sade. Lighting a straight cigarette, Danny took it and read, laughing in the appropriate places. Good old California. Strangely restless now, not wanting to be unoccupied through sleep. Looking up on finishing the volume he was amazed when he switched off the lights to find the room permeated in the soft grey light of Californian wet season dawn. The wet season and for half an hour it then dutifully poured rain. Literally hammers of wet. The hour before dawn. The hour when young love wakes on its white shoulder in every second bedroom during term on every campus and pad, California. Only he'd managed to miss all this.

He dressed in lighter garb and walked down amongst the dripping vegetation past the duckpond past the Spanish style faculty buildings with such graffiti as Support Chavez— I will do that—to the ocean. The Pacific Ocean ocean of his forbears. Hearing now through overtiredness in his ears the sound revisiting of a conch sounding now like pipes of Pan to him he returned to his room in time to see his roommate, a spotty lad from Bristol England emerging from the adjoining room in a singlet a towel around his neck and a toothbrush in his hand. Spot of breakfast he said, no thanks said Danny, I just arrived, telling lies, tired out fell onto the bed. A smile upon his face, for no good reason he realized when he woke around eleven or twelve by the clock and thought back over the vagaries of the night and the early dawn. Travel, ah travel, it does things to a man, makes him restless for one thing. Especially the venture back. The venture back is filled with joy, the venture forth is filled with dread. And yet the final outcome could well be contrariwise—could well be. He thought this out but briefly as, seemingly a biochemist again but against his better judgement, he studied the day's program of which he had already missed a good half.

Chapter 10

The sessions, on the first day all plenary lectures, were being held in a large lecture hall at the back of the Chemistry School, and when not listening to speakers, ie., between speeches, it was the delegates' habit to stand around outside the hall with name tags of each delegate stating home institution prominently displayed, laughing, sipping coffee and soaking up the sunshine. When Danny arrived for the afternoon session on the Monday morning having missed out on lunch as well as breakfast, he saw the last of the regular delegates to go into the hall making ready to shut and lock the door. Not wanting to let any of these informations leak out to the public at large. He stopped, and let Danny in, taking note of his name tag. Some delegates were wearing suits, most outmoded sports clothes. Danny a pair of jeans and a sweatshirt. There was only a sprinkling of postdocs, also a few local graduate student observers. These sat in the back rows. On a cursory glance around Danny couldn't see anyone from his institute. Placing his name tag in his pocket, he sat in the row immediately in front of the graduate students. Smiling at them, he noted that they did not smile back. Too terrified of making any misalliance. And also he was probably looking as tired and odd as he felt. He hadn't even shaven. Probably took him for an interloper of some description, it's cool, he said with another smile, but they said nothing. Wearying of them, he turned front, straining forward in his seat to hear what was going on and being said. Someone with an East Coast accent held the stand. Difficult to decipher his speech above the roar of the ocean—no, not really difficult. Just a matter of concentration.

The topic of the day was rates of enzymic catalysis. Many problems in explaining these rates of enzymic catalysis. Many problems also in justifying the celerity of chemical models as illuminative. Some of these problems were being raised and glossed over by the speaker, essentially a physical organic chemist. Someone had drawn a reaction coordinate on the blackboard during the morning session, and it was still there. Someone else had drawn a transition state diagram, horse radish peroxidase judging by the look of it, and it was still there too. The speaker was discussing the way in which he had cunningly obtained monumentally rapid condensations of certain sterically hindered aromatic acids with suitably hydroxylated side chains, very fast lactonizations, that sort of thing. He had a whole lot of slides and he was making a whole lot of statements that Danny felt were wrong and fatuous. And before he was even really sure of what was happening Danny found himself on his feet and saying out loud and clear but to no one really in particular— in fact interrupting, a major breach of conference etiquette, especially at a plenary session—in the broadest, most nasal voice he could muster too, now you wait a minute man, just hold on a minute there, before you go any further I have a few points I'd like to raise. As a body, the convocation turned, sea of blood-lustful faces annoyed by his arrogant manner as much as by the fact of his interruption. Also eager to see which institute had so disgraced itself. Some would recognize him, Berkeley, MIT, his own institute. But his name tag was in his pocket. He took it out and held it up as he spoke, rotating it slowly so as all their craning heads could get a good look. An audible groan arose from a few rows in front and he recognized the groan as that of his old adversary Institute heavy Aarons. Oh Christ, Aarons was saying to his neighbour, he's going to make fools of us all.

Which of course he did. He knew the speaker was wrong in what he was saying, but when pressed, couldn't really put his finger on *why*. The speaker, scenting blood and anxious to humiliate his interrupter, kept pressing. Groans and heckling, mutterings of shut up and sit down. Thought he recognized amongst them all a Bristol accent. Take care of that later. Most of what he wanted to say he learnt had been discussed at exhaustive length during the morning session. Finally, he was completely cornered by the speaker, who demanded loudly to know the basis for his gravamen. He paused—just long enough to allow the expectant hall to become silent. He then said, well there are two opinions on this. Aarons said, yeah, yours and everybody else's, and got a good laugh. Highly revealing of these curs that they had never read their Thoreau on the matter of the majority of one. But what if he was wrong? He certainly had no basis he could think of. Finally, in a very loud arrogant but somewhat desperate voice he said, well if you want to know why I think you're wrong all I have to say is that my intuition tells me so. He then sat down amidst, of course, momentary uproar—laughter, deprecatory clucking—Fermi over in Chicago used to say that sort of thing and get away with it, everyone would listen respectfully to Fermi. But of course, he was not Fermi. Several myopic individuals in front still asking who in fact he was. He heard the voice of his preceptor as the speaker called for his next slide, ahem, some dumb arse postdoc of mine I regret to say, forget it, never knows when to shut up. Exit Harris from the international biochemical scene. On account of a peccadillo, solely on account of a lack of respect for this armadillo on the stand.

Of course *he* would eventually be proven correct, of that he had no doubt, and the speaker wrong. He was equally certain that everyone in the hall *also* knew or felt the speaker to be wrong, just didn't have the gumption to get up and say it. Need the right data to do that sort of thing. Full marks however to the speaker for having had the *data* man, *reasons* man, for going about everything in an orderly, logical, punctilious if incorrect fashion. Whereas being right through intuition, a big demerit. Why do we need data anyway waste all our time on data when it's only ideas we're interested in? Make up the data, might as well, we're not interested in the truth, the sooner we find the truth the sooner we're out of business. What's the difference anyway between doing what I just did sticking my neck out and getting it chopped off over nothing and sticking your neck out a mile over some trivial, inconsequential and probably quite wrong or at least soon to be outmoded piece of data? After all, my intuition *is* data: I'm made of molecules so my molecules should be capable of empathetic understanding of all other molecules intuitively. Heresy you say? Remember Galileo. And forget Aristotle with his fucking either or. What sort of a dumb arse science is this we have here today no room in it for intuition? Why I could work out why this bastard's wrong given half an hour with a pencil and paper but why should I bother? Guess I should have been a theoretical physicist, oh well, my bad luck. He made all these points quite explicitly to the students behind him in continuing asides, reaffixing his name tag in order to lend himself a little authority, only to be told eventually by one of them on behalf of the others, perhaps they thought he was drunk or stoned, shut up, as they were trying to listen to the speaker. Everyone in the hall trying to listen to the speaker. That did it. He leapt up, vaulted into their row of seats and seized the offending student by the scruff of his neck. A smallish student he proved to be, with a Pecos Pete moustache long hair and prayer beads. Trying to pose as a hippie and don't even believe in intuition, I'll teach you he said raising his fist in a threatening gesture. But noting that he had once again disrupted proceedings by his behaviour and that a group of Notre Dame type biochemists were moving purposefully towards him from several directions in the hall he left, not wishing to cause any more trouble. Carefully and quietly shutting the door behind him. What an anti-climax. Took out his name tag and studied it. Yes, it had been him all right back in there. The enormity of what he had just done had suddenly dawned on him. And then the enormity of its lack of enormity. Perhaps overtired, it had all been an hallucination. Perhaps he'd found a plug of hash the night before and was on some gigantic bummer.

No use. No use to work out why the speaker had been wrong. Maybe the speaker had been right after all, difficult to see clearly through his haze of facts and misbegotten data. He immediately lost interest in the matter. The sky too clear, the gardens too fixed for that. He strolled down to the sea near the Marine Institute and along the shore awhile, then dropped into the campus post office to send a postcard to Sylvia. Went back to his room, shaved, dressed respectably in sports coat and trousers. Anxious to get out before his roommate should return. But no hurry until the doors opened on the last session. He sat in a chair and looked through the list of participants. Noted that there were two Australian delegates, now that must have cost a pretty penny. Practically unrecognizable from his earlier debacle and speaking in his Harvard accent, he found them from their name tags and edged in beside them as they queued for dinner with trays in the student cafeteria. Mind if I just ask you about job prospects back home at present in Australia. My wife is Australian you see, and I thought I'd ask . . .

Very tight. Try the ANU, might pick up a research fellowship there, but it's only a postdoc and you should stoop so low. Great deal of inbreeding throughout Australia, most biochem departments not worth a pinch of shit. Full of bacterial cultures, plants in greenhouses, you wouldn't believe it. Also a great many local products overseas stranded on postdocs trying to get back home. Small country overproducing in the field of pure science for reasons best known to itself, no national science policy . . . Thanking them, he walked away. Heard it all how many times before. Not necessarily in reference to Australia of course. He noticed glowering eyes directed at him from his own institute table, but did not pause to exchange the time of day. This was it. Checking out. Wondering not for the first time why visiting Australians always spoke in stage Australian accents with continual interlarding of stage Australian idiomatic expressions. Stone the crows. Fair Dinkum Cobber. Surely not all scientists were sons of fettlers in chains on that be it never so egalitarian continent of his forbears? His mother had told him his grandfather still spoke with an Australian accent; and his grandfather's accent was nothing like these mens'. Inferiority complexes maybe? A desire to please more likely. He saw their eyes fearful upon him as he left reminding him of quadroons attempting to pass in a Southern cafeteria. One had a crewcut, the first crewcut he'd ever seen. Strange country all right. Speaking of his grandfather, that's where he was headed, a pattern was now beginning to emerge from all this idiocy and embarrassment. Ordeal of fire. Well nothing worthwhile comes easy they say. Not like a Ph.D. now. Clear of that easy *summa cum laude* territory now and for all time. Good. He appreciated a challenge. Managing to avoid his preceptor he went back to his room and fell asleep overcome by great weariness.

Next morning he lay in bed long after breakfast feeling no longer any compulsion whatsoever to attend the conference, which also had night sessions he had also failed to attend. Not wanting to line up with those grey and potentially grey eminences on their long postbreakfast strolls across the campus for one thing. Feeling he would no longer particularly care if he never knew how any enzyme worked. All the data's in anyhow, it just doesn't answer the questions. Feeling that all science might prove this way in the final analysis. Much head scratching ahead. How pure and beautiful and innocent those few undergraduates that were still on campus looked when compared with the older generations of spotty scientists, all loaded of course with hangups so deeply repressed they wouldn't even admit to them anymore. And with what ill concealed scorn and contempt they regarded the students, and the students them. Pretending it to be indulgence on the one hand, fear on the other. His generation probably the last generation to be conned by all this logic. How ashamed he was of his own generation, now he had to look to those younger than him to show him the path. It was a disgrace. He pulled his slides out from under his pillow and carefully watched how the celluloid or whatever it was peeled away as he prodded at it with the hot end of a cigarette. Then he dressed—his roommate was now as anxious to avoid him as he was to avoid his roommate— and wandered back down onto the beach again. Various plans suggested themselves. Whip down to UCLA find Castaneda get Don Juan's current address. Feeling deeply the need for a new guru. Dismayed to find on the sand in a sort of nest of kelp a negro staring out between the oil rigs in a full lotus. Dismayed at the health and strength and purity of the individual rather than his colour. A younger man than himself he adjudged him. After all, his generation the last generation to place a premium on so-called intellectual development at the expense of health and strength.

This return to sanity was pleasing to behold. He thought with distaste of the disgusting physical condition of so many fat biochemical Aarons. He had stood up before the multitude and said—body is mind mind body, that is all ye need to know. And they had kicked his arse out of the temple anxious to get back to their pig dealing, scribes and pharisees of our times. Where is our present day Jesus to scourge these bastards, get in amongst them with the knout they so richly deserve? Abbie Hoffman? Jerry Rubin? Tom Hayden? Improbable. Give them enough rope they'll hang themselves. And all the rest of us with them. However, personally in need of a creed he continued to wander around the campus all afternoon, amongst all the beautiful and sane young, hoping whatever it was they had was contagious, ashamed

of his own generation, turn your back five minutes and
there they are dragging out that Golden Calf again just
can't seem to help themselves; their gutless apostasy, their
total sell-out despite misgivings. For a great many had misgivings. That much he knew for a fact. Get them drunk and
hear the puffers spill out their misgivings, that is why they
won't get drunk, generally disguised as academic bitchery
but it goes deeper, plea trying to make itself heard body is
mind, mind body. These are your enzymes speaking, cease
interference forthwith or take the consequences. *You* are an
enzyme old yellow enzyme. The alchemists have been misunderstood and their art perverted.

Ok, fine state of affairs—first of all the priests walk out
of the church, next of all the scientists walk out of science,
the army won't fight—what's going to become of this country? Answer: Who gives a fuck. Recollect first synthesis of
insulin—out of Shanghai and you think *that* didn't take the
boys a little by surprise a few questions asked in the upper
echelons—guided by the thoughts of Chairman Mao we
attached the A chain to the B chain in the following
manner . . . back to alchemy. The shape of things to come.
Recapitulate now. Find a Chinese philosophy and work your
way up. Only thing was, Danny couldn't hack Zen, it was
far too practical for him. He was more Indian than Chinese.
And he couldn't sit still for more than ten minutes. Except
when under the influence.

He walked across later in the day into the student off
campus area, past the big co-operative organic garden into
the record shop. Spent a long time in there looking at all the
record covers. And this was their provenance. Weasels
ripped his flesh.

Graduate students still exist in the physical and bio-
physical sciences but their numbers have decreased alarm-
ingly over the past academic year . . . he asked the saleslady,
a beautiful big breasted and bra-less soul-eyed student
number where he could obtain a joint—and was taken aback
by her disdain. Looking down, he saw what she saw, for the
first time clearly, an undercover cop passing, effect of a
rhino in a lion suit . . . I can't help my age you know, he

said with a nervous and distasteful smile. But did not press
the point.

Back wandering around the shop it was just like on a trip
anyway just to smell the girls, the Pacific air, look at the
record covers, the posters.

He saw it.

That poster over there, that one there next to the authentic portrait of Sitting Bull—what is that. The saleslady
though still not liking his pitch answered from the catalogue,
that is from the Koya Museum, ascribed to Yeshin Sodzu,
shows Amida with the twenty five Bodhisattvas on violet
covered clouds and to the accompaniment of music welcoming a pious soul into the Land of Purity.

The Land of Purity you say?

Yes.

What are you doing tonight?

Going home to my husband impious one.

Tell me what you know about this Land of Purity.

The Pure Land teaching, together with Zen, were the only
two surviving sects of the Mahayana in China prior to the
Cultural Revolution. Apart from that nothing. That much
I remember from Suzuki, he goes into it somewhere.

Is that so? I'll take the poster. Where would I find some
relevant data on this Pure Land teaching?

Book store specializing in the occult right across the
way . . .

Oh, it doesn't sound too occult to *me*—the Pure Land
teaching that is. And don't sound so bored, for Christ's sake.
After all, I'm human—even if you have got a husband.

She smiled a nicer smile. Maybe her old man was out of
town. He wasn't in the mood to follow this up. Took the
poster and went across to the bookshop. Nothing there.
Actually, he wasn't altogether sorry, didn't want any facts.
Facts spoil things. Bought Suzuki's Essays Third Series
anyway to reread back in his room. Sylvia had taken him
through the complete Suzuki quite early in his course of
home improvement. He understood it all at an intellectual
level. Which, as he understood it and as Suzuki himself took
pains continually to point out, was worse than useless. Like

understanding perfectly what is a fuck or a glass of water happening to be thirsty. Bristol came in on him and spoke nary a word. Final excommunication. Save when he was leaving, to go out to some communal natter in someone else's room, I see you're on tomorrow; spose you'll be wanting to 'bone up' this evening so I'll leave you in peace.

Certainly, said Danny slipping easefully through his Suzuki.

Nothing. Just an occasional and tantalizing mention in passing of the Pure Land teaching. The Pure Land. The Pure Land. Laying down Suzuki he unravelled the poster and hung it in Bristol's room where he would see it when he came in. The poster was one of the illustrations in the Rider Third Series Suzuki edition, no doubt that was where the poster company had picked up the idea. No doubt a considerable demand for such a poster throughout the Bay area. The Pure Land. Left the poster for Bristol, essence of the Mahayana faith to enlighten others. Doesn't do to take too much stuff like that onto the road either, Feds don't like it. Suspicious of all Buddhists. Checked out; I am leaving the convention early owing to some personal matter which has cropped up, handing his room key back to the student desk clerk. It should have felt more dramatic: perhaps it had already actually happened years before. Took the last bus down to the highway in Santa B, having emptied the remains of his slides into Bristol's wastepaper basket. Hoped he'd understand that gesture. Hitched a ride back to LA. Standing on the freeway a head with a van full of electronic impedimenta and wearing dark glasses in the night stopped for him. They drove.

Wouldn't have a joint would you man?

Back of the glove box.

That's uncool.

You don't have to take it man.

Roll one for you too?

Please.

Meantime back at the ranch enzyme structures in 3D and living colour.

Chapter 11

The next day he went out to Hollywood after spending the night on the floor in his benefactor's pad, sleeping but fitfully, full of dreams waking and sleeping of Amida and his retinue of Bodhisattvas on purple coloured clouds welcoming him into the Land of Purity to the accompaniment of the dolorous Ravi Shankar raga that his benefactor played all night long on the hi fi. Overtiredness and hunger was now his customary state. He felt he could soon eke out a subsistence if needs be in a trance between sleep and waking nourished only by nettle soup. He was certainly making progress. He wondered if his grandfather would not be proud of him.

He found it difficult to say actually—when the time came.
His grandfather, unused to saying anything much but perhaps Hare Krishna, seemed to blink in the Hollywood
daylight as though unused to it like a sleepy owl. It was a
brilliant, sunny day, or would have been over the Mojave.
The smog over LA was getting beyond a joke. It seemed
that day worse than he could remember it. For a while they
exchanged pleasantries together, sitting in the garden under
the trees catching their breath in the acrid air. A long time
since he had seen his grandfather, whom he understood had
worked as a photographer of some sort in Australia in his
youth, prior to coming to America. He was surprised to see
how old a man he had become. His head was a mass of
bones and carbuncles.

In a rambling manner he told his grandfather as best he
could that he was in the middle of some sort of spiritual
crisis he took it for, and that he wanted help, and that he
had felt his grandfather was the only person spiritually
suited to advising him. Thus, he had come all this way out
to the West Coast solely to ask for advice. His grandfather
said nothing. He then said he wanted to leave science and
become a monk. His grandfather laughed out loud, but still
said nothing. Look, he said finally: if there's some sort of
dialectic going on here that I'm missing with my talking
and your laughing—forget it will you? You're only wasting
your time, because I'm not *enlightened* enough to understand that sort of thing yet: I'm just *looking* for the Ox,
you understand?

Hare Krishna, said his grandfather. He asked about the
Pure Land teaching, and his grandfather smiled. Said he'd
never heard of it. Suddenly in tears he got up: you're living
in some sort of fool's paradise here pop, and made to leave,
walking away across the lawn.

Wait. His grandfather asked him to come back, sit down,
don't be hasty he said, said he had not been certain of his
identity. Unused to the outside world you understand.
Asked him what he had done in life. He told him, it didn't
take long. Omitted details of Sylvia and all the rest, Jake,
Jean, and his grandfather didn't ask about them.

A long pause. Frankly, his grandfather said, your prospects of attaining religious enlightenment do not appear to me to be all that good.

Why not, asked Danny.

You will be too accustomed, if what you have told me can be taken as any indication, to logical thinking. Takes a long time to learn to live and compromise after too much logical thinking. I never suffered from this disadvantage. Most here —he gestured across the grounds—and I only say what I say through knowledge of them, are of your type. Intellectuals. People like Christopher Isherwood, I understand an author of some standing.

Hopeless?

Too cerebral. Too discontented. Now, as you put it, it is something to feel the *need* for enlightenment. But unfortunately most people who feel this need need to keep feeling the need. They do not want to take the next step, the first is so novel and they feel they have come so far anyway that there is no further need to travel. But to see the existence of a path is not to travel it. Frankly, they are scared of attaining enlightenment, scared of committing themselves to the path. Scared of finding it too dull. Back home, I had a lapse of this nature and then I came over here and saw the error of my ways. It means giving up on everything you know—are you really ready for that? At your age I doubt it. Usually you need to have everything taken away. Like me. It's easy at my age to renounce carnal pleasures, they don't exist for me any more. But you're young.

Oh I don't know grandfather; I think there may be one point about the Mahayana teaching you've missed. You see, the Bodhisattva is *supposed* to deliberately hold himself back from ultimate enlightenment so as to remain in the world and save all beings.

Well, that teaching would not suit me, I would find that a very odd religion, said his grandfather. I don't know what's meant by ultimate enlightenment, unless annihilation. I think we should aim at our own salvation personally, at a strictly personal level. After all, multiplicity is supposed to be an illusion.

I think you would find the Hinayana teaching more congenial. Anyhow; have you attained salvation here?

Of a sort, yes, I believe so. In reference to our last point however, it is usually the case that in their early stages all religions are concerned only with personal, individual salvation. There is not much concern amongst the devout for those who are not devout. After all, these will be born again, or if they are not, it need not trouble them. A concern for the welfare of the community at large usually arises later; in my opinion, when the religion has allowed itself to become debased and secularized. But then, as to my personal salvation again, you must realize that I am a simple minded man, and it was not difficult for me. Equally, it may be that I am easily pleased or deluded.

But you also felt the need? At around my age?

No, later. This country forces one to mature earlier. But ah yes, eventually I did. In a far less cerebral manner than yourself apparently.

Oh, I wouldn't say that. I don't know about that at all.

He thought the interview was over so long was the silence that followed these remarks, and he didn't want to say anything or go, but then his grandfather said to him all of a sudden:

May I give you one piece of advice?

Please, please.

Get out of this country. It's going to the dogs. Go back to Australia. It was a mistake my ever leaving it, I see that now. Especially now knowing what you are going through. I am afraid, I have always been afraid, that I was too harsh on the place. This may be the very point of your discontent. Perhaps you are simply a displaced person. Go back there and re-examine your religious fervour anew. You may find it to have disappeared en route. It's the only way you can be sure. You may simply be in the wrong environment. I have at this time a strong feeling that you should return to Australia. It's the last place, you know.

Is that right?

Absolutely. The very last place. How well I remember . . . apart from that, I can't be of much help. But it will be easy and congenial for you there. You see: *you* will be going down.

What do you mean, grandfather, going down?

By going down, I mean from a more advanced to a less advanced culture. I mean travelling into the past. It will be a relaxing experience, you may even grow bored there, as I did—to my eternal discredit. See if you can not grow bored in Australia. That will be your test, yes, that will be it. You will have to find something there to do to earn a living though: I suggest some form of manual labour, you seem strongly built.

I understand: you're saying Australia may well be the Pure Land for me, after a fashion. Do you think that's possible? It can't be just all coincidence, can it. I mean it all has meaning, hasn't it?

I believe so. I had to come up. Into the future. Up to the United States. It was a shock. But in a way I've made your necessary spiritual pilgrimage far more easy for you. On the other hand, had we remained in Australia you might never have experienced the need for enlightenment. Very few Australians that I remember seemed to. Assuming you would have been born at all. On the other hand, you may find it very difficult, I may just be thinking of myself again. I don't know you very well, do I. I never think of anyone. I know nothing of science. I don't know what this country has done to you, assuming you are essentially me at an earlier stage of development. Back in Jersey City, you remember our house there Danny? By the way, how's your mother getting on these days?

Oh, fine.

I think you're telling me lies now. But it doesn't matter.

Hey you know that's exactly the way I'm beginning to feel about it? Facts aren't the truth—the truth must be something else entirely! I *knew* I'd find you sympathetic!

Well—we have the same blood after all. I can't pretend I understand what you're talking about. But I'm not really surprised that it has come to this. For you, I mean. You must have found it hard going keeping up your pretense for so long.

Only for the last few days. Until a few days ago it didn't seem a pretense.

That's the way it hits you. You take me back. I must say I find it extremely difficult though to envisage any descendant of mine as a man of logic. Although admittedly we all wanted you to be a doctor—but that's not quite the same thing is it? Anyway, you will find it all so much clearer in your Land of Purity I hope.

I'll bet I will.

He left his grandfather saying to himself under the trees, a strange country, misjudged the place harshly never really understood it. Ah well.

It could have been himself talking. What's a generation or two when you have continuity of bloodline? And yet look at the way they debase the institution of marriage in this country they don't seem to understand the fundamental importance of anything. Have to leave this country now as a matter of great personal exigency.

Oh. One thing he'd meant to ask his grandfather was, in his opinion, should he not take it upon himself to put an end to the bloodline by failing to reproduce? He did not even bother going back so strong was his empathetic feeling that his grandfather without so much as a moment's hesitation would reply yes: I think that would be a very good idea indeed. I made a mistake, you rectify it for me, where's the point in going on? Mistakes eventually rearise, no one knows how or why, but it is so.

Standing outside the Ashram all he had left was the suitcase in his hand, a credit card in his pocket enough to get him back to the East Coast and a newly burning ambition to get across to the Pure Land. Fancy having been instructed by a bloodline guru and card carrying nonintellectual to see if he could endure life in a Land of Purity. It would be like taking candy from a baby, strange when you think of it the way things pan out enough to restore a man's faith in causation.

Chapter 12

On the road—he ended up on the road—Danny either thought to himself or talked to his companions, and more frequently the former than the latter people being what they are; concerning his decision. Because it was not a decision until he found himself on the road. Why could he no longer continue as a scientist? He must still have had a fair bit of scientist in him he reflected, inasmuch as he was not content to let the decision rest, as a truly wise and confident man might have done, but had to rationalize it. Of course he had no great argument with the Scientific Method—it was generally in accordance, at its height, with what could be

arrived upon intuitively as shown from the ancient sutras
—he just saw it as an inferior, perhaps even harmful, technique. These days. For example, the wave particle paradox,
insofar as it is still seen as a paradox, puts paid to the
Aristotelian either or but this does not seem to have leaked
down to the bench biochemist.

Supposing he found himself next to an articulate van
driver, or in the back of some van with a group of articulates
interested in debating the matter—LA to the Bay Area
only—although, unlike him, they generally didn't see any
need to discuss the undesirability of science, taking it for
granted intuitively no doubt having prejudged it through
hearsay—just let him ramble on through politeness no doubt
not even listening—he'd say right: you have two methods
of looking at the universe, in the limit. a, you separate yourself rigorously from it and proceed to examine it as though
you do not exist in it except as an objective observer, a
method which is ok insofar as it goes—and it went a fair
way within limitations—but in the nature of things it means
by now that each individual scientist—your average scientist, let's leave Pauling Einstein and Bragg out of this for the
moment—spends his working life fossicking away in one
miniscule corner, he can't even understand the man in the
ditch next door, can't remember any more why he is described on his diploma as a doctor of philosophy—shouldn't
this be more than merely titular?—and so on. Philosophi-
cally, not much chop you must concede. He prefers games,
power struggles etc having forgotten his original objective,
assuming he ever had it—*understanding*, which is *not* just
the manipulation of materials the construction of rockets
and transistors and so on—these are merely side issues, tan-
gents—ever see the public so unmoved as by the landing
of their bloody man on the moon? Just couldn't get it to
sink in could they, no and they never will—it will never
sink in, because there's nothing there to *sink* in—what
willing nature speaks what forced by fire, let me recommend
the lending of your ear to the former and not to the latter—
please learn from my experience, I'd be really proud if you
did—his means are now his ends. It happens to every

academy with monotonous regularity over the years, and it is once again time to pitch the academicians out on their arses. You can set your clock by it. Also, this method in the final analysis leads to an impasse, I refer you to Heisenberg and Heidegger. So what, I hear them saying back at the bench, and not unnaturally I seem to have aroused their ire; I've got five hundred grams of acetic anhydride sitting here right in front of me and you're telling me I can't be certain of what I'm looking at? Friend, that is *exactly* what I am telling you. The problem being of course that your average scientist (and I'm speaking here believe me from abundant personal experience) is not much more nor less than an animalcule, an infusorian in his wretched system. Now, with this travesty fresh in your minds take by contrast the second approach b. By contrast we start *here* with the *a priori* feeling—perfectly reasonable, and even backed up if you must by physical evidence, radiotracer studies etc have demonstrated to I think universal satisfaction that your molecules are in a pretty close to continuous state of flux with your environment—that you are in fact part of a continuum, there *is* no observer and no observed, no discontinuity whatsoever, it's an undesirable postulate in fact this observer, the primordial trap in fact, read Suzuki on Genesis I promise you'll find it most illuminating—and that by *realizing* this (the aim of all religious enlightenment is to bring this realization forcibly home) you can become one with the Godhead of your choice in much more than a merely physical fashion. You are now in a position to *arrive* at understandings through sheer molecular empathy. And so the lowliest priest or artisan knows more of eternity than the lowliest scientist can ever hope to know, let him spend never so many hours at his bench and at the blackboard and on the phone, which is the point of my personal defection, which is why I am wandering around here these highways and byways instead of being back home on the East Coast attending to my work. The West Coast is a powerful hallucinogen, useful to show the way but bound to be discontinued in the interest of future wellbeing. That's my level I fear, the lowliest, and since I'm in this business for

myself alone, and since life is short and time so very
precious, is it any wonder I have had to take stock of my
situation and drop out? Isn't that what you would have done
under the same circumstances? Wouldn't you rather build
your own clumsy tower than stick one brick in the Great
Wall of China?

Yawn. Yeah sure man sure. Well I mean I *guess* that's
what it's all about. Got to get yourself together some time.
But don't be so uptight: if you really had it as as-is'd as
you think you wouldn't need to talk about it so much,
would you.

Yes, well of course I *could* spend my life as could anyone
else accumulating a whole load of useless knowledge (all
partial knowledge being of itself useless) without having
the time to enrich myself in the process—I can't deny it
would be very convenient in so many ways—but I won't
do it, I'm too selfish. I'm an all-American boy at heart, just
like yourselves, *I* don't want to become a mere cell in a
larger social unit wiser collectively than I am; and so I
guess if I wanted to be logically consistent I'd have to
enlist in our next incursion into communist territory; but
fortunately I don't particularly want to be logically consistent any more; as a matter of fact I want to try to avoid this
as far as possible; I *do* know now that if I just sit quietly
amidst this crumbling social structure of ours refusing to
lift so much as a finger to stop its crumbling—which as you
know would be very time consuming—all that knowledge
or the better part of it will just *float* in. Make sound sense
to you people all of this (supposing he just happened to be
speaking)?

Looking at them closely—have a happy life people they
would say to one another stumbling from the rear of the
van totally as-is'd; strangely enough he no longer personally
took marihuana seeming to feel no further need for it—he
sometimes wondered about them. It also distressed him
that in the course of his disquisition, as they had pointed
out (and frankly, it was all in his head he suspected and
not a disquisition at all) he had had to pose an indubitable
either or. He knew it was so easy to be misunderstood;
they had probably found him a total bore; for example

Zen some people have taken that as carte blanche for practically anything. As the bold sensualist uses the name of philosophy to gild his crime. And frankly, most of the people in the backs of these vans didn't look all that enlightened to him. Always the same problem. Standing at the top of the normal distribution curve (somewhat like the hillock of the transition state in a reaction coordinate) front and back look pretty much alike. Down. There is a sense of height and distance but not direction. This sense of confusion will be eternal to the molecule wondering which way to slide. Perhaps they *are* identical: Han—Shan, Shih-Te, Pu-Tei—a favorite subject of the Zen painters the Zen lunatics, and no doubt for this very same reason. The path of human existence being A, B, and A with a reason again. He'd come over the hump B° himself. A with a reason always confused with mere A with no reason, ignorant A as yet not up to your B°. That's youngsters. Not too many Ginsbergs around, most of the kids in the backs of these vans travelling forever travelling to nowhere in appearance are actually looking for a convenient point of disembarkation. Many will end up working in banks. They seek a destination, they do not seek to cast themselves adrift at all. Most adrift will drift back. As has always previously been the case. And after all, had it *not* always previously been the case, then society would have collapsed long ago.

Thus one looks on from the back of the van with somewhat bated breath. Can the grand experiment continue (what does it adumbrate?)? Will the centre hold? Where are all the old sailors?

First thing after leaving LA he went up to San Francisco in the back of many vans. He'd thought he'd just keep hitching until the urge to be amongst the young, the West Coast hebephrenia, wore off. Then he'd probably catch a bus back home. Selfdisgust filled him. He felt totally lifeless. The idea of travelling further than San Francisco didn't really come until somewhere just the other side of Santa B when the van driver at the time stopped to pick up what turned out to be an army deserter (in mufti), complete with more gear than one man could possibly carry and simultaneously walk with—all his material possessions—and a dog. Danny became particular friends with this deserter, a youth of about twenty-one or two, a college dropout redrafted AI heading for the Canadian border from his base in Wisconsin by an exceedingly devious route he had decided to take a chance (and what a chance he was taking), one last, lingering look at the United States before crossing the Canadian border into permanent exile. It struck Danny that this wasn't a bad idea, that there were many parallels in their respective states, that there were many scenes in the United States judging from tourist brochures worth seeing that he hadn't seen either, and since he would soon be a self-imposed exile himself (in his Land of Purity across the sea, although he no longer thought of it as such, just a torch this had been to light his way), he thought he might go with the deserter as far as the border, taking in Oregon and Washington along the way, and then perhaps wander back to Sylvia taking in Montana and all those other states and places he so yearned to see, depending upon the weather. He wrote several long letters very early to Sylvia from Los Angeles and San Francisco, explaining as best he could what had happened and what he was doing and why, all just a tangled jumble of guilt and rationalization really he didn't even believe it himself, but because of his itineracy and uncertainty Sylvia could not write back. Fortunately, he had his credit card and he was not short of cash. At LA airport before commencing his journey he managed to sell his return air ticket for $100. And of course he had a little money on him anyway. He wondered what Sylvia's reaction would be, but had so much else to occupy his mind that Sylvia and his own motivations in doing what he was doing became lost, and his epistles, in the absence of any possibility of an avocatory directive from Sylvia, the institute or the NIH, merely conventional road poems. And because he felt it didn't mean much coming in unless it all went out again onto paper—wretched legacy of science—he ended up keeping a sort of diary which he posted as letters to Sylvia. For example, one of his earlier letters, before his jaunt as he'd intended it really began, read as follows:

Dearest Sylvia,

I think I wrote you last letter from San Francisco how I have teamed up with a young deserter and his dog who are at present heading for the Canadian border. He is so pitiful and vulnerable in his plight that everyone sympathizes with him who picks us up (and perforce me as well, we are at present indetachable)—he is inordinately candid incidentally—and even Republicans have taken us into their homes overnight. It is thus the best unguided tour of America that one could undertake, reviving as it does some sense of pride in the core of the American people—at least those who pick up hitchhikers, perhaps not exactly a representative sampling—and since I want to have a look at the place myself, just as he does, before we both leave and since I have nothing much better any longer to do as I have already explained to you I fear at great length; I am making the most of the opportunity, virtually at his disposal. I am useful to him as a companion and also my finances are in a more healthy state than are his. We spent last night at a house in Oakland and tonight as I write this we're some place on the outskirts of Portland. We camp up the coast to avoid Sacramento and the possibility of cowboys (one of the few things odd as it may seem able to strike terror into the heart of my travelling companion—I have undertaken not to divulge his name through the mails as you can well appreciate this could be prejudicial to him—the outcome anyway as far as I can gather of an unfortunate incident earlier on in his peregrination, concerning which it does not turn him on to talk)—and I'm glad we did. To see the redwoods again always had a revivifying effect on me, I remember back even to my student days, and I was pleased to find that I have not changed so much that I cannot still enjoy these old pleasures. We had a short time by the side of the road on the Oregon side of Eureka early this morning (we left Oakland well before dawn—we don't get much sleep) and I took the dog for a walk down the beach while he sorted out something, I don't know what he was doing actually. It was an overcast, pretty cool morning, raining on and off. The beach was as rough as hell, and in the night a

man who was fishing nearby off some rocks told me you
could hear sea lions barking or whatever it is sea lions do.
The dog seemed to want to swim and so, despite the cold
and ignoring the man's warnings of a dangerous rip, we
dove in and played around for a while (I kept my under-
pants on so as not to scandalize the man too much) with the
froth breaking all over us. It was freezing cold but very
refreshing, and with my clothes on once again and walking
back up to the road I felt invigorated physically (ie. mentally as well, that old ignored nexus you know) to an extent
I can hardly remember. Like a cold shower after a night
in bed with you, if you know what I mean. The dog kept
shaking itself and racing around like a mad thing the way
a dog will do when it's wet. Later on from a car on the road
again not far up the road as a matter of fact we saw a herd
of deer amongst a stand of redwood trees and, once in
Oregon, not far past Crescent City, we hit snow. Amazing
to think how one can swim and strike snow all in the same
day. We had pretty conventional lifts all the way, it's pretty
late now of course, though the guy who brought us up as
far as Trinidad was some sort of stage assistant with a
Shakespearean Company somewhere up here in Oregon of
all places apparently. He had to go visit an auntie. They're
all nice guys. There seems to be quite a tendency amongst
the young people in Southern California to move up north
into the less populated states. I guess they'll strike a little
local opposition at first, but they're all so eager to live a
quiet life, not exactly aggressive, I doubt if their neighbours
will persecute them too much. I tell you what, even if we
weren't going to Australia, we should come out and try this
type of life. If not California (either way up in the north or I
think you'd have to go really far south, probably into
Mexico to get away from the smog and all the crowding),
then Oregon looks great to me so far, and I'm sure places
like Idaho, Montana, if you could just find some place that
suited you. I don't see how you would want to go back east
again. You've never been up this far I know. I tell you, it's
absolutely nothing like the Bay area. The air is so clean.
My companion keeps talking of going up into the backwoods

of British Columbia (BC he calls it), I don't know what he thinks he's going to do for a living, but I'm sure he'll make out fine.

I've made up a little story about myself that I keep telling everyone (I'm a great liar now you'll be pleased to hear), I keep saying I was born in Australia and my family moved to the States when I was very young. It's not really much of a lie, is it. Somehow when I say it to anyone I feel it's more the truth than the truth is. You'd be surprised at the interest everyone shows in the place, of course they don't know much about it, the mere mention of it however, particularly the kids, it's all kind of frightening really. I hope they all don't get it into their heads to migrate! That's the last thing we'd want. They ask me what I can remember, and I tell them of the Sydney beaches, Bondi and so on, and the Blue Mountains, mainly what Jean told us, but they keep asking about the Outback. It's the bloody Outback that interests them in particular. I tell them it's all desert and stuff they wouldn't like it at all, but it's all they're interested in. Frontier mentality scratch the surface just a little. I suspect they'll end up depredating any place they go to, they just won't be able to help themselves. Other countries should legislate to keep them out.

Well. Just about ready to shut up shop for the night. Amazing how little sleep you need. I never got as little sleep as this (even with you in the bed) when I was supposed to be in the thick of a project—and now I'm doing nothing yet I feel a sense of urgency I don't know how to account for on any logical basis. Sends cold shivers up my spine. When I'm on my own again—I won't go into Canada—I may get a bus back, depending on the weather through the badlands. Not really the best time of year to be doing this sort of thing of course, it's so goddam cold. Still, something about winter I'm beginning to like, it lets you know you're alive in a way summer doesn't seem to. Snow everywhere. I might have to fly. I think I might continue writing to you pretty well every night, that's if you can stand it—and of course I've no way of knowing if you can't, telephone conversations are strictly against the rules, after all, this is our

*year of the lord eighteen seventy . . . you might keep the
letters though, it might amuse us to read back over them in
years to come from our Land of Purity . . .*

*It's funny how much younger I feel already. Did you ever
used to do much travelling around when you were at Bryn
Mawr? It has this effect of making you feel younger—
proud of your own courage I suppose, although you're safer
out here than walking down almost any street in South
Philly—maybe it's just the West Coast magic. That beautiful
Pacific. They're all mad out here of course, you have to be
in it. You know I used to feel like some relic from the past
when I was at Berkeley? I can't imagine a tour of Pennsylvania having the same effect somehow: but I know I mustn't
insult your beloved East Coast Atlantic Seaboard! I know
how you adore that East Coast of yours!*

*The only thing I'm missing in this new life is you. You're
my wife. You know that. Please don't worry about my
personal morality out here on the road, there aren't any
women, and even if there were I'm sort of not thinking
about sex too much. But if I do, it's only ever you. You'd be
an impossible act to follow, Sylvia, I hope you realize that.
For other reasons now as well, as if I didn't have enough
before, I want us to be legally married. I'm sure there'd be
no problem once we got over in Australia—and if anyone
should ever find out, we could always pretend we were
hillbillies from the Ozarks, we didn't know any better! I
shouldn't kid about it. It would mean so much to me. Anyhow, don't even think about it if you don't want to at this
stage. I guess it's only a piece of paper, not too important.*

*Must sign off now, am making other people restless in
the house with my writing. Maybe they're illiterates: I don't
see any books anywhere,*

Love,

Danny.

A week and several letters later he was back in Philadelphia fumbling at the door. Some story of having had to
fly out of Seattle, snow storm right across the country he'd
been advised. Every magnanimous gesture forever ruined.

Chapter 13

Why hello there, said Sylvia when she heard him making his way into the hall that night of his return year of the lord eighteen seventy. Fancy you back here so soon. It was about eight pm and she was already in bed watching a program on the television set that stood at the foot of their bed. If she had not expected him, then she seemed remarkably self-composed at his return, Danny could not but think as he closed all the doors quietly behind him and moved up into the bedroom so as to preserve the warmth in the house. But he wasn't in much of a mood for thinking, as his lust to empty himself, both physically and emotionally (if there remained any more such a distinction) into Sylvia, after so much travelling, was by then acute. He stood leaning beneath the lintel of her door, and pulled the extension plug of the TV out of its socket with his foot. He leaned back against the door post, looking at her and waiting—a smile, an unfolding of her arms towards him, an unbuttoning of her nightgown—any such gesture of invitation would have been eminently acceptable.

Instead of which she watched the residual spark of light on the tube until it died. He leant forward to watch it with her. Intending irony. Like a dying star it was. Why did you do that, she asked eventually, somewhat icy in her manner towards him. Referring to his having extinguished the spark. Pretending to be interested in the program more than in his body.

Oh, I don't know, he said. Already chasing his air of sexual savoir faire was an apprehension over her icy manner. She could be very icy. That was what made nestling into her bosom such harbour. Blinded by lust, tactless, discounting her mood, totally ignoring his higher instincts which said to wait, he ventured forth the back of his hand intending only to stroke her face; only to have it slapped down with great violence. She continued to stare with a petulant expression at where the spot on the screen had last been seen. As though his image was equally dead to her. He seemed for a moment to catch her implication, but then dropped it. Intent upon watching the red imprint of her fingers fading upon the back of his hand trying to read the meaning of them fading.

Have I worried you, he asked at length.

Yes you have.

I'm sorry, he said, moving towards the bed, every fibre in him supplicatory for the instant removal of her nightdress.

You're not sorry, she replied. You're a fucking liar. Her face, however stern, was no match for the ineffable softness of her breasts. Danny could not dispel the great tenderness he felt towards her, a woman he had screwed and screwed so often and so thoroughly, a proprietary feeling which gave him in his own mind perpetual carnal rights over her forever, gave him even the right to wink at her most asexually dignified stance if he so chose, crumble her into dust in so doing if needs be, a detestable intimacy indeed from her viewpoint if to her he was just a cold, dead fish that never was . . . knowledge that she could never again conceal her flesh from him even on some public thoroughfare on the arm of another man, his X-ray eyes.

You are looking at me as though I were a piece of Californian tail, she said.

You are the juiciest piece of tail on the East Coast, he answered, as if that was any answer.

Furious with him at this, she jumped out of bed grabbing for her robe where it lay on a nearby chair. He, however, was only aware of the movement in her breasts, and she caught him watching them. She tossed her hair and tied her robe across so as to obstruct his view.

You insulting sonofabitch. Don't look at me like I was Miss USA. We've got other matters to discuss you and I.

Can't they wait? I can't be lucid until I've had you Sylvia. Wait until after I've had you. It's been too long.

You've never had me brother, I've had you. What do you think this is Danny? Some sort of East Coast airport cathouse where you can empty your load while waiting for the next flight out? You may never unburden yourself in me again. I've been thinking about you and I while you've been out on your so-called road. You great Dharma bumpkin.

Did you get my letters then?

Oh yes thank you. I read them many times. I couldn't believe them at first you see. They seemed just a little out of character with what you'd told me you were going to California for. I thought that you couldn't possibly have written them. I even went so far as to compare the handwriting in them with yours. But I understand them quite well now. You're pathetic.

Well she had to go and say it. Danny felt his libido die his penis detumesce and collapse like a cannon with metal fatigue.

What's the matter? Did the letters upset you or something?

Some of them did. I didn't bother opening the last ones. And I suppose there'll be more coming in after you've gone. I'll send them on. I can't say they made interesting reading, I kept getting this sensation of—*deja vu*, you know?

Sylvia—I'm not planning on going anywhere without you and never did.

But that's not what you say in your letters. You're on your way back to the 'Land of Purity', isn't that what you call it? Can you see me in your Pure Land? Every Buddhist with his bride? Would you like me to show you your Pure Land letters? Want me to get them and read them back to you? Or perhaps that would be too cruel do you think. I'll give you one of my pink ribbons to wrap them in before you go, you can rub it between my legs if you like . . .

Sylvia, I don't understand . . .

I know you don't. Anything. But you will. I'll make it my business before you tuck yourself in on the couch downstairs tonight to see that you do.

Why are you doing this to me?

Poor little Danny boy. No one understands you. Because sooner or later someone has to. You go fuck off to Australia, go on. Go now and you won't have to listen. By the way, before you do you should get in touch with your supervisor at the Institute. He seems genuinely concerned about you. He's been here several times asking after you. He told me about your performance at the conference. I had a hard time deciding whether your account and his coincided. He thinks you've had a nervous breakdown. Have you? What's your account? I showed him your first letter.

You *what!*

I showed him your first letter. Well why shouldn't I have? After all, you said yourself it was supposed to be a manifesto —said I could nail it up on the Institute notice board if I wanted . . .

Someone's voice saying yes but it was just for you, I didn't think you'd go that far. His. Gentle arms on his shoulder. Hers. You weren't really planning on going anywhere right? You can fuck me now if you want to. Come on, fuck me good so I stay fucked Danny.

Everything ok again once they have you at a disadvantage. He wasn't listening anymore. Surprised to find tears staining his eyes. Shameful, cowardly tears. He put his arms around his so-called sister, mechanically letting her head come to rest upon his shoulder. Not wanting to look into her tear-stained eyes. Not wanting her to look into his. She was really quite naïve, imagining that all their differences didn't matter in bed, of course it was precisely there they mattered most.

Why shouldn't we go back to Australia Sylvia?

He felt through his scapula rather than heard her reply. Oh darling you wouldn't like it there. God's honour, it's a terrible place, really it is. I've read about it. Old Manwaring, what does he remember. Ask yourself. The Pure Land, oh for God's sake Danny . . . he felt her shaking with either tears or laughter probably both . . . do you know it's the most urbanized country in the Western world? They have a lifeline runs direct to them from the Northern Hemisphere. Nothing of their own whatsoever. All brought in. Anyone with brains or talent leaves as soon as they're old enough to get a passport. Besides—she looked at him her eyes wide and her little girl face with corners of the mouth drooping, tears moistening her eyes, well and truly ready to be taken now all right—and yet he was no longer sure he wanted her in any shape or form—why I'll bet they don't even have any Rousseaus in their art galleries.

The room dislocated.

Goddam Yankee bitch, he said. You think Rousseau was an American? How dare you talk like that and pushed her away roughly. She fell. By the way if you think that Shirley Temple routine sounds sexy, think again. Making a bloody joke at my expense out of Rousseau!

Ok Danny—tone of voice changed again (we are in a nasty kaleidoscope here, watch out for all that broken glass at the bottom of the cylinder each time we revolve), her B grade Hollywood long suffering crone tone of voice—let's not make it a night for hurting one another tonight Danny! Because I can hurt you a lot more than you can hurt me.

Then why is it you who are crying, sister.

Because of—*you!* She spat all over him. Ppth. Ppth. Ppth. You goddam *fraud!*

And so away she went, etching every vitriolic word meticulously into his brain where she hoped it would stay with him the rest of his days.

You can't make the grade here Danny, so you're running scared. You're running, not chasing. Back back back. I heard about how you ran out of that conference with the shit practically running down your legs. A flop with some big-titted Californian broad and in your post-fuck ecstacy with a roach hanging out your stupid mouth and a nineteen-twenty Suzuki essay in your paw you think you got enlightenment. Marihuana—Whoopee! A walk along the goddam fucking beach like in a Marlboro ad. En*light*enment! Don't make me laugh. What is it with you Danny that you can't cotton onto anything until ten years after the rest of us? Don't you realize how stupid this makes you look? And don't you see it makes you just a painful laboratory joke and a sickening embarrassment to me? Zen heads went out with button down shoes Danny. What are you? If you're interested in the fashions, then for Christ's sake keep up with the fashions. It ain't dogged as does it in this arena Danny. But you can't keep up. You're incapable. Half of my adult life I've wasted thrusting the modern world down your reluctant and constricted craw. I've concluded it takes ten years to penetrate that bony head of yours. And I'm so sick and tired of your pathetic gesturings . . . I hit you on the head with a mallet and a week later your leg pops up. What am I supposed to do? Applaud? You're like a kitten dragging in a mouse with this enlightenment garbage Danny. You want to hear the truth? Your letters made me *laugh* . . . you were so pathetic. And God only knows, for some reason I love you enough, I tried not to laugh. Where'd you get this gee whiz golly gosh attitude Danny? All these little self preservation thingies? Have you been reading *Catcher in the Rye* again? I told you what I'd do if I ever caught you with that book again didn't I . . . Momma's big bubba huh? Here, come on, over here, look, I've pulled out this big tit for you. I know how you love them. Come and have a suck at your sister's tit one more time before you move on Danny, you goddam motherfucker. Shit scared Danny, that's you—you creep—belong back with the Stutz Bearcat and the warm hipflask. That's your vintage and you've got hangups to suit. Well go back to your shit country, go on, who knows Danny, they may still be showing clean decent family entertainment over there. That's if they've got moving pictures yet. There you go, you can spend every night at the pictures just like you've always wanted. Perhaps it will suit you, only don't write me any letters from your Land of Purity Danny, I hate yokels, please don't write me any more of your goddam fucking letters.

You're the one that's doing all the crying Sylvia.

That's right. Ever think of trying to work out why? You heartless *shit!* Because I love you like you can never love me . . . Oh Jesus . . . I'm just a big symbol of something to you, progress, something you want but can't have, you're all scare Danny, envy, fear, jealousy, all that sort of disgusting crap that decent people don't feel anymore. Oh I just don't want to *think* about it any more, why you have to be the way you are . . .

No, Sylvia. I look at you. It was never any other way. You don't even know I exist. I see that now.

And with her echoing 'I see that now, I see that now, Oh Jesus Christ give me strength, help me God' and her ululation and sobbing erasing in its ugly huskiness whatever ardour for her he might have had left in him, he walked out, feeling once outside that he had escaped by the narrowest of possible margins a mantrap of the greatest possible deadliness. Who knows? She might have had him back in that institute inside a week. Sucking all the goodness vitality strength and resolution out of him eternally, unfecund Venus of his declining moon. If she wanted to laugh, then let her laugh. He felt about him and breathed in deeply once again the crisp winter air. His mistake had not been in the resolution—although he still didn't properly understand that—but in the having spoken about it, still prematurely as it seemed, to a denizen of the East Coast, rotten people of the East Coast certain to misconstrue every pure and undevious gesture made before them. His Southern star called him still—and the more she reviled it the stronger it shone.

Although there was no doubt something in what she said, in fairness he was conscious that there did exist some sort of phase lag between them, nevertheless she didn't seem to realize that a genuine gesture remains none the less genuine for being late. The last flower of spring is not the inferior of the first, or necessarily its imitator. They just happen to look alike and the one came before the other. The universe being as it is a sine wave and not an arrowhead. But she was right; in that a suck of the sister's tit cannot compensate eternally for a crest when you're in a trough. Two generations, and still this gap extant. Two generations is all the time any experimenter can afford. The experiment had failed, he saw it walking in the general direction of the deserted ticket shed a dismal failure. And he so effete somehow, so ineffably tired. Small because weathered, like an antique mountain range. But a woman's tears always accompany the birth of a man. What did this mean? Take his own birth, for example. In an orphanage, he might have stood a fighting chance. In his heart he warmed towards Australia, seeing it anew in his imagination as the orphan of the Western world with himself as its freshly appointed paladin. An environment at last fully concordant with his needs. He would be forever unable to bridge that ten year gap between his own consciousness and the East Coast-West Coast conspiracy. And besides, what can grow strong or worthwhile in such fetid air, such polyglot halitosis? Best travel therefore ten years into the past. He would be forever unable to satisfy Sylvia, ten years after her multicoloured but sterile orgasm would come his own monochromatic effort, perchance pullulating though with slow, dismal life it would seem to her. He revived their life together and saw it the attempted mating of the tortoise with the hare. It would be hard not to take his own exit as a defeat indeed. But he was going to try to. And even if one moves from defeat to defeat to defeat everlastingly, then that can only mean that it is only through defeat that one is to be nourished. Nettle soup for some.

It was so totally unfair of Sylvia. After all—how explain the emptiness in Sylvia in a vast area where he himself was vital and large and full to overflowing, and which he could not convey to her, or even properly to himself, because he'd learnt to speak in her rotten language from the cradle, her language which by design only talked of those things where she was full and he empty? And as she herself had pointed out, *she* could constantly evade him and replenish herself at his expense so that he could never even *hope* to be full on her terms—as long as he fought the battle, the battle in which she had him preordained loser, on her terms! So he thought, I'll fight this battle in the future on my own terms, even if my advance looks like a retreat to her, and my emergence like the burial of a once mildly promising head in the sand of the great Outback.

And so resolving, seeking in his mind for new coordinates, he broke open the window of the deserted ticket office and lay down to sleep soundly.

Chapter 14

On arriving in New York he found there were no passenger ships sailing from the East Coast to Australia, unless one cared to go the long way round via Europe, which he certainly did not care to do and which was anyway financially out of the question for him. He could have gone by air, but he wanted to enjoy the real sensation of distance—he wanted to watch every inch of water passing under the bows of his ship, if that could be. There were a few freighters that made the route he wanted to sail and carried a limited number of passengers, say, six to twelve, but all were booked out seasons in advance. He learnt this early at the travel agencies. He had with him his life's savings (which amounted to his last twelve month's savings, a little under eight hundred dollars, meant for a holiday with Sylvia and which he could never have saved at all without her active complicity) in travellers' cheques, and he was travelling light, prepared to carry nothing, prepared to abandon even his last suitcase, which he carried only for the sake of appearances anyway as it was next to empty. He had decided against contacting anyone at the institute—they might not understand. The only course left open appeared to be to work his passage. He had come up from Philadelphia in the train with his eyes all but shut, fearful of hitchhiking on the Jersey turnpike, which was also proscribed, and knowing no desire to revisit his birthplace and childhood home Jersey City.

Stiffening himself for possible premature death or disfigurement he made his way on his second day in New York (sleeping the first night at a Manhattan hotel, too nervous to go down at once to the Y) down towards the docks where he sipped drinks—whatever seemed to be the drink of the house—in the bars of several waterfront taverns, the walls of the taverns in many cases covered with portraits as it seemed of sporting and seafaring men—in order to find out how one would go about working one's passage aboard a ship, though too nervous initially to say anything for fear of being beaten up. Also, he could not be certain of who were longshoremen and who were seamen. Eventually, tired out, the day nearing its ending and his eyes already beginning to weep in the acidulous air made worse by the smoke of the smokers at the bars, sufficiently drunk eventually to fear nothing any longer, he asked an obvious seaman, a young drinker with shoulder length hair, golden earrings, a filigreed leather jacket and a decidedly Slavic appearance, where one would go to find about working one's passage. In stumbling English the seaman, apparently not comfortable in New York and overwhelmed at being accosted by a stranger making only a friendly enquiry not involving drugs or perversion, told him with utter candour that the unions in New York being so extremely strong there was no way of getting aboard an American ship at all. On the other hand, foreign seamen (the seaman described himself as 'foreign') did desert ship in New York, and one could occasionally get a ship, but only at an hour's notice or less, by waiting in the merchant seaman's engagement office for a desertion to be reported—which was never any more than an hour before sailing time, because seamen are so very often late to board their ship—and generally not at all, for seamen frequently miss their ship through unforseeable circumstances not intending to desert. The seaman asked him what he was experienced in.

Nothing, replied Danny.

Too bad, said the seaman—it transpired from subsequent conversation that he was fourth engineer on a Dutch freighter—the merchant navy is less and less the place for unskilled people. Have you ever worked in a restaurant?

No, said Danny.

Better call yourself a steward just the same, said the seaman, anyone can carry a tray. Where do you want to go?

Australia, said Danny, ordering them both another drink.

Australia, said the seaman. But that was all he could say, never having been to Australia, except that you must, of course, have all your papers in order.

Danny, having overlooked the necessity of a visa, made the next morning to the Australian Consulate. He applied (he already had a passport, having attended while still a student at Berkeley a conference in Stockholm) for an immigrant visa. However, withering later in the day under the questioning of the inquisitorial satrap assigned to screen him, not wishing to discuss himself, he changed his mind and in mid-interview asked instead for a tourist visa. This vacillation did not much impress the man, who was also unimpressed by his rather tattered and unshaven appearance, his diffidence in divulging his vocation and its high improbability when he did; who in short took him more than probably for a hippie, and in any event for an undesirable immigrant. As he was aware that his mother and grandfather had entered the United States under false papers, he felt he could scarcely mellow down proceedings by claiming in his journey an element of repatriation. Eventually they gave him a tourist visa. He said he intended flying out from the West Coast. On being asked did he have the price of the return air fare he said yes, but could not prove it. Inspecting the visa they issued him once out in the snow of the streets again, he saw it was good for twenty one days only, and conditional upon Australian Customs being satisfied that he possessed the financial means to quit the country at the cessation of the prescribed period. He thought this harsh, but reflected that it was probably a long enough period to see what had to be seen and then kill himself. Because he was very depressed by this time, totally adrift it seemed in the very worst city to be adrift in, unable any longer even to use his prefix 'doctor' to keep the rough and harsh realities of everyday people at a respectable distance. Remembering the chill of the dockside bars where he had entered carrying about him all his improbability like a short change artist's aura of deceit brought fresh anguish to his mind as he made his way into the merchant seamen's engagement office.

He sat for three days on a bench, during which time he received only one offer, and that for a passage to London. Provided he ran to a certain berth and climbed in through a hawsehole. He declined the offer and leaving the office on the third day, bought a paper for the shipping movements. A freighter was sailing in three day's time for Auckland and Sydney via Panama, and he determined to be on it. He decided he would stow away, and offer his fare when apprehended, throw himself at the captain's mercy in fact, as in sea stories. Having no more idea of how to go about stowing away than of how to throw himself at another man's mercy with any semblance of sincerity, an act which would involve he knew swallowing the arrogance with which he had always ruined his interactions with other men, though intrinsically less an assumption of superiority on his part than a protective measure—he went down to the Y and lay there on his bunk for three whole days and nights, except when the cleaner told him to shift his ass cleaning the dorm mid-mornings, only stirring to satisfy nature, hardly eating though eliminating a great deal, and on the third day, a last journey into the Museum of Modern Art where he spent as it seemed to the suspicious attendant and himself both an inordinately long time staring at The Sleeping Gypsy with its Picassoesque guitar. His favourite painting. His own guitar. Usurped and preempted by everywhere imitators, the original gesture, clumsy at the time, totally out of time, and everywhere swamped.

For example at the Y he knew that if he cared to ask around there would be at least half a dozen young post-doctoral dropouts, down and outs from the East Coast, all awaiting trans-shipment to their Lands of Purity. Desperately seeking chiefly silence, wearied of words, he did not speak and nor, mercifully, did they. What sort of people, he lay and asked himself deeply in his mind, in strictest silence, over and over, what sort of people in this city that can draw comfort in the existence of so many millions in every respect themselves.

Out on the town he finally walked, town where Madison Avenue expires in a squalid heap of black garbage and icy winter winds are bisected by the Flat Iron building. Brushing aside difficulties and possibilities as though they were a bore on the dock, he walked straight up the gangplank of his chosen freighter, dressed only in a seamanlike turtleneck sweater and a pair of old jeans and carrying nothing except his passport and his traveller's cheques, jumping into the first lifeboat he saw. The ship seemed deserted but not long after he came on board he heard voices and became aware of motion. Peering under a flap of canvas he looked up through the haze at the lights of the Varrazane Bridge as the ship passed through The Narrows and out into the Atlantic. He'd chosen the only one of the four lifeboats that had any canvas in it he later discovered. Not that that signified anything.

In the morning he came out, and even had to walk onto the bridge to attract anyone's attention. The captain, initially mildly surprised, took his money, checked his papers and established to his satisfaction that he had enough money left to get to either Portuguese Timor or New Zealand prior to the expiry of his visa (and that Australian Customs would therefore be obliged to let him disembark), admonished him in a surprisingly mild fashion, and then put him to work as a deckhand, all after a radiotelephone call to the shipping company's New York offices, the cost of which Danny noted was added to the fare. He wondered, it was all so easy, whether what he had done was not fairly common practice. His New York depression he was pleased to feel evanescing as he walked down from the bridge to the forecastle; he saw it at once for what it had been, a US artifact.

He found, with the passage of time, that he enjoyed the performance of his duties, and even the initial raillery of his fellow seamen which soon were good-naturedly off, very much. As far as his duties permitted it he preferred to work on deck, and as close as possible to the ship's rail, so that every so often in what he was doing, generally swabbing, he could look up and watch the water. Eventually his fellow crewmen could no longer pick up even Florida radio on their transistors, and there was at last a silence for him to work in, broken only by the sound of water being passed through and the ship's engines. He did not feel enlightened, but he certainly felt no regrets. Just a sense of profound inner numbness, as though the episode was intended only as an interregnum, too painful to explore. Why rip off scabs. He did not feel afraid. The men found him good company, because he listened while they spoke temporizing where necessary, and this they took as a sign of intelligence in him. No one tried to beat him up, rob him or rape him. He did not tell them of his background, and they didn't ask him; although the captain must have noticed that the old Swedish visa on his passport was for some reason accompanied by a stapled NIH statement of the purpose of his trip to Stockholm. He noticed that there were maybe half a dozen passengers on board however, middle aged people who strolled the deck in coats, breathing deeply and talking in his presence as though he was not there, and several times early in the voyage he had to fight off an urge to stand up in front of them, introduce himself, and announce that he was in actual fact a Doctor of Philosophy, a graduate of Berkeley and MIT undercover. But it dawned on him that there would have ensued no applause at this disclosure, rather a shocked silence either of disbelief, incomprehension, or even disappointment that anyone upon whom so much taxpayers' money had been expended could abuse such a background by taking work as a deckhand. And also, that the gesture, in its pitifulness, would destroy his fresh life. He felt proud that he had been made a deckhand, and not a steward. He worked so hard that at night he fell into his bunk too exhausted to think. Probably contrivedly. Physical labour, he must have realized even then, can make so much lifegiving discontentment seem so transparently artifactual. He did not know what the ship's cargo was, and never enquired. After all, he never went down into the holds, but was permitted, at his own express request, to remain at work on deck, or if not on deck, then in the companionways.

It was the voyage of voyages for him, the high point of his existence, and he knew it at the time.

Chapter 15

In a sea land filled with shipping they sailed through the Caribbean, between Cuba and Hispaniola, to Panama. Docking late in the afternoon at Colon, the Caribbean seaport of Panama, they had to wait until early the next morning for a passage through the canal, and so the crew had a night on the town. Danny went with them, about eight pm they left the ship, noting many duty free stores on the way from the docks where the passengers would be able to pick up cheap goods. Colon, once outside the Canal Zone—caveat Americanos—appeared to consist largely of bars and brothels. The indigenous population appeared to be entirely black. They all went straight to one particular bar evidently well known to them, and began to drink Rhum Negrita, tossing back drink after drink of neat rum, which made Danny feel very seamanlike until the negroes around them seemed to be absorbing all their light and sound.

So as soon as he was able to do so without causing his shipmates undue offence, about eleven o'clock local time, he left, murmuring something about wanting to do some shopping before the duty free stores closed for the night, out of the door into the stunning tropical heat. Wanting in fact as always to be alone and to recapitulate and to enjoy in particular the sense of impending tropical rain. After all, it was to be his last night in the Americas with any luck. He paused temporarily in a sidestreet over a gutter to vomit up some of the overpoweringly sweet rum, then walked on, a humid storm already beginning to spit at the dust of the backstreets where he walked, not really knowing where he was or who he was or why.

A fat black slut came up to him in an otherwise deserted street, so humid the air that her face was agleam and aglisten with greasy moisture like after a hard night in bed, moisture from the air appeared to have condensed on her pinguid and ample lips and mechanically he licked his own, certainly he did not want to let her treacle glue them together, for one thing he felt about as much like sex as an old turnip, and for another he had noted the evil stench of her black skin, a cunt like the canal in all probability with a comparable count of faecal bacillus and swimming in the dreaded gonococcus.

You want a cheap fuck, she said.

Yeah, why not, he replied. I don't think I've ever had one of those.

She laughed at his slurred riposte in a high pitched shriek that carried her out of her sordid black shape for a split second soaring like the shriek of a tropical bird right up their deserted street. It was a gift, he could always make the ladies laugh. Albeit with cabbage leaves or what he took for cabbage leaves putrescing in the gutters, all the shops in this particular street locked and barred, and he was thinking as he took the arm she offered him how lucky that he had left most of his money aboard and had all but spent what he had on him, for he was just a drunk ready for the rolling that no doubt awaited him back in her room. That's if she even had a room, for just a hustler was all she was, in a knitted beanie too with a surly accomplice around the very next corner laying in wait no doubt like an ant lion for any seaman drunk stupid and unfussy enough to find such a disgusting specimen of womanhood alluring. And yet here he was going with her, taking her proffered arm in fact. Notwithstanding his cogitation.

But, although drunk, he was far from unfussy. And so as he laughed along with her he sent a disengaged arm around her rolls of brassiere constrained fat to grab her free hand on the backswing and twist it up sharply behind her back, at the same time forcing her (with a strength and resolution she must have found remarkable) into a nearby shop doorway where he closed her mouth ready as it was poised to emit a high pitched scream with the full force of his fist, drawing blood. After this action, which had seemed to fly involuntarily from him, she was quiet, and, not a bit chagrined, he forced her onto her knees, kicking her once or twice in the process and saying repeatedly without cause (for she had said nothing) shut up, shut up . . . her eyes looking up at him with those imploring eye whites seemed from the deep South like old Aunt Jemimah on the pancake pack, he could scarcely help laughing; Ok he said, unzipping his fly, get down on that. To his great surprise he saw he actually had an erection. She made an attempted protest or two, and wouldn't open her mouth at first. But he kicked her again, really hard and said open up or I'll knock out all your teeth blackbird, now get to work. But no sooner had she got to work and he his eyes closed in dreamy anticipation, he felt like a whiff of an incipient decollation the sweat of a strong arm at or about his neck which was certainly not her arm, opening his eyes he saw a black flash of vengeance from the corner of her eye no more, he sensed muscle with plenty of black phosphocreatine on the ready, and a cosh or more simply a forearm drove down on his neck so hard that he simply sighed and collapsed, no doubt ejaculating, if at all, somewhat sluggishly sometime later into a cabbage leaf or banana leaf, in the gutter where they threw him after kicking his guts and teeth in.

The slut scratched bit and gouged him viciously on the cock, while her accomplice (perhaps he was just a well-intentioned passer-by) hove in as though intending to mess him up really badly; but maybe they both realized in time he was an Amerikanski—maybe from out his pocket had tumbled his pack of Lucky Strikes—and maybe because they did not want to antagonize his fellow countrymen and invoke perhaps large scale reprisals from the Canal Zone they eventually gave him a few last sporadic kicks in the region of his kidneys (both wearing sharp pointed shoes he noted that had gone out of fashion in the States years ago), and the slut clawed his face a few more times for good measure, spitting on him as she was dragged away, wanting as she put it to shit all over him but her accomplice insisting that they had not the time—so he got off lightly. He wasn't even completely unconscious.

It seemed in the gutter to him that he had been righteously punished by the Lord God Almighty, and he could feel no ill will towards his assailants. Whom, after all, he had provoked. He noticed after a time that he could not get up out of the gutter unassisted, and that his bashed in mouth was bleeding considerably, either because he kept automatically sucking at the stumps where his front teeth had been, or else the rain kept washing his blood away (his mouth being open to the sky), depleting his fibrinogen reserves in accordance with Le Chatelier's Principle. He rolled painfully on his bed of leaves to turn his head into the gutter, intending either to drown in the torrents of water there or go to sleep and be washed away; whereupon shortly afterwards he felt himself being shaken and eventually assisted from the gutter by men who turned out to be members of the crew from his own ship, all rotten drunk and exuding Rhum Negrita, though very full of sober indignation at the treatment their crewmate had been subjected to. Evidently they had deliberately come looking for him, as some were carrying chains and knives, fearful of the worst. They shook him, slapped him, tried to make him act sensibly, wanting some of them to go on an immediate rampage and beat up every man and woman in the Republic; fuck all the women too; but he said it wath all my fault guyth, I went looking for the fight; so they merely swore and smashed a nearby window that had too few bars on it, eventually helping him back to the ship. And what a long way away it seemed.

Look at that, said one seaman as they laid him on his bunk, why those motherfuckers must have tried to cut his pecker off with razors; noting that his fly was still unzipped and its contents bloodied. Aghast at what the natives would not stoop to, they stared at him in silence. No, no, he replied, they had a lady with them who thucked me off while they beat me up the ath to take my mind off mythelf. Ath a matter of fact I'm not thure I wouldn't like to line up for a thecond helping; and so amidst general laughter and relief, and adjudging him not seriously injured—which was in fact the case, all his injuries proved superficial—they left him to listen to the greasy rain on the ship and the harbour while they went back ashore, now certain in their minds that they were in the midst of a really good night.

Carefully and painfully, he pulled himself to the porthole after they had gone and watched the hard rain falling on the craw of the canal making it difficult to delimit sky from land and water. All Colon seemed from the din to be tin roofed. The rain lent the port a romance and majesty he no longer felt inclined to entitle it. They had left him a bottle of Rhum Negrita to ease his sufferings, and he shoved it into his mouth as he set to watching the rain, dislodging yet another loose tooth in the process. He spat the tooth out the porthole into the harbour, a gesture which, taken together with the earlier imbroglio and the seemingly relentlessly pathetic and unoriginal nature of his everymost gesture, made him start to sob with laughter. And the sound of this strange laughter sounded as if prerecorded. Even pain was not painful enough. There must be a film crew around somewhere, he felt, filming a cheapie (all your own stunts) something early from the pen of Conrad or Melville or Lowry. Yet still the ship refused to sail and set him moving once and for all out into the uncharted regions, away from the stinking Atlantic and all these Amerikas. What am I here, he thought and drank until he was as drunk as ever he had been, some fucking half arsed Lord Jim from the turn of the century? Can I invent no new gesture? Ashamed at his monumental lack of credibility even in the midst of all this drunkenness and blood, he felt again for his blood, it oozed from all over him, to make sure it was real. Dislodging here and there scabs in the process. It did not feel real and it did not look real. And yet he had no option but to consider it as real. Lose enough and you're dead, you have to take the sciences as gospel in some matters. Wrapped up in a cabbage leaf in the gutter of a banana republic like a red pupa in a cocoon, he could not even emerge into the real world with dignity. The first physical beating he had ever received taught him only that martyrdom itself could not arouse in him any sense of having lived. Therefore, he reasoned, what is the point in proceeding any further into this 'real' world? None; except that it possesses anaesthetic qualities towards other, truly lethal ones. With some reluctance, he therefore crossed out in his mind with the assistance of the last bottle of rum the last remaining cell of the matrix, which he had provisionally labelled 'reality': real existence, romance, travel, sex, improbable occupations, blood and violence. There were no more cells that suggested themselves. He seemed, at the age of twenty-six, to have exhausted all the possibilities of his life. And yet still the rain fell and still he looked at it, preferring it to the cabin interior.

Why?

In the morning they made through the canal and out into the Pacific. Yet still there persisted ships in their sea lane. Danny, excused from duties for a few days, watched them from the deck. Where could they be making for and from, he wondered. The Galapagos?

FOUR

Chapter 16

Dearest Sylvia,

Once emerged from the grey of night we made this morning into Sydney Harbour. I went without incident through customs, though, being virtually toothless since Panama, I speak at present with great difficulty. Which is why I find it easier now to write—I must very soon find a dentist.

Later the same day. I went to the Dental Hospital on the advice of the chaplain where I'm staying—(for some reason I am imagining to myself that you are very concerned over the state of my mouth)—and they said they could fix me up, but it's going to take a few days. So I'm staying at the Mission to Seamen, which is nice and comfy and centrally located in downtown Sydney, not far from Cadman's Cottage practically under the pylons of the Harbour Bridge —I'm a regular seaman Sylvia, now I've got these discharge papers the captain gave me I might sail out on the next tide (twenty-one days time), the boys said I might become eligible to join a union now, I intend to look into this— meanwhile, my time's my own to explore the city when I'm not up at the Dental Hospital.

Well I won't keep you in suspense any longer concerning the city itself after such a prolonged silence:

It was a fine, sunny day, with the dawn just breaking as we sailed into the harbour through the Heads. Curious bushland could be seen—it's the beginning of March now, that makes it autumn here, though the trees being all eucalypts they don't lose their leaves. You'd never know it was autumn (fall). It's quite warm. Just like Cali.

There are plenty of bushland trees that you can see on sailing down the harbour, it's a magnificent harbour, apparently the best in the world. Many harbourside suburbs with elegant housing, and we sailed past the celebrated Opera House under the celebrated Bridge to our dock. I don't know what I expected—whalers perhaps, full-rigged ships, Aboriginals leaning on spears? The city reminds me most of San Francisco. On a clear day like today, the same breezes blow right amongst all the city buildings. Imagine my horror when walking up town after lunch I saw a meretricious horse drawn vehicle with Old San Francisco Restaurant or some such thing written on it! And no one throwing stones! No doubt the brainchild of an enterprising fellow countryman of ours—don't they make you proud of them? The people here look strange to me. Very healthy, but strange. I don't know what it is about them, but you can tell they're not Americans. Equally, *they* can tell you *are* American, even before you open your mouth—which, in the condition my teeth are in, I try as far as possible to avoid. Their attitude towards Americans is apparently somewhat ambivalent. Would you believe me that the city is full of

GI's on R and R from Vietnam? I met one today, stopped me in the street, said he knew I was a Yank, just like that. And without me even speaking. He said it's just like an occupied war zone here. The chicks love you, the guys either love you or hate you and generally both at the same time, everyone wants to rob you. Well, I may never know about all this. Nothing is ever what you expect.

It makes me uneasy to be American though. To start with, I feel I should be Australian anyway, on the other hand I'm not sure I shouldn't be grateful I'm not. Looking around, I feel somehow confident as I walk amongst them, though it's difficult to explain why. A load off my back. Big fish in a small pond maybe. Grandpa warned me to expect this. You did too. It *looks* like nineteen seventy, that's the date on all the papers; but somehow you know it really isn't. They seem scared Sylvia, I don't know how else to put it. Scared of being caught on the wrong foot or something: The wrong attitude on recent events, girls caught in outmoded fashions: and you're looking right through them with those cold X-ray Yankee eyes of yours. Exposing them. Making them look foolish. I don't know what to say, after all, I'm back in there with them aren't I? Or am I. Shouldn't look a gift horse in the mouth like this though I guess, most unseemly.

Take, for example, women's fashions (something for you to identify with Sylvia, that's correct). Now, it's not like in the Bay area with everyone doing their own thing—they seem to *care* here. Yet they look so ridiculous in their Mother Hubbard smocks, so serious somehow, you need a certain kind of *nonchalant face* to wear one of those. An American face do you suppose? Anyway, they don't have it. I guess I could say they all look pretty stupid, but that wouldn't be fair, because whatever it is it's not their fault. I shouldn't say they're stupid. But I was pleased enough to talk to that GI who accosted me, man from Omaha, an enlisted man and all, and there was I pleased to see him, a bloodied Vietnam volunteer, and me describing myself as a merchant seaman. I'll have to watch this tendency of mine towards criticizing the place here, things are bound to be different here, after all—*I* should talk about ambivalences; and it's like a second marriage for me, I have to make allowances. Thanks to you.

Sorry Sylvia. Sorry I ever left you at home. There's no one here I want to lay, I can tell that just looking round. I'm scared. I feel already I'm being squatted upon or laid upon by some great, fat, suntanned, ignorant Bondi lady in this city. Like a nightmare, when I open my mouth to scream she can't hear me and won't move. I search her for malignancies but she's clean. Slowly turns her uncomprehending eyes upon me. I better head for the hinterlands I think. The great Outback.

Later. It's the next day, nineteen to go. I just had breakfast. I have my first dental appointment this afternoon, to make things fresher I'm taking my little pen and diary along with me, so as I can speak to you dear sister whenever the occasion moves. By tonight I hope to be drunk. (After all, you must realize I'm a bona fide sailor now, and of how many other Berkeley Ph.D.'s of my vintage can that be said? Who's left who behind now huh?)

Here I am in the Botanical Gardens, just taking my ease here, and I'm truly happy and contented for the first time in Sydney, I see that now. It's the bush you understand me? The bush—Sydney or the bush (local coloquialism). There's only me here, and over the sea wall I can see the harbour. This, my Sydney Guide informs me, is Farm Cove, where the first farm in the colony was established. A pandanus palm is on my left, shooting adventitious roots in all directions. It has my sympathy, I know just how it feels . . . Two hundred years ago—nothing. It's a very young country Sylvia—why then does it seem so old? So worn out, so effete . . . geologically of course, it's a withered crone amongst continents. Old withered crone comes through all the fresh young faces in the streets.

It's nice here in the Gardens. I just can't believe that this is fall (autumn). At one stage during my perambulations I found myself in a rose garden and just outside the fence was a white building with some modern built-ons, that my guide book tells me is the Sydney Conservatorium of Music, originally designed as a stables by a convict architect. I don't know how they planned on getting their horses up those stairs. But the music coming out made me sad. So what did I expect? Didgeridoos and dancing sticks? It was cacophonic Western music Sylvia, out of the practice rooms. And women singing Lieder. I have to keep reminding myself I'm still in the Western world. Or rather, I keep being forcibly reminded. I wish I was a musician Sylvia, suddenly I have this great yearning to be a good guitarist. Maybe I'll just walk right in and enrol, why don't I do that right now.

I didn't enrol. They couldn't teach you guitar here. Just a minute ago I came out of the Mitchell Library, it's across the road from the Gardens. There is a big map of the continent in the foyer. Inside, many books, all around the walls. I found some Australian authors. I read a little, but I can't read much of it, Sylvia, help me; help me to know how to approach the literature of this the Land of my Forbears. It's incomprehensible, and when it's not—God help me. Outside the sun is still shining brightly—what was I doing anyway in this musty old library? Why did I come to this country? Not to visit libraries on my twenty-one day visa, that's for sure.

Stop press. Now *here* is something finally worth reporting. I am writing this from inside the Art Gallery, which houses a pretty abysmal collection by international standards, and I say that being used as I am to the Philly Museum and the Guggenheim etc., but I don't want to be churlish because first things first, bread before art I fully concur. To get here I walked from the Mitchell Library (where there is apparently a lot of Australiana upstairs but after all, I recalled half way up the stairs, I'm not a tourist in this place, I came here to escape my strait-jacket of tradition, not trade in my big and roomy one for a small and constricting one, no, better by far to remain ignorant of all this, have to watch this scholarly predisposition of mine like a *hawk*); I walked straight back down to the foyer—over a stretch of land called The Domain (I take that to be English), where the roads are lined with giant fig trees—they also had these in the Gardens, Sylvia, Moreton Bay figs they're called—

but enough of the setting: I'm in the Australian section of the gallery here, the modern Australian art section, and I'm so *excited*—but I had some curious experiences here at first, let me tell you about one. I saw what I took to be a *Chagall,* never knew Chagall had been in Australia, but on closer inspection it turned out to be a painting by a man called Boyd. Then I saw what I took to be a *Rousseau!* Ha, ha, I hear you say. But I'm standing in front of it now. Still standing. Pretty Polly Mine it's called, and it's by a painter calling himself Sydney Nolan. *Sydney* Nolan, how about that? I like that. Wait a minute though—sorry, it's Sidney Nolan. Sidney. Is that a common English given name? Anyway, the reason I must have thought it was a Rousseau is that it has a man in it who looks identically like black suited Rousseau (complete with chapeau—or was it beret) in that self portrait he did of himself down by the docks (only without the artist's pallet of course), standing centrally, next to a mine shaft in the Australian Outback. In the upper foreground are some upside down parrots, or one of them upside down, a direct steal from Klee's Garden of Birds, but that doesn't matter, that doesn't worry me a bit. So it's all very derivative, what the hell. The important thing is this: this artist Nolan, whom I am now determined to find out more about, has felt *Rousseau* had something to say similar to what *he* wanted to say. And after all Klee was also a great admirer of Rousseau, this painting's one for the in-crowd, you get it? And I'm one of them. After only two days I'm one of them. The point is—if *this* is what Australia does to you (particularly the Outback), then I've come to the right place, as I'm sure you would be the very first to admit. I will write a further report of this when I track the matter down in the city. Later from the great Outback, you watch me.

It is sometime later. I am now in the city. The other Australian art, though I examined it but desultorily, didn't turn me on. I asked a custodian about Nolan (mumble, mutter) and it turns out that Nolan is a very highly regarded painter, apparently world famous! C. P. *Snow* owns a painting of his! Wow—C. P. *Snow!* I guess there's just no limit to my ignorance. I am at present in a downtown bookshop (I'll have to rush to make my dental appointment, but first things first) and open before me I have a coffee table art book with some of Nolan's paintings in it. Yes, I managed to find a book without any difficulty. Yes, the Rousseau element early on is very heavy. They say writing is fifty years behind painting. And this country twenty years behind the rest of the world. It all checks out if I did my sums aright (a thing I was never noted for), Rousseau painting around the turn of the century, me writing in this diary today, one in spirit, correct. One painting of Nolan's that particularly entrances me features this same black Rousseau-like figure (Nolan?), most incongruously of course (but that's the whole point, you get it? Now, you're quite *sure* now ... sorry for all this Sylvia) in the Outback, the effect comes off very well, I think I begin to understand yes I am beginning to under*stand* Sylvia—there is alienation here mate, if there is alienation anywhere: alienation of the artist just another myth, I quote from a chapter entitled 'The Plastic Parthenon' by John McHale in a nearby collection entitled 'Kitsch'— just another Yankee know-nothing: I swear I opened the page at random too—can it be that strange things are at long last beginning to happen? This time Rousseau's standing next to a river, the Murray River. I am going from this bookshop to buy a big map of this continent, and tonight when I get back from the Harbour View after a good night's guzzling of that famous Australian beer (makes all the American pisz like Pabst and Budweiser seem quite *ersatz*) I will write you another letter, essaying to explicate the art of Sydney Nolan, and in particular Rousseau at the billabong, in greater detail.

At present, I am off to get some teeth replaced. From now on, I hold my *peace* in any public drinking house no matter how provoked; of that I assure you,

Love,

Danny

PS. Just before going off to the boozer—this is a strange, relaxing country, and I don't know if I've brought it out sufficiently in the text of this letter. After all, I'm just a neurotic, I'd be miserable anywhere. I ask that this please be taken into account. American tensions are already melting. Australian tensions already taking root. But let me tell you one thing, I personally would exchange *any* cultural advantages for clean skies and decent beer and victuals. Actually, there is a fair bit of smog over Sydney, but I didn't want to mention it as I am speaking already of the high mountains (three thousand and something feet high the Blue Mountains I learn from my comprehensive map—like going back to some childhood play place to find the scale of everything much reduced. wouldn't you say?) and the massive hinterland Outback of course. I shall sleep tonight dreaming of the Murray River. Goodnight sweet lady. This is no place for you.

Chapter 17

I don't think there's much point in me detailing this city, meaning this inner city, any more. I've already described the choicest spots to you. I've haunted the Gardens and The Domain for a couple of days now, getting drunk every night —trying spasmodically to remember what it was I had to do here before I left for Katoomba. Did I tell you the captain paid me wages? In case you're wondering where all the money's coming from. Well now, I've remembered. Hunt up my maternal grandmother out in Bondi. How could I *ever* have forgotten this? My memory, Sylvia, once well-nigh perfect, is now beginning to fail me badly. What does this signify if not incipient alcoholism? So frequent and so complete was Jean's description to me of her mother's home in Bondi when I was young (ie, before I met you)—etched in with all the freshly remembered detail of homesickness following her divorce from my infamous father—that I believe I will find it with no difficulty. The house I seek is a brick cottage with a red tiled roof, a cement drive on one side to a disused garage, a small lawn with snapdragons, marigolds, poinsettia and frangipani in the flower beds, and a small front fence partly of picket and partly of wire. The house, like its neighbours to both sides, will consist of one storey and contain a large bay window, heavily draped. Once admitted to the house, I will not fail to recognize it by its ochre ceilings (though by now these will be virtually black), its distinctive floral wallpaper, and a large grey cat answering to the name of Whiskers. The house is in a street that runs down to the beach somewhere near the Bondi Public School, narrowing the area of my search still further. The weather is indeed remarkably fine here; and since I will have all my teeth back again, oh so necessary to conduct an enquiry with, after my final dental appointment at nine this Friday morning (the more I drink at nights the earlier I seem to get up in the morning, my nights are again shrinking into nonexistence) I am heading for Bondi Beach. By bus. I see there are no longer trams here. Some things apparently do change.

The same night. There must be ten million Bondi houses answering to the above description. I have to go out again tomorrow. I caught a bus that let me off in Old South Head Road, near to a golf links, and as I then walked down towards the beach certain things that I saw came back to me via my mother's memory with a strange and second hand vividness. A sensation of *deja vu* for instance as I walked down a street from Old South Head Road with cannas growing in plots in the centre of it. Like playing a child's game of cold and hot. I kept to the boulevarde of cannas as long as I could, and eventually found Bondi Public School. After a very long time. So I was close, I was hot. But there were very many streets there, all very like one

another, and not a few, in fact a good many of the houses
have frangipani in their front yard. All are brick and have
red tiled roofs. And I don't even know my grandmother's
name—isn't that remarkable? From time to time I stopped
and knocked at a door chosen at random. Introducing myself
to the lady of the house as a GI on R and R searching the
area for a long lost Australian relative. An aunt. A likely
story, would have been my own reaction to this. But how
many compliments I received from the elderly, and even not
so elderly ladies, for protecting them against the Red Peril!
How many cups of Bushell's tea I downed! And such was
my alcoholic desiccation I did not mind, I drank every one
of them. This then, was my introduction to surburban
Sydney. I found the people friendly. A vastly more friendly
people than suburban Philadelphians. But with perhaps less
to fear from their Red Peril than suburban Philadelphians
from the wolf already at the door. But I have not yet traced
my grandmother. One day more I will give it, this quest
of mine. It is not a quest that troubles me overmuch any
longer. Details and particulars are no longer too important
to me. Tomorrow, a Saturday, will see me back out on the
streets of Bondi. However, I felt I had to report back to you
this evening—knowing your concern—thus far not very
many pennies.

The following night. Everyone in Bondi was out washing
their car in the sunlight and all the husbands were home
this morning, it being a Saturday, an accredited holiday in
this country, shops here do not open on Saturday afternoon
or Sunday at all. I accordingly knocked on very few doors
this morning Sylvia. Around lunchtime the men all departed,
as appears to be their habit, for sporting fixtures, the local
pub, or bowls which is a combination of the two. Nicely
dressed the middle aged and elderly men in white flannels
and blue blazers off to bowls. I felt very out of place, very,
extremely out of place. Also all this drinking has been
catching up with my bowels, drinking beer all the time
instead of whisky made for a very uncomfortable time for
me today. I spare you no details of my quest Sylvia. I
found myself continually moving between the boulevarde

of cannas and the school. At about my fifth pass of a certain
intersection, however, I noticed for the first time specifically
the large number of streets that fed into it. I felt an
immediate response from within. I counted them. Seven
streets. 'Seven Ways'. The seven ways. Like a detective.
My mother, of course, had spoken to me often of the seven
ways. I knew then my street was one of seven. One of seven
streets that were one street removed from the streets that
ran into and constituted at their conflux the seven ways.
For this much my mother had told me. But I was able to
eliminate six of these streets in my own mind, in that the
seventh ran almost directly down upon the public school.
And so I had the street, and only about one hundred houses
to choose from. Of these, perhaps twenty had frangipani
in their front garden. Of these, perhaps ten had poinsettia
as well. Of these, none I regret had snapdragons, or even
marigolds. But the odds were growing shorter. Of the ten,
five had young families, or very young people in them. These
I excluded. Bold now, I walked up to the house of my
choice. About midway up the street, it stood with a cement
driveway to one side of it as required. In fact it all checked
out. My *intuition* told me it was my mother's mother's house.
I rang for a long time at the doorbell, watched by several
curious children from the house next door, our driveways
contiguous, at whom I smiled but did not speak, wishing to
conceal from them my nationality. Having noted their television antenna. Could it be that no one was home? Impossible. This, I refused even to entertain as a possibility.

And the believer is always rewarded. I could have gone
time and time again; instead, I chose to stay and keep
ringing. Anyone else would have been not so persistent.
At length, the door was opened slightly, or as much as a
chain affixing it to its doorpost would permit, and I glimpsed
what appeared to be a little old lady standing on the other
side. Regarding me with suspicion. Ah, good afternoon
ma'am, I said. Ah'm an American serviceman (gasps and
whistles of approval from the children at this disclosure)
and Ah'm searching for an Australian relative of mine whom
Ah believe to be in the area. In fact, in this house. (For

some reason I find myself tending to adopt when nervous in this new environment an accent like a Georgia peach.) She made promptly to shut the door, but I cunningly insinuated my foot into the aperture.

Ah—could you perhaps tell me then where the *previous* occupant of this dwelling is to be found?

In a voice I could scarcely understand, Scots, she said Mr and Mrs Fisk ha gone away to Bateman's Bay.

Bateman's Bay, I said. Oh—(with surprise in my voice, even consternation)—Ah guess she's *remarried* then?

I swear, I'm certain the woman said yes. Bigamy.

And could you just tell me before Ah leave, I added, her Christian name? So as Ah may be sure Ah don't have the wrong lady?

Dulce and Tom Fisk, she said, but they wouldna be who you're after. They'd ha na to do with Americans.

Well thank you for your trouble ma'am just the same. Thank you kindly.

She slammed the door in my face. I had withdrawn my foot.

So there it is Sylvia. Dulcie Fisk my grandmother is posing as, and she lives in Bateman's Bay. I have already satisfied myself that this is a South Coast seaside resort. Never one to let the grass grow beneath my feet. I can already hear your protestations Sylvia, something is it about a lack of rigor in my researches? Well can it Sylvia, will you? Dulce Fisk. A good strong name. Bateman's Bay. It'll do me, I couldn't take another day wandering around Bondi Beach. Ah, the joint depresses me, all those red roofs, I too, would be inclined to move away to Bateman's Bay. The kids next door chased after me, asked me why I wasn't wearing my uniform and service medals. Why I don't know what you're talking about I'm sure, I said to them in as pure an upper crust British accent as I could manage. But they persisted. Did I know Hoss, Little Joe? Of course, I said, yes, certainly, both personal friends of mine. My ploy succeeded. They ran home to improvise autograph books at the suggestion of the eldest, affording me the opportunity

to disappear on the run into the public bar of the providentially handy Bondi Rex.

Tomorrow I check out Sylvia, head for the high mountains. Got to get to the headwaters of all this flowing,
flowing . . .

Chapter 18

Dear Sylvia,

Arrived in Katoomba today, this morning—caught an early morning train having ascertained that The Fish Jean used to speak of is a commuter train coming down in the mornings and departing five fifteen pm from Sydney's Central Station—no use to me that, in these winter evenings when it's dark by six. It was another fine, breezy, cloudless day (I don't think I've seen a cloud bigger than a pocket handkerchief since I've been on the continent. The weather pattern over the past few years has apparently settled into the typical Southern Cali wet summer/dry mild winter) and I was amazed to find suburban Sydney extending practically nonstop fifty miles to the foot of the Blue Mountains (where they call a halt more than anything else, because it creeps up the eastern escarpment as well), rivalling in size LA to say the least. The line is electrified beyond Katoomba these days, and the journey only takes about two hours. No steam trains anymore I was disappointed to find (is there *no* stopping this pernicious phenomenon progress?). And what can I say about the mountains. They're beautiful. They may be short and unprogressive, but they have a rugged, uncaring, untamed, prehistoric look about them, uncaringest mountains I, speaking as a white man, ever did see. I prefer them to the Sierras. There is no snow. There were occasional yellow flowers about by the side of the railway line, looked to me like daisies, and now and again I saw flocks of parrots, crimson and blue. I asked about the parrots, they're called crimson rosellas, and apparently they abound. There are other birds too—I wouldn't mind becoming an ornithologist in a small way, make it my business to see and know by name all these mountain birds. The naturalist's is the only scientist's hand I wish anymore to shake. I got talking in the train to a man who got out low down in the mountains (innumerable mountain towns, at every one of which my train stopped: The Fish, apparently, being a crack express does not stop until Springwood, a strictly upper mountains affair) and when he found out I was a Yank—I told him I was on R and R, the usual story— he started explaining about the valleys to me, told me of the first crossing of the Blue Mountains etc, in the matter of *fact* though I would rather just have looked out the window and formed my own conclusions, but I listened politely as I could. Also, I opened the conversation, asking him about the parrots. Or was that another man. When did I first see the parrots? It would have been a severe test of my patience though had he not got out when he did.

I noticed a wind building up the higher we climbed (I should explain that Katoomba sits, or lays, or how you will, virtually at the peak of these mountains, very old and weathered remember, and with what must be a pronounced plateau; though of course the first road, and hence all the settlements today as well as the railway line, followed the ridges—periodically from the train you get to see your views across sweeping, bushy valleys), a *severe* wind, and by the time we got to Katoomba it was stiff and cold enough to blow me nearly off my feet. It must come out of the west. I can understand how old Dulce could have hated this town though if this wind is any indication. She must be a good age. Although not necessarily, because she could have been a whole lot younger than Manwaring, couldn't she? When you're cold in this country Sylvia, you're cold. There is no central heating, the people making very little provision for the cold climate. In this hotel I'm in for example (just at the top of Katoomba Street really) I'm freezing my ass as I write this.

Well the discovery of the day, after I'd found myself some accommodation, was that the Paragon still stands, as does Mount Saint Mary's Convent and Hinkler Park, those three places so well beloved and remembered of our poor old Jean. I walked all around the town, specifically enquiring for them. The Paragon is a real period piece, you should see their soda fountain. Mount Saint Mary's, well I can only suppose in respect of it that if you've seen one convent you've seen them all. I can't praise the place Sylvia, some modern built-ons of course (I've come to expect these from every old building I see), and Hinkler Park appears to be smaller than Jean remembered it. My grandfather's photographic workshop apparently no longer exists; at least I could find no trace of it at the top of Katoomba Street where it should have been. The Astor Flats are still here though. Jesus Christ, they look cold. I might enquire about leasing one—but how far, I am asking myself, can I afford to take this ancestral nostalgia? What's my point in it anyway Sylvia, do you remember what I'm here for? I don't—did I plan on spending the rest of my life here? Was that what I was going to do? I'm not sure I don't want to get the hell out of here back to sea. Maybe if I just sit in the *bush* long enough though, find some quiet valley, even Hinkler Park might do me, at least I'll recognize the trees there . . . I'll survive. I'll have to do some meditating pretty soon, I've the constant feeling I'm putting *off* something. But what is it? What can it be?

I want to get away from people. I want to be alone. You know they hate Americans up here? You know they *laugh* at them? My accent? What should I do—tell them to get fucked? Tell them Manwaring was my grandfather? I tried that—no one remembers him. I'm beginning to wonder if he ever really existed. Disorientated's just not the word to describe the way I feel. Too much change too fast do you think. I'm going to get an ulcer if I don't watch it. Constant indigestion. Constant drinking, gulp my food, scared to stop. There's also the problem of my visa—so what do you reckon; you think they'll form a posse and come up here after me? I don't think so, I doubt that—I think if I just had a job they wouldn't even care. Just lie low maybe. They won't bother me. But that's another thing—jobs aren't exactly a dime a dozen up here either. There's no work— what if I can't even manage a bloody *job*? I better go back down to Sydney do you think, see about that seaman's union business? Get on a ship out? I should have struck while the iron was hot on that issue. While my captain was still around, you know, he was very friendly towards me that man. I grew to like him very much. But they'd have sailed by now. In a way I wish I was with them. I don't even know where they went.

I don't know much Sylvia, I'm just so *agitated* I can't rest, I dream all night, hiding, seeking, who knows what I'm doing any more. I get cold chills when I think of what I've done. It's all so irrevocable—if it ever really happened, that is. Did it ever really 'happen'? Pins when I stick them into my flesh don't even hurt. I have no sense of reality you know, in the midst of all these escapades. Jesus, if I never felt loneliness before I feel it now. I never felt so lonely in all my life. I guess that's what I'm here for though, after all; I came of my own volition. Surely I was lonely back home though—I've felt this feeling, perhaps attenuated, before, I know I have—it's no use, I can't work anything out.

Next day. Last night I couldn't sleep, so after writing to

you I went for a walk down to Echo Point. I came up here
Monday, it was going to be Sunday, but I made it Monday,
superstitious I suppose, wanting to start all ventures on a
Monday—today's Tuesday, I don't even like to think about
my visa. I can't imitate the Australian accent worth a damn,
people that speak to me at all only want to know all about
America, Vietnam etc, the real low down. I feel like a
walking talking recruitment poster. I hate this being a
professional American stranger! Down to Echo Point, no
one walks around the streets at night here when winter
approaches anyway, they've got more sense. But I'm inured
to the cold and the dark. Stumbled down a bush track and
looked across the alien Jamieson Valley to Mount Solitary,
Orphan Rock, oh fucking Jesus, how long can I keep this
up? I don't get any sleep. I'm obsessed with nightmares
about rejected papers (I keep dreaming my last paper got
rejected—I guess I'll never know and I'd never be game to
ask). I'll have to do something Sylvia, the puritanical work
ethnic's got me in its dreaded grasp. If only I could just
meditate. But what in God's name am I going to meditate
on? I better go off to the quack and get myself a script for
some valium or something instead. Better yet, let me find a
job. My tensions will disappear do you think when I get a
job? And my money can't last forever.

Today I went to the labour exchange—nothing doing.
Being as how I'm so obvious a foreigner anyway, and with
a lot of the local Australian workforce unemployed (Katoomba Street looking a bit like Germantown Avenue in the
extent of the unemployed males all slouching about), they
won't exactly be breaking their necks to find me a job will
they. Kept asking embarrassing questions too about my job
experience etc. Eventually they're going to get nosy about
my visa. And that'll be the end of me. Also, why did I tell
all those lies compromising myself around the town saying
how I was a Vietnam veteran? I've turned into a goddamed
compulsive liar. Don't say I came all this way to find I can't
even get a bloody *job*! I remember my grandfather saying
to me, *get* a job, work, a menial job, calm down. Oh, he
was so right. Panic of not having a job is terrible—the

captain was a very wise man, you know that? He took my fare, then he put me to work. He just created a job, it wasn't really necessary the work I did, but it took my mind off myself didn't it. So far all this sitting around amidst alien bushland has done is put the shits up me well and truly. I'm chain smoking too. God help me. Going to pieces. Falling apart. Having achieved my objective, I see it for what it is. Such an attitude.

The next day. Saved, in one respect only. A job. Wouldn't you know it there'd be another Yank in town? They're everywhere. They stand out like a crimson rosella amongst a bunch of pigeons, maybe it's just they're so conspicuous makes them seem so abundant. I saw his advertisement in the local paper (loudly advertising his nationality of course; but lucky for me he did), I was having morning coffee in the Paragon at the time. He runs a fuel yard, and so I looked him up (on the run), explained my situation (I forget how the story ran), but national affinity runs thicker than water Sylvia, and though he had no vacancy he said he'd give me a job. I guess he thinks I'm the type'll be moving on pretty soon. Of course, in his case it was the old expatriate story of being fed up with lack of scope, spades (I swear that's what he called them—no he didn't, he called them negroes, I said that just to be nasty darling), inflation etc. But what is it in my case? Indeed. Probably the same story when all's said and done. Oh, I don't like to think about this, I can tell you. I don't like to think about it at all. Nasty moments of truth. My grandfather—my grandfather —his spirit is haunting me. He said when you get there, *reexamine* your religious impulses.

What religious impulses?

I need to meditate. Need to relax. If I wanted manual work, well, I've got that now, everything always goes well for me looked at from the other eye, the other angle, menial labour in a fuel yard. I was so grateful . . . but sir, I said after my pleading had met with such marked success, do you mind very much if I don't start work until next Monday sir? Boy, he said: I don't give a fuck if you don't start at *all*, I don't *need* the extra labour, I'm just doing you a favour, you understand that boy? Thank you sir, I said.

So you know what I'm going to do? You know what I've got in my stupid head to do now? I'm going to squander what's left of my money (now that I have the security of prospective employment—just keep the shit in the fan or out of it about the old USA depending on the prevailing wind, that's about all I need to do to hold this job—I think I can safely do that, and I think I can forget about this visa thing, once I've been in a job a while I'll present the immigration people here with a *fait accompli*)—a trip to Bateman's Bay. Did you guess? And then my roving will be done, or at least I hope so, as I'm all through roving Sylvia, all that I can't do at nights or on the weekends at least. And then I will settle down calmly into my new life, I am tempted to say my fresh life, here, in this alien town, in this wilderness, a life picked out of a fucking hat.

Why oh why is it no one will ever give me a job where my labours are really *needed*? Is *all* work in this world apart from subsistence farming just a great con to keep people like me from going totally insane and making anti-social pests of themselves? I keep rubbing disbelief at myself like sleep from my weary eyes. What am I going to do here at *nights*? It may shock me into some great personal discovery. Failing that Sylvia, it may lull me (manual labour is very lulling, which is why it has enjoyed such popularity, and always will, even when there is no longer any cybernetic justification for it)—into a high bush languor of some sort in which I will no longer care about anything. Besides, I have things to do here. I have to find some of Manwaring's old photos. I have to have something to pore over at nights. I have to stop rereading the local tabloids. Then I have to learn to meditate up here. Perhaps I need a metabolic starter of some sort—fact is, I'm lost without my hash. For the rest of my life I have to meditate up here. That is my lot. Sylvia—I'm sorry this device is so excessively crammed with rhetorical questions.

Chapter 19

I'm a little resentful to say the least that I have to live up here when I could be living down by the Pacific. Preferably Crescent City. If only the Australian people were different! If only they were Californians.

My unaccustomed back is sore, my mind has all the consistency of an Appalachian patchwork quilt, but I don't resent the physical labour. I can make believe I'm really alive only when cording wood with the wind ripping through my clothes.

My visa has expired. Can I go do you suppose to the US Consulate in Sydney and ask to be repatriated? I think repatriation means that I will never again be issued with a passport. I don't think I could face that prospect—what if I want to go fight in some war of liberation? One just never knows what one wants to do does one. Also, it would be an admission of defeat. I'm not quite ready to admit defeat. But it may not be long away.

As my muscles strengthen, so does my equanimity at this cosmic plight of ours, if that does not sound too audacious and arch, and I've not the slightest doubt it does, but I'm tired of tying myself in knots of self-apology. No security in this job of course, but the older you get the less that concerns you. You don't care about comforts. Time flies. I've aged aeons in the last few months. I'm telling you things I know you think you know already, but they're new to all of us. I bought myself a car to go down the coast in, got my licence without any difficulty. They drive on the left hand side of the road here. Facts and more facts. The car is a clapped out bomb cost me $A150, an FH Holden (General Motors Australia—wholly owned subsidiary), it's blowing smoke and about to lose what little compression's left on all four cylinders, but I keep pushing it up and down these mountains. I can hear the tappets and rings slapping around. Particularly up from and down into the Megalong Valley (choice Aboriginal like Nullarbor), a nearby valley I like. These last two weekends I hired a horse from an outfit down there and rode up and down the icy Megalong Creek. Was tempted to swim, but didn't. Times like these I feel I can stick it out—that in fact I must, that I have no real alternative. This is the end of the line for me, you see. But the weekdays, or more especially the week*nights*, are terrible to endure. I'm so tired, the temptation for me is every night just to fall asleep, but I don't want to do this. It would be dangerous. Because if that's enlightenment, I don't want enlightenment. I think my job is secure. There's a picture theatre here, but it only changes programs once a week. And they're pretty dreadful programs. Last Wednesday I saw 'Easy Rider'. Nothing but bowdlerized American shit. Australian television I can't bring myself to watch. Australian films don't exist. Australian books I can't bring myself to read, other than those purely factual. All right: so why don't I make my own entertainment? Poems, with one exception I am going to take a chance on and exhibit, I can't bring myself to write. And it's no use telling me to get out of the room, because I can't come at the local snatch—sexually, I'm beside myself, get out of the screwing habit long enough and it deserts you. Have to make overtures, and I wouldn't know how to go about them. Don't know the local mating rites. I'd be the laughing stock of the place anyway, with my fat American accent. On the other hand, although I dream of it believe me, I know I can't go back to the bench. Hands are shaking so much these days I couldn't synthesize an aliphatic ester given a million years and the full facilities of the Noyes Laboratory. I accordingly try not to think of home. I try to feel that *this* is home. But it isn't. And neither was my home my home. Soon it's going to be wintertime here. And that's going to be hard to take, that's going to be a real test. Winter upon winter. Tahiti was my half way house. I developed excruciating sunburn there. I ask you. I wish I had some profound observations to make. I'd like to talk like a wise Chinese, but all I can make is a sigh, maybe of profound relief, as I relax back down in to the quagmirey masses. In a way, it'd be an interesting experiment—any life is just an experiment—to marry some ugly, stupid, bare-legged mountain girl, and have half a dozen ignorant, ugly, stupid, bare-assed mountain brats, all pregnant or off to reform school at sixteen, speaking in accents forever alien to their dad—so then I could *really* get to see how the other half lives at close quarters. There's supposed to be a lot of poetry in their lives, or is it rude, animal vigour they enjoy, some quality at any rate that I know we people don't have and could well do with. Frankly, I'd settle for either vigour or poetry at this point. A little more vigour and I could break away, a little more poetry and I could accept what I've got. It'd be better still to have no kids—I fear I'd enjoy neither poetry nor vigour. This turning of one's back though, it would be preferable I'm sure to be turning *towards* something. Even Manwaring had his photographs. He may not have been enamoured of them, but they were there. I just can't find any. I have a book of Australian birds, and on the weekends down in the Megalong I try to identify all birds I see. But that can hardly be an existence in itself.

As I don't spend much money, I've still got money left. This coming Saturday I'm going down to Sydney, and I'm going to look up some of my R and R friends and compatriots, and I'm going to buy as big a lump of hash as I can afford, it's around, I can smell it from here, and the following day the Sunday I'm going to roll it all into one sweet ball wrap it up in Tally Ho papers with some Log Cabin ready rubbed, and I'm going to smoke it right down in the Megalong Valley behind some tree where no one'll see me. You might see this as defeatist, but I've decided boozing is bad for my health. I have an ulcerated gut. I need some euphoria badly. And boozing, well it only depresses me, makes me want to piss all the time. And frankly, I'm all pissed out, I don't want to have to look at my poor, shrunken, vestigial prick ever again. I wrote a little song for my guitar last week, you want to hear it? Just sit back and shut your eyes pretend we're kids and playing our guitars in our room together and listen: it's called Blue Note. It was meant for you.

Actually, I don't think I'll include it.

Chapter 20

I am still going and have a hot tip on where I may find some of my grandfather's photography at last. Do you know I've searched this town and I can't find a single photo? I'm full of clarity now, last weekend worked wonders on me. Chopped wood so far all this week like a fiend, and Saturday (I live for weekends, a thing I never remember at home, there life proceeded an uninterrupted if corrupt stream like the Delaware below the Walt Whitman Bridge) I'm going to hunt around a few local museums, there's one at Wentworth Falls, another at Mount York—in the hope that the custodians will be able to help me in my quest. Will report back later.

Success, success! Saturday evening and success! I haven't even opened the packet yet—bundled everything in without looking too—I'm going to write it all down all my impressions as I look at it. The Mount York Natural History Museum has trunks full of old photographs it never displays, generally dumped on it by anonymous entities, I was allowed to look in the trunks and in one trunk I looked into was a bunch of old glass plates, looked like negatives, together with a lot of sepia prints and oddments, some of the plates had A. Manwaring written on them in white ink, also titles, and a stamp A. Manwaring Katoomba, copyright, was on the back of those sepia prints, the majority, which turned out to be postcards (POST CARD: correspondence/address only, also a little square where the stamp goes KODAK along the top AUSTRAL down the sides). He exists! He exists. I have them out on loan. Perhaps these will give me the clue I have really been seeking on this quest—what made the bastard go to the States in the first place when he had everything going for him up here?

I'm pulling them out now—I took a random selection only of the sepia prints and cards, not looking at them, the plates, all stacked away in Kodak cardboard boxes were too heavy and cumbersome, and I'm sure I have a representative sampling here—taking a swig at the recidivous bottle of JB I have had on order at Gearins and which I picked up this afternoon on my way back, especially brought in for times of acute stress and excitement and hope—here they come, tumbling out, I'm going to describe them one by one. And here I am selecting them, totally at random. Evidence of my past at last.

1. Postcard. 'Chimney Cottage' Mt Wilson copyright in white ink. A roughly constructed cottage with a large stone chimney occupying half of the facing wall, a sort of lean-to with cane chairs and a table, perhaps for visitors. Some trees in the background, some hewn logs in the foreground. A nice little garden around the cottage, from what I can judge.

2. Postcard. 'Log Cabin Mt Wilson' could be the same cottage from another angle, but the lean-to's not there.

3. Not a postcard. A bunch of old buses lined up in front
of a brick building bearing the inscription '1936' up the top
and 'Blue Mountain Transport Pty Ltd' underneath. The
bus destinations as shown are, from left (and no two are
alike), Minna-Ha-Ha (!), Katoomba Stn, Mount Victoria,
Echo Point, Gordon Falls, Govett's Leap, Lithgow S.A.F.
(Small Arms Factory, my own addendum). Well, well.

4. Not a postcard. Scene of a hotel I do not recognize,
under a rose arch up a garden path from in front of the
building, a couple of what look like T model Fords parked
on the gravel. A sort of hedge and a couple of cupids bearing
arrows at the front steps. Perhaps a defunct hotel, there are
many of these, now mostly convalescent homes. No white
ink anywhere.

5. Not a postcard. Interior of a church with wooden walls.
Obviously Catholic, big statue of the Virgin Mother. No
inscription. No. 12 written on the back. My guess 'Catholic
Church, Mt Wilson'?

6. 'Mt Wilson'. Not a postcard. 444 pencilled on the back.
Looks like a private residence, with a lot of giant tree ferns
growing outside it. Eerie effect.

7. Not a postcard. No inscription anywhere, front or back.
The sweeping gravel drive of a hotel or private school. I do
not recognize it. What could be a covered ambulatory lead-
ing to another building on the left.

8. A small photo, not postcard. 'Linda Falls, Leura'
printed as though by stamp, on the back. A waterfall falling
through a ferny glade, into a rocky pool. A large tree fern
in the foreground. I have not yet myself been to Linda Falls.

9. A ring-in. A piece of advertising. Whether taken by
Manwaring as business on the side I cannot say. A card,
containing the portrait of a rather dreamy, self-opinionated
looking man, and beneath, the following: 'Billy Preston,
World's Champion Endurance Dancer. Established at
Katoomba Casino-de-Luxe. Danced from 9 am April 9th
till 9.50 am April 14th, 1928. Actual dancing time, 120 hours
50 minutes'.

I wonder if this record still stands.

10. Not a postcard. 'Monument, Mount Boyce—he fre-

quently does not close his quotation marks; and then the Manwaring copyright I have noticed when he does not put in his full name, so: M

11. Not a postcard. A brass band at attention, in the background the Carrington, obviously a parade of some sort, early model cars parked beside the road, I can just make out banners reading '2KA' and 'Parramatta Branch'. On the back, a circular stamp, printed HARRINGTONS KATOOMBA on the circumference BY in the middle.

12. A really rotten photo, all blurred, with VELOX VELOX VELOX all over the back. Manwaring himself in the foreground. Manwaring leaning on a tripod, bespectacled, looking down, standing on an awning I would say, above a blurred parade with blurred banners marching down Katoomba Street. Probably the awning under the Astor Flats. Taken I would say by Dulce or more likely Jean.

So Manwaring was really here.

13. A postcard. 'The Katoomba' Miniature Golf Course. M The less said about this the better. Miniature Harbour Bridges like at Glenbrook Station constitute hazards. In the background is Sans Souci, now a convalescent home. I can't work out where this course could have stood.

14. A postcard. The same dark-braided brass band as before, led by a smallish and youthful drum major in white, crossing the railway line at the top of Katoomba Street. I know this because there is a sign (not there now) saying 'Beware of Trains' and the tracks can be seen. Women are standing on the fence.

15. A moustachioed digger in serge drill and slouch hat nursing a little girl. Not a postcard.

16. A postcard. Singing columns of diggers marching in what looks to be the Middle East. Not a Manwaring original, I wouldn't think, no Manwaring copyright either, the first postcard without one. And Manwaring never went to war. Also, I thought he was supposed to be in the USA during World War Two. I guess this is World War One.

17. A postcard. Manwaring copyright. 'Swimming Pool, Blackheath'. Many people swimming and picnicking.

18. Another postcard 'Swimming Pool, Blackheath'. Ano-

ther aspect of the above pool. Children in wide-brimmed hats and braces and baggy pants.

19. A larger, but in every other way identical, version of 4 above.

20. Another version of 5, only now the celebrant is there, raising the chalice wearing his chasuble his back towards the camera. I'm not surprised. Is it permitted to photograph the mass? I should think not. Could interfere with the transubstantiation. I now also observe a more than life-sized Christ which I did not previously observe, hanging from a giant cross above the altar.

21. Some eerily illuminated gum trees. Not a postcard. On the back, some ink writing. Above the stamp 'A. Manwaring, Katoomba' is handwritten 'from' and below it 'Flood-lit Trees at Katoomba Falls Reserve'.

22. A congregation of people as viewed from the awning over the shop below the Astor Flats I would guess, watching a parade. No doubt the same parade. Copyright Manwaring and printed by Harringtons. Women are wearing cloches. Armistice Day?

23. 'Mt York Blue Mtns' M Manwaring's favorite mountain I think we may assume, or was that Mt Wilson. A picnic table on a bluff with a dome over it, higher up a rocky path under a tree a man with a suit and a hat and an obelisk at the summit. Nothing on the back.

24. A menu. On the front a photograph of the Carrington in about a foot of snow. 'Winter, Carrington Hotel, Katoomba M Copyright M 'Making doubly sure of this one. All in scribbled white ink contrasting markedly with the inscription on the back of the photograph, which is as follows: Menu (in florid scroll), Souvenir of Easter, 1932. Easter Sunday Dinner, March 26th, 1932: Pailletes au Parmasan, Consomme Pompadour, creme d'Asperges, Fried Filet Whiting (Sauce Tartare), Pailettes de Boeuf (Moderne), Sweetbread Patties a la Reine, Roast Baron Beef a l' Anglaise, Roast Valley Sucking Pig (Apple Sauce), Roast Saddle Lamb (Mint Sauce), Larded Filet Veal with Seasoning, Green Peas, Baked Tomatoes, Potatoes Varies, Roast Turkey with York Ham a la Broche, Baked Young

Gosling, Cider Sauce, Roast Spring Chicken with Bacon, Roast Aylesbury Duckling with Dressing, Pommes Saratoga, Asperges au Buerre Fondu, Steamed Turkish Pudding, Queen Merengue Custard, Cherry Tartlets with Cream, Chocolate Eclairs, Tutti Fruitti Sundae, Dessert, Nuts, Queen Olives, Cafe Noir.

Now that's the way to celebrate the Ascension. Not one indigenous dish. I think I'll show it to the proprietress though, see what effect it has just on the offchance.

25. Postcard, no white writing, but it's that swimming pool again.

26. Nothing, back or front. A tree leaning at an acute angle from under a cave, where there is the inevitable picnic table. Some ferns, higher up. Could be anywhere.

27. Close up of the ornate little lovers' summer house in the front garden of the Carrington, still there by the way, on the back ROUGH PROOF ONLY.

28. '26th Inf. Bde., Katoomba 22/8/40' Soldiers marching. And I was born in 1944. On the back A. Manwaring copyright.

29. Unveiling the obelisk at Mount Boyce. A postcard. There's a headmaster in a trencher, a dignitary with an ear trumpet, a crone in a cloche, assorted scouts, a chaplain, and a group of upper mountain people beneath the flowering gums.

A procession of people, including young girls in veils about to be admitted to their first communion, Gordon Falls Reserve Leura, same old holidaymakers taking their ease and grinning at the camera that never lies, 'Chimney Cottage', the pool again, Memory Park Blackheath with a little reservoir and incongruous firs and summer houses absolutely ridiculous in all this bush, oh and here—'My daughter Janet'.

We may have had more than one compulsive liar in our 'family' Sylvia. Perhaps one fewer Jew.

•

Words have failed me. But I'm going on. Osbourne College Blackheath a group of young ladies in a fencing pose,

floodlighting at Katoomba Falls, The Mall Leura, an obelisk
bearing the inscription Pass of Victoria: constructed under
the direction of Sir Thomas Mitchell Surveyor General,
opened by Governor Sir Richard Bourke October 23 1832
R.A.H.S., marching soldiers, Wishing Chair Mt York, soldiers
chatting with a man in mayoral robes, presumably, though
not necessarily I should caution, a mayor, a family portrait
of assorted poorly posed boys, the back verandah of a
weatherboard house with a wickerwork reclining chair,
Janet again—Rocking Stone, Silver Cascades, Reid's Plateau,
Convict Pick Marks made in widening the first road Mount
York 1814, the Blackheath waterhole again, the altar etc.
etc. Leura Golf House, obelisk obelisk obelisk—I'm going
to burn the lot right now.

They're burning.

Why oh why did my mother tell me lies? You know what
I think?—I think she probably met up with old Manwaring
in Jersey City and they developed some sort of ugly relationship between them there more hideous and ugly by far
than anything sexual, and as a result lost her mind and
turned into a compulsive liar got hold of a few of his old
mountain photographs and passed herself off with his complicity as an Australian the rest of her days. The facts don't
add up. I swear she told me she came over to the States
when she was thirteen and I was born in 1944 and here's
a Manwaring photograph taken here in Katoomba in 1940
and she was older than seventeen when I was born unless
I'm a very poor judge of a lady's age. Lies, lies—*Lies*!

I am into my bottle of JB neat, and I am very naturally
thinking over what are the implications of this sordid discovery, if any. I am wondering if it is possibly God's final
way of testing me with respect to logic or of dealing with
compulsive liars and apostates like me who turn their back
on facts. If Manwaring was *not* my grandfather—then can
I be really sure that 'Jean' was my mother?

I have decided there are no implications. It's cool. I have
kept two of the pictures as momentos. (Actually, they fell
out of the fire and are both charred.) The curator at Mount
York will be very angry with me for having burnt the rest

do you think. Not to mention the proprietress, you should see the hole in her carpet. I think not. I think he will be glad to be rid of them. I think they are rubbish by any photographic standards, past or present. And their historio-graphical value, as I have just demonstrated, is nil. One is of the park called Memory Park. The other is of a pretty little girl called Janet next to a tree fern in some valley.

Well, she looks a little more like Jean to me now she's all charred and I'm so drunk. She could be Jean. Perhaps I just can't add, I think she's probably Jean. I've let facts lead me astray too long to take any notice of them now. After all, I'm quite sick of tying myself in knots over facts.

I wonder what I'm going to do next.

My Land of Purity may well await me just around the very next bend.

I don't know how to end this—I can't believe it's really ended.

More about Penguins and Pelicans